SPIRIT OF THE HILLS

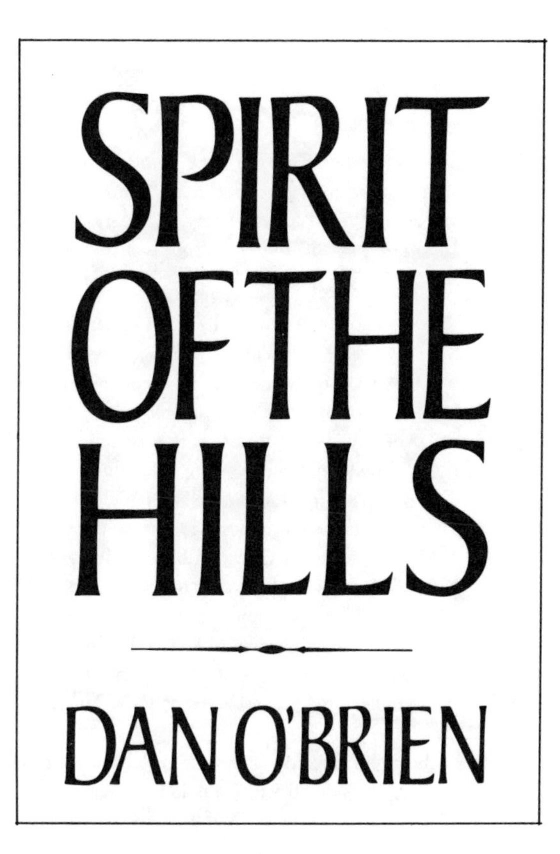

CROWN PUBLISHERS, INC.
NEW YORK

PUBLISHER'S NOTE: *This is a work of fiction. The characters, incidents, and dialogues are products of the author's imagination and are not to be construed as real. Any resemblance to actual events or persons, living or dead, is entirely coincidental.*

Published by Crown Publishers, Inc.,
225 Park Avenue South, New York, New York 10003,
and represented in Canada
by the Canadian MANDA Group
CROWN is a trademark of Crown Publishers, Inc.
Manufactured in the United States of America

Library of Congress Cataloging-in-Publication Data
O'Brien, Dan, 1947–
The spirit of the hills.
I. Title.
PS3565.B665S65 1987 813'.54 87-3311
ISBN 0-517-56727-X

10 9 8 7 6 5 4 3 2 1

First Edition

For Kris

SPIRIT OF THE HILLS

Prologue

Jimmy McVay was still alive when the man kicked his hand away from the envelope filled with hundred-dollar bills. But he felt nothing. Earlier, the force of the three shots had sent him backward, twisting in what seemed to be slow motion. His shoulder had hit the wall behind him, and he slid to the asphalt. He lay trying to remember what it had felt like to be shot. All that would come to his mind was that his brother, Tom, had been in the war and had never been shot. That fact seemed more significant than any of the rest. It was not important that he had forged his mother's name to the transfer at the bank, that he had withdrawn the money from his account as if it was his own. It did not seem important that he was lying in a growing puddle of blood. It was not even important that he was dying.

He assumed he was already dead, that it was his spirit that watched the man pick up the envelope. He had read about dying and knew people who had been brought back told of watching themselves from above. That is what it was like to watch the man stuff the money into his coat pocket, then snap the pistol away in its holster hidden in the small of his back. But Jimmy was not looking down on the man, he was looking up. It felt like his eyes were open, but he could not move them.

There was no pain. There was the feel of blood, but nothing hurt. He thought back, trying to remember how it had happened. They had met just the way they had planned. Jimmy had brought the money the way he had said he would. It seemed so easy. He would have tripled the money, had his mother's money back in her account before she knew it was gone. He remembered the car he planned to buy, the clothes, the new apartment, just like Tom's. But he had screwed up. It had been the simplest of mistakes. The man had asked if he had brought the money, and he had said yes, and patted the envelope in his jacket pocket. He knew it was wrong as soon as he had done it, but it was too late. Trying to keep the deal going, he asked the man where the marijuana was stored, but the man was not listening, he was reaching behind him for the pistol. What would Tom have done then?

He would have brought a gun of his own, never tipped the man off that the money was in his pocket. Tom would not have had the money in his pocket. He would not have taken the cash in the first place. His brother, Tom, would not have gotten into a deal like this, would not be lying in a puddle of his own blood, unable to move even his eyes. He certainly would not have let a punk kill him. But Jimmy had.

The last thing he remembered was how the three shots had sounded in the alley. They had been much louder than he had expected. It had surprised him that they had actually made him fly backward. Then he saw himself lying in this cold alley in the warehouse section of Toledo, the man walking casually out toward the street. Cars moved on the streets in every direction as if nothing had happened. He watched the man's Ford pull from the curb and move slowly into the traffic. Then, just for an instant, he saw the whole city. It sparkled, pulsing with streetlights and the lights from people's homes. In the middle of the lights, lost now, lay the body of Tom McVay's little brother.

Part One

The sliding glass doors of his daughter's kitchen looked out into a small, well-kept backyard. It was early morning, and the colors were all too pale. Spring had come weeks before, and the grass had begun to grow, but still the color of the earth was only a yellow-green. There was a small brick patio just off the kitchen that was edged with some kind of Japanese evergreen. Bill Egan had asked the name of the shrub when he had first come to live there, and his son-in-law had told him. But now he couldn't remember what it was called. He did remember that last autumn both his daughter and son-in-law had made a big fuss over trimming it. They called it "pruning" the shrubbery. The evergreen limbs were cut flat on the top and the sides so that they looked like one giant rectangular bush surrounding the patio.

Today, as Egan looked out of the kitchen from where he always sat, he saw that one tiny branch had caught the spirit of spring and broken away from the lines that the bush had been trimmed into. The branch was pushing its way out of the rectangle of shrubbery toward the gray Illinois sky. It was only a few inches long and looked thin and weak. Sitting in the kitchen chair, drinking his coffee, Egan decided that he wouldn't mention the branch. He would let his daughter and son-in-law discover the renegade on their own.

He sipped at the coffee and listened to the sound of someone beginning to move in the back of the house. It was nearly six o'clock. They left for work about seven-thirty, and Egan knew that they would be out moving around the kitchen soon. In a way they would ruin the morning. But it was their home, and he was grateful to them, he supposed, for letting him stay there. It was an easy way to live: the house was warm, the water always came out of the faucets like it was supposed to, and there was a convenience store just two blocks away. He couldn't complain about any of that. And he couldn't complain about the way they treated him. They acted like they were glad that he was there. But still it was a poor way to live. He felt a little like the branch must have felt while it was trimmed in close to that long rectangular shrub. He felt useless and bored. He had sat there in his chair a thousand times and figured it every way that he knew how. Every time it came up the same, he would sit there being bored for a few more years and then die.

It had started with a simple visit. He had a job lined up with a big rancher in the panhandle of Nebraska. It wasn't much, but it was a place to sleep and three squares a day. The ranch was a big operation, and all he would have had to do was trap a few coyotes and poison prairie dogs, with some of the greatest country in the world to look at. He glanced back out into the backyard. The sun was higher now, but things had not gotten much lighter. He shook his head. Why had he come to this rainy, overcast country? The whole place was like a sponge, always wet. There was never a real winter, mostly freezing rain and clouds. But he came back to visit before he went to the new job. That was at Christmas three years ago. He never made it to the job. His daughter had taken over. Egan knew that it had been a mistake to come to Illinois, but his big mistake was letting his daughter talk him into going to the doctor.

It would have been possible to get away if the doctor hadn't filled her head with worry. Sure, he was weaker, had a little trouble breathing. Hell, he was an old man. The doctor had listened to his heart and taken a long time doing it. When he finally finished listening, he looked up at Egan and pulled the stethoscope from his ears. "You ever have rheumatic fever?" he asked.

Egan nodded. "Sixty some years ago."

"Well, you've got a couple of weak valves on the left side of your heart. That's what's making you short of breath and energy."

Egan quit listening at that point, but his daughter, who was right there, listened to every word. He was sitting on the table with his shirt off. The doctor and his daughter went on talking like he wasn't there. He slid off the table and put his shirt back on, all the time thinking that this was going to mess up his plans to take that job in Nebraska. He stood for a minute and watched them discussing his health. It was a little like he was already dead. Then he heard them talking about rest and taking it easy, and he knew they were talking about someone who was still alive, but barely. He slipped out of the examining room and went to find a chair in the waiting room. His daughter found him just as he started an article in *Popular Mechanics*. She smiled at him but looked upset. Egan knew she would want him to stay in Illinois.

And that is just what he had done. There had been some discussion, a few tears, then a couple kinds of pills to take, a new bed moved into the guest room, his own set of keys to the house, and Egan was part of the family. But he never had any use for the set of keys. If he took his old pickup out into the country, he was always back before anyone was in bed, and although he was part of the family, he never felt like he belonged. It made his daughter feel good to think that she was taking care of him. She often said she was glad he had chosen to live with them. But it didn't suit him.

There was more activity in the back of the house, and Egan knew that he had only a few minutes left to try to enjoy the morning. He glanced around the tiny yard once more. One day, he thought, it would be nice if he could look out there and see a cottontail rabbit or a squirrel. He closed his eyes and imagined that his daughter's backyard was an endless expanse of prairie. The Japanese shrubs turned into a dry gully filled with buffaloberry bushes, the neatly clipped blue grass to grama grass and forbs. In his mind, Egan turned the yard fence into the distant horizon, and then he started to walk the same way he had walked almost every morning since he had come to stay with his daughter and her husband. He moved out along the flat-topped prairie with an easy, tireless stride and jumped a jackrabbit from its hiding place behind a yucca plant. He stopped and scanned the horizon, then started to go down into the thick gully. But this morning it felt different. For some reason he did not want to go down into the gully. He moved slowly along the flat above and watched the land ahead of him. Keeping his eyes closed, he moved his head slowly from side to side, pretending to look around. He had imagined this scene a thousand times, but this morning something seemed odd. It was the old feeling of being watched. He came to a stop overlooking a long, flat valley. Although the scene was imagined, the feeling was real. Today there was something alive on his prairie. Something was watching him. Something was going to happen. He scanned the prairie again, moving his head from side to side. Finally the feeling was too much. He opened his eyes, knowing that the tiny backyard would reappear and suspecting that the feeling at the back of his neck was his daughter, standing at the kitchen door, watching him, wondering what he could possibly be dreaming of.

There was a light burning on the second floor of an old apartment building on Revere Street. Tom McVay was sitting in his pickup truck parked against the curb in the outskirts of St. Louis. The number on the apartment building matched the address written on the scrap of paper he held up in the streetlight's glow. McVay looked at the address for the tenth time. He knew he was at the right place because he had been inside the building, moving unheard on the stairs and in the halls. The light he was watching burned in the apartment whose address was written on the scrap of paper. He was hoping that the light would stay on until the street was clear.

At 12:15 the light in the apartment was still on. No one had driven past McVay for twenty minutes. A friend of Jimmy's had told him that the apartment had four rooms. The door opened into the living room.

The kitchen would be on his right; the first door on the left was the bathroom; the second door was the bedroom. McVay figured the light was in the bedroom. He took a last look up and down the street, and in easy motions opened the pickup door, stepped out onto the street, reached behind the seat, and pulled out a brand-new ax handle. He closed the pickup door gently and began a casual walk toward the front door of the apartment building.

When McVay reached the top of the stairs, the light was still on. It shone beneath the door as he stood in the hall, leaning against the wall across from the apartment. He held the ax handle by the very end. The other end, where the ax head would be, touched the toe of a combat boot polished to a mirror finish. His eyes were calm, and he took a few deep breaths. Then he bowed his head, and the breaths became deeper. Finally the head came up, and he took one last breath of air. The eyes were intent now. They stared at, and through, the door across the hallway. His free hand pushed off the wall as the air expelled itself. The door broke in three pieces when McVay's shoulder hit it.

There was no hesitation. His momentum carried him to the partially opened bedroom door. He was right. The light was in the bedroom, and in a fraction of a second he was standing at the foot of the bed. A naked woman was scrambling to get off a man lying in the bed, and the man was reaching for a pistol on the bed stand. The ax handle moved in a lightning-fast arch, and when it hit the outstretched arm there was a tremendous cracking noise. The man screamed, and the pistol spun off the bed stand and onto the floor.

Then there was silence. The woman was standing frozen against the wall, and the man, naked also, twisted into a ball, holding his arm and gritting his teeth. The woman began to tremble. "Don't kill us," she said.

"Shut up," said McVay without turning his head toward her.

He was looking at the man. "Does the name McVay ring a bell?" he asked.

The man's face was a snarl now. "Never heard it," he said, and before the last syllable cleared his throat, the ax handle came down on his rib cage. The man and the woman cried out together.

"Jimmy McVay. Small-time, easy mark for you creeps. My

brother." This time the man didn't answer, but McVay could see that he was listening. "You did a real bad thing to him." The woman was crying now and slid down the wall, sitting cross-legged, her head down and her hair touching her thighs.

"It wasn't us," she said.

The man hissed at her, trying to keep her from talking, and again the ax handle came down across his ribs.

"Well, he was supposed to meet you two in Toledo with twenty-five thousand dollars and came home in a box with nothing but three forty-five slugs in him." McVay flipped the pistol farther away from the woman. It was a .357, not the one that killed his brother. "You folks were supposed to sell him dope. You were the last to see him alive, and I'm going to beat on you until I get some answers." He reached out with the ax handle and poked the woman, who was sobbing softly. "The money really didn't belong to him," McVay said. He poked her again and saw that the man was watching. "I need to know who owned the forty-five."

He slapped the woman's back firmly with the ax handle and watched the man's reaction. "I don't have all night," he said. The ax handle slammed hard into the wall above the woman, and as plaster rained down on her, he heard the man mumble something. "Louder," McVay said, and dislodged another piece of plaster above the woman.

"P.J. Billion," the man said.

The ax handle hit the wall again. "Where?"

"South Dakota."

"Where?"

"Medicine Springs."

"And you two didn't have anything to do with it?"

"We just put them together," the woman cried. "We never even saw your brother." She made her way to the bed and wrapped her arms around the man. They held each other tightly for a long time. When they looked up, McVay was gone.

In Bill Egan's mind it was bitter cold. A late spring blizzard had piled six inches of soft, light snow against the sagebrush and the fence posts and glazed, thick as a hammer handle, the single strand of barbed wire that ran gradually uphill and out of sight. Then the wind had begun to blow, gusting to sixty miles per hour, and the temperature had crashed. The snow blew into tiny slivers that flaked off the drifts in crystals, tumbled into the night, and now in the stillness of morning, the landscape of Egan's mind was sparkling.

It was a rare, destructive storm. The kind that came too often to the prairie in April. It would all be gone in a day, and the grass would benefit. The ground might stay green into August. But now, there was only white, hard and frozen. Half-grown lambs and calves lay rigid, buried beneath the drifts. The next two days would be difficult for other animals—more would die.

Egan was in his daughter's garage, going through the tools of his trade. His traps and tarps and the old .22 express rifle were laid out on the tailgate of the pickup. It was warm inside the garage, and Egan was dressed in only a white T-shirt. But in his mind he was wrapped in a down-filled coat with a western hat pulled close over his eyes. It was impossible for him to know if it was a dream or a memory. But he knew that he had come up the backside of the butte where the wind had blown most of the snow away and stood now above a flock of sheep, breathing thick, white clouds into the still prairie air. Egan counted carefully, looking hard around every ewe, trying to see if their lambs had made it, looking to see if any were in trouble. They were in a bad spot. He had been trying to get to them since the snow had stopped, and the top of the butte had been the best that he could do. They were still nearly half a mile away, huddled in a small, treeless gully. It would take a good saddle horse to get there.

Egan squinted into the sun and around the horizon. It was going to be a clear day. The storm was over. Now it was just cold. He rubbed his chin with the back of his glove to warm it. Then, from the periphery of his vision, he picked up a tiny movement along a draw. It could be a lamb separated from the flock. It could be a thousand things. But now he saw nothing. The draw led into the gully where the sheep had taken refuge. Then there was another movement further down. This time he was sure. He picked a spot fifty yards ahead of where he'd noticed the second movement and concentrated on seeing anything that moved across it. He had almost given up when a large dark silhouette passed slowly across the spot. The silhouette looked more like it had been painted on the scenery than a natural part of it. He watched farther down the gully, and it appeared again. This time it was in the open and moved steadily toward the sheep. Egan pretended not to know what it was. But when it started its rush, he leaned over and took the .22 express off the tailgate of the pickup. He did not shoulder the weapon but, instead, looked down at the warm, oiled stock and remembered a thousand impossible shots that he had made with it. From a small box on the tailgate he took a single cartridge and slid it into the chamber.

When he looked up, the animal was huge against the snow, jogging after the floundering sheep. Egan could see the long red streaks in the snow where the lambs had run trailing their insides. There were at least three down, and a fourth had been separated from the flock. Easily, playfully, covering twenty feet in a leap, the animal caught up to the lamb and neatly nipped its underside. The lamb tumbled in the snow and was on its feet again. Another nip and tumble, and blood began to stain the snow as the lamb tried again. The third attack finished it. The lamb's insides hung from underneath as it righted itself. It stepped on its own entrails and could not run. It fell, bleating into the snow.

When Egan slid the safety off the rifle, the animal stopped and looked directly at the old man. It was a wolf, and it sat down in the snow within easy range of the .22 express. They looked into each other's faces, and though Egan knew he was in his daughter's warm garage, he felt a chill. He looked away from the wolf toward the horizon and studied the seam between the white bareness of the snow and the blue of the prairie sky. Then he turned the rifle toward himself and looked down the barrel.

He was jarred back to reality by the sound of his daughter opening the garage door. He pointed the rifle away, slid on the safety, and pretended to be cleaning it.

"Dad?" She smiled when she saw that he was there. "There's a call for you."

Egan questioned her with his look. There had not been a call for him since he came to Illinois. But she nodded. "Yes, a Mr. Simmons from the Forest Service. Long distance from the Dakotas."

Egan stared at his daughter but still held the rifle gently in his hands. Now her smile seemed forced. "Do you know him, Dad?"

Egan looked at the rifle. "I used to," he said, then laid the rifle down on the tailgate and slid the bolt back. But he did not take the cartridge from the chamber.

Tom McVay had no idea where he was going. He stopped at an all-night gas station on the outskirts of St. Louis and bought a map. Medicine Springs was at the edge of the Black Hills of South Dakota, and mentally he traced his route across Missouri, the corner of Kansas, and the diagonal of Nebraska. He had not wanted to come to St. Louis, and he didn't want to go to South Dakota. Medicine Springs seemed an unlikely place, a tiny dot on the map, at the western edge of the state, not far from Wyoming. He shook his head and looked up at the road signs, trying to figure out how to get onto the freeway heading toward Kansas City.

Westward. It was very late, and only a few cars shared the freeway with him. He did not pass the cars traveling in his direction, but put the speedometer on sixty miles per hour and held it there. The driving relaxed him, and he began to think about what he was doing, about his brother, Jimmy. In a way, McVay thought, the last ten years had been harder on Jimmy than on him. Things had been hard on everyone. Some people just took it better than others. They simply recovered faster. McVay didn't think much about those years. He didn't have the problems that other veterans he read about had. Basically he had forgotten about it. But Jimmy, who had never had to go, hadn't seemed to recover from the sixties: long hair, happy-sad, nerves edgy. And now, just as Tom had always thought, there had been trouble. Jimmy had been a nice kid. It was only a matter of time until someone took advantage of him. Their mother had told him about his younger brother. She had called, and McVay had known immediately that she wanted him to do something—she wanted Tom to make it all better. That's the way it had always been. Tom will make it better. Tom will do something. Tom will DO. Jimmy was the one that never did anything, the one stricken with inertia. Too much thinking, Tom had always said. Not enough thinking, Jimmy would say of him. And maybe Jimmy had been right.

The call had come early in the evening. McVay had just finished eating and was washing the dishes. The apartment was new. He had moved out of his mother's house only a few weeks before. Most of his things were still there. Now he had his own place, but it didn't seem right. It was as if he expected the call. At the hospital, minutes later, he had found nothing that he could do. He left his mother sitting outside the emergency room where they had taken Jimmy's body. It didn't take long for Tom to find out what had happened. One of the guys Jimmy had been running with told him everything. Two hours after he heard of Jimmy's death, he had a St. Louis address scribbled on a piece of paper and stuffed in his jeans jacket.

Their mother was exhausted, and the grief had silenced her, but she watched with a deep dread as Tom brought the duffel bag from the garage and began to go through the gear inside. She made him self-conscious. He wondered if he'd known all along that the duffel bag had been put away only temporarily. Did she realize the homogeneous nature of the equipment in the bag? He remembered hanging it up on the wall in the garage and laughing, saying it was just a bag of souvenirs. Now the boots and fatigues and binoculars and flashlight and backpack lay spread on the floor, along with things that he was sure she could not identify.

He had already said that he would be gone for a while, that funerals were not for him. Now working calmly, steadily, he realized that his mother had not seen this in him before; she had only seen his pleasant side, never the cold calmness that he'd learned. It was something he couldn't help. The best he could do, after he'd gone to the closet in the den and taken out the military .45 and rifle, was to turn to her, smile like the boy she remembered, and tell her not to worry. It was a silly thing to say, one boy dead and the other checking the bolt of his .45. But she didn't know everything McVay had found out. She didn't know that Jimmy had lost not only his life but also $25,000 that had belonged to her. That was what McVay had meant when he told her not to worry. A silly thing to say. Even if she had known, it wouldn't be the money she would worry about. She wasn't the kind to worry about her future; she worried about her boys.

Now McVay was in Kansas and trying not to think about his mother and brother. The decision had been made, and now he had no choice. He was getting tired. It was after three o'clock in the morning, and the darkness of the Kansas night had made him sleepy. There was a motel sign at an exit, and he took the turn. An old man finally came to the office door in a robe. McVay tried to be nice, but the man was mad at being awakened, so Tom took the key and left as quickly as he could. He was tired, but once he was inside the room and lying on the bed, sleep wouldn't come—he was *too* tired. Finally he pulled on his pants and jacket and stepped out into the moonlight.

It was a beautiful night, and even though the country was barren, the motel had a nice setting. Hills of grass rolled up behind the building, and in front the land was flat as far as the moonlight would let him see. There were no lights on in the motel. McVay wondered if anyone else was there that night. There were a few trees, obviously planted by man—they were in straight rows and all of uniform size. McVay stepped around the corner of the motel, and a cat leapt from where it has been hiding, pressed against the back of the building. It ran out into the moonlight in elongated bounds, and McVay was captured by the rhythm of the movement. He watched its silhouette rise from the ground as its shadow moved out to the side, then the two smashed together as the cat touched the ground and made another lunge for the trees. The silence of the scene gave the illusion of slow motion, and McVay watched, amazed at the beauty of such a simple thing. He had no idea that a cat could move like that. It did not occur to him that the cat was terrified, running for its life.

But an instant before a second shadow caught the cat, McVay shuddered, thinking, Yes, God, yes. The shudder came before he knew what he was watching. The cat and shadow made one last, sideways leap and met at the exact point where the owl claimed its own shadow and nailed everything to the ground. There was one long terrible hiss and a low moan. McVay stood motionless, still hidden in the shadow of the motel. The hiss and the moan were the only sounds he had heard since he frightened the cat. He moved out toward the owl, picking up a tree branch as he started to run. But the owl flew away before he was within twenty feet of it. It rose toward the trees, slow and silent, hanging on floating wings. McVay looked at the branch in his hand, wondered what he had intended to do with it, and threw it down. The cat lay dead where the owl had left it. There was no blood. Just the cat, lying dead as if from old age. There was nothing McVay could do. He could feel the owl watching from the darkness as he took the cat by the tail and carried it back toward the motel. He found some boards to hide it under and put several bricks on top of the boards. Then he looked back to where the owl had flown, and suddenly the night came alive. For the first time he heard the night sounds that had been there all along. They forced him back into his room, and he stood for several minutes watching the night through the crack between the curtains. He imagined the owl, twisting its head, drawing long black talons across the bricks, scratching at the boards that hid the cat.

Part Two

For a week the prairie will be soft. The antelope and deer will stay on the highest ground, and the pickup trucks will not leave the graveled roads. Then it will start to dry, and by August the ground will be as hard as the bentonite flats four miles north of the town. The easy times are about to begin on the prairie. The young fox and coyote pups will be out soon, and then the other young of the year will start to move. They will be preyed upon. The fledgling birds, young prairie dogs, gophers, mice, and the flightless ducks will nourish the predators that can catch them. Then, for the strong will come the mule deer fawns and the antelope kids. And for the very bold, the crippled and savage, there are lambs and calves in abundance. The animal population of the prairie is beginning its annual explosion. Within the next four weeks the population will quadruple, then it will begin its decline again. It is a time of plenty, a time of movement and some confusion. The pine-covered hills that form a backdrop for the prairie in this part of the world loom dark in the distance. They are sterile in comparison to the prairie; the timber is deep and black. Since the beginning of time the hills have supplied a place of refuge for the hunted, an impregnable sanctuary for predators of all kinds.

Mel Simmons knew all of that. He knew perfectly well how the prairie worked. As Chief Forest Ranger for the Black Hills National Forest, it was his business to know. It was always busiest at this time of year. People begin to move on the prairie in the spring, and they notice things. They see the predators competing with man as he tries to beat a living out of the land. It seems wrong to them and they are all experts. These self-proclaimed experts know predation when they see it and are quick to jump to conclusions. In his first seven years as chief, there had been two sightings of tigers, three lions, six bears, eight wolves, three crocodiles, and a hyena. All of the sightings proved to be other animals, or, in most cases, overactive imaginations. Simmons made it a rule to be polite to people who called about such sightings. He talked to them gently, agreed where he could, reassured them, and when the conversation was over, forgot the whole thing. But this time it was different. Of all the nonexistent animals, wolves were the most commonly seen, probably because, to most people, they look a great deal like coyotes. The old gray wolves of the prairie, long extinct, did not in fact look like coyotes. They were twice the size of a big coyote, and unlike coyotes, had no qualms about killing the property of man. They were used to preying on buffalo, and when the buffalo were gone, they turned naturally to sheep and cattle. Simmons had seen four in his early life. They were tall, light-colored animals, very bold. He had been in on the very end of their extermination. They had been difficult to trap. The process of selection had bred into them an almost supernatural cunning and a haughty contempt for man. But they were all gone now. The very last one had been trapped in the 1920s. The prairie was a much tamer place now than it had been back then. There was nothing really wild out there anymore.

But something had the people around Medicine Springs stirred up. There had been a dozen sheep kills in that area since the end of winter, and the ranchers were starting to bring political pressure to bear. Simmons had sent his top coyote man out, and still there were sheep lost.

The man had trapped several coyotes but apparently not the right ones. It was calving season now and the ante was up. Cattle prices were high, and if ranchers started losing calves, it would be at a price of over a hundred dollars a head. Then the pressure would really start. Somehow it had gotten into their heads that it was a wolf that was doing the killing. Simmons and everyone else in the department knew that it couldn't be a wolf, but the public could not be convinced. It reminded him of the farmers who plowed every square inch of the land, then insisted that Simmons do something because hawks had killed all the pheasants. They never thought that they had destroyed the pheasants' hiding place. Their minds could not be changed. Simmons was sure that it was a coyote doing the killing around Medicine Springs, or more probably a group of coyotes—maybe a bitch feeding her pups. But someone had gotten to a state senator and Simmons had received a call. The senator, too, was convinced that it was a wolf and suggested that Simmons send an expert out there to look the situation over.

The senator made a good point. He said a good wolfer could settle the thing by looking at a couple of kills. He could tell the people exactly what was doing the killing and show them why it wasn't a wolf. It made sense, and Simmons would have done it weeks before the senator called, but the fact was that there was no one on his staff, except himself, who had ever even seen a wolf—certainly no experts. He had seen four wolves, and that had been in some very remote mountains of New Mexico forty-one years ago. He knew everything there was to know about wolves that could be learned from books, but Mel Simmons was smart enough to know that wouldn't help in the field. As a kid he'd gone to work for the old United States Biological Survey, which had since been changed to the Bureau of Sports Fisheries and Wildlife. He'd been eighteen and wanted to be a trapper. He'd helped set the traps that had caught the four outlaws. But he had made none of the decisions. Bill Egan had made the decisions. He had been the Survey's top wolfer and been all over the western states trapping wolves. He knew them, could think like them, and had caught more than anyone.

By the time Simmons met Bill Egan, the wolves were almost gone. He was trapping only renegades then, the ones no one else could catch. Those wolves were legends. Their kills numbered in the hundreds. They were given names like Three Toes, Whitey, and Bags. They were a super race. Average wolves were no challenge for Egan. He, too, had become a legend. When the wolves had all been killed, Egan dropped out of sight, like the animals themselves.

But that was all history. Simmons knew that he had to come up with at least a token wolfer. Simmons was old now; pressure was something he didn't need. His first thought was to bring someone in from upper Minnesota or Canada where they had a few of the smaller, tamer timber wolves still around. But that was useless; there weren't even enough left to give anyone the experience to really *know* wolves. He thought of sending a biologist from the university, but a biologist's word would not mean much to the people of Medicine Springs. That would be his last resort. Finally he tried a long shot. He tried to track down Egan. He knew that he'd be old now, maybe even dead, but if he could still move about, he'd have authority enough to ride around and look at a couple of kills and tell the people that it was not a wolf.

Egan had been hard to find. He had been let go from his job in 1944, had served in the states during the war, but Simmons could find nothing on him until he showed up in a V.A. hospital in Pueblo, Colorado, in 1946. Then he slipped out of sight again until he turned up in Springfield, Illinois, living with his daughter. Simmons found him alert and eager to take a look at a few kills. When this wolf idea was out of everyone's head, Simmons would send a couple of airplanes out there and hit the coyotes hard. That would make life a little easier for the lambs and sheep around Medicine Springs and would get the ranchers off his back.

It was politics. The whole thing was politics. Simmons was tired of trying to keep everyone happy. He was tired of people's happiness taking precedence over sound wildlife management. But he was almost done. A few more years and he'd be gone, retired with a good pension. He didn't need a controversy now.

Boyd Knutson was one of the ranchers who had had sheep killed. His boy, Harmon, told him that there wasn't any reason to get excited, but Boyd was nervous. Sheep were only sheep. Cattle were something else. Boyd Knutson had never seen cattle prices so high, and high cattle prices meant losing cattle was costly. The price of dead cattle came right off the top of the income sheet. But Harmon promised he'd either catch or shoot whatever it was that was getting the sheep before the calves started to come. He said he'd have it before the state had a chance to get its expert all the way out there. Boyd wasn't as sure as his son. He had seen a lot of sheep killed in his lifetime, had caught up to a few of the culprits himself, and knew that sometimes it wasn't as easy as it seemed. But he certainly didn't discourage his son. The more people out there with guns and traps the better, as far as he was concerned. He had already lost over $500 worth of stock, and the calves would be starting to come any day. If he lost any of those, it would mean big money.

So Harmon spent a lot of time on the prairie. He was twenty-two years old, drove an old Dodge four-wheel-drive pickup, and carried his .30-30 in the back window. Harmon was a tall boy, six feet two, and starting to fill out. His Scandinavian blood showed through: his hair was blonde, and his eyes were very pale blue. He was a good shot with the .30-30, a hard worker, and he'd ridden a few saddle broncs.

It was Harmon who first said that what was killing lambs around Medicine Springs could be a wolf. Everyone else simply assumed that it was a coyote and that, like most coyotes, it would make a mistake and would be caught. But Harmon pointed out that if it was a coyote, it was ranging farther than any coyote he had ever heard of. There had been kills all over the county, some of them twenty miles apart. If it was a coyote, it had to be more than one. When the state trapper arrived, he was full of answers. He said that he'd have the killer in four days. Harmon went with him and learned a lot about coyote trapping. They caught five coyotes in those four days, and the state man was pleased. He stayed two more days and picked up one more. Everyone assumed that was the end of it. But the day after he left, Jim Martins lost six head of ewes and lambs in one night. It was then that people started wondering if Harmon Knutson might not be right. The people around Medicine Springs started calling whatever was killing their sheep a wolf. The Thursday after Jim Martins's sheep were killed, the *Medicine Springs Recorder* came out with an article listing the kills that had taken place that spring. The article referred to the culprit as a "Killer Wolf."

After Junior Bailey read the article in the *Recorder,* he slammed it down on his desk. "Shit," he said, and he swiveled in his chair, taking his hat from the top of the gun case. Junior was the sheriff of Lindon County. He was thirty-seven years old and serving his second term. The job would be his as long as he wanted it because he was a good sheriff. Some people didn't like him, but everyone agreed that he was honest, fair, and didn't put up with nonsense. The *Recorder* article was nonsense.

Bailey pulled the hat down as he came out of his office and into the sun. Spitting out the splinters of a toothpick he'd been chewing, he walked down the street to the *Recorder* office. Jerry Stockton, the owner and editor of the *Recorder,* was sitting at his desk. He started talking as soon as he saw who it was. Bailey held up one hand, but Stockton didn't stop. He was going on about several things at the same time, and none of them were of any interest to Bailey. The sheriff kept one hand in the air and raised a finger from the other hand to his lips. He made a loud hissing sound, and Stockton stopped talking and looked up as if he was startled. Bailey pushed his hat back and sat down on the corner of Stockton's desk.

"Good morning, Jerry," he said.

"Morning, Junior," Stockton answered.

"Now what did you go and write a ghost story for? Couldn't you find enough news?" Bailey asked. That set Stockton off again, but Bailey quieted him with hands in the air. "Jerry, don't you know that that sort of thing can make everybody spooky? There's twenty grandmothers in this county that can remember being scared of wolves when they were little kids, and every one of them is sitting in her kitchen right now reading that dumb article of yours." He hushed Stockton before he had a chance to start. "You see, Jerry, these people don't have a lot to do. That kind of story gives them something to do. They start worrying and running around the countryside with guns, shooting at noises."

Stockton made a face. "Oh, Junior, you're always jumping to conclusions about the effects of things."

"And you're always jumping to conclusions about the facts."

"Bull! The facts speak for themselves. Didn't you read the article?" Stockton said.

"Afraid so," Bailey said. "I should have shit-canned it."

"Oh, now you're going to get nasty," Stockton said. "I suppose you're going to tell me that I can't write any more articles about the wolf. Well, I've got news for you. I'm no fool. I know you can't silence me about the wolf."

"Jerry"—Bailey leaned over the desk and patted his cheek—"there is no wolf." Bailey stood up. "And stop writing like there was." It was then he noticed old Johnny from the hotel, standing quietly in the corner, his eyes wide. "Oh," Bailey said, "morning, Johnny."

"That's a violation of my rights," Stockton said.

"Oh, shit, Jerry."

"It is. We have the right to a free press in this country."

Bailey pulled his hat back down as the rush of words came at him. He rolled his eyes and turned toward the door. "This is how it works," Stockton was saying. "A small paper like this finds a story, and pretty soon the public becomes aware, and the word gets out. Then a big paper finds out and sends a reporter out here from the East somewhere."

Just before Bailey walked out, there was a pause in Stockton's tirade.

"Go ahead, then," Bailey said quickly, "scare the hell out of a bunch of kids and old ladies." He looked closely at the man and gritted his teeth. "And if there's trouble, you'll be as responsible as anyone." He pulled his hat down hard and closed the door firmly behind him. He tried hard not to slam it and resisted the urge to scream when he was out on the street. But, looking down, he saw that his hands had rolled themselves into fists. Stockton and he were friends, but Stockton was from a big city somewhere. Sometimes he let his education and big words carry him away. About twice a week their meetings ended like that. He could still hear Stockton exercising his jaw at the closed door.

Old Johnny, standing in the corner, was getting an earful. Bailey pulled his hat lower against the sun. He crossed the street to the Top Café.

When Bailey stepped into the street, the old man, who had been listening quietly, turned to Stockton, then moved closer to the desk. He looked at Stockton and smiled as if the two of them had a secret. "'Spose the *New York Times* will send someone all the way out here?" he asked, and smiled a toothless grin.

It was ten o'clock. Half the town was in the café rolling dice for coffee. Bailey was waved to the main table where the banker and the grocer and three ranchers were shaking dice from the café's leather dice cup. Bailey was handed the cup and rolled them out as he sat down. A pair of fours. He picked up the other three dice and rolled again. No fours. He tried again. Still no more fours.

Harmon Knutson had not read the newspaper that day. When the mail had been delivered, he had been probably five miles across country from the ranch house, a mile north of where they had lost lambs two weeks before. The pickup bounced slowly over the broken prairie and sank in slightly where the sun hadn't gotten at the spring moisture. He'd been out every morning and most evenings since the lambs had been killed, looking along the ridges and in the washes for some sign of what had happened that day. It was all mixed up. Harmon knew that he was not good at reading the prairie. It irritated him. It was like reading a book that had fallen into a puddle. Everything seemed to be there, but blurry. He had read it wrong somewhere and trapped two badgers the first two days. But he had reread, and backtracked, and put himself in the killer's place, and tried again. The night before, he had felt confident and made a set in a cut bank just like the state man had done. He had worn gloves, knelt on a canvas, spooned the soil out with a graden tool, placed the smoked and waxed trap carefully, and sifted the soil back on top. Then he had carried the extra soil away in the canvas and dumped it a mile from the sight. The next day the signs had been clear: coyote tracks up the gully and in a circle around the trap; then, clearly, the tracks of a coyote backing up; and centered perfectly on the traps' trigger pan, the coyote's stool.

He had four more sets out. They were along the ridge just ahead of him, and he had a feeling this time. There was a temptation to speed up, but he knew that he must take the bumps slowly. There was no rhythm to the prairie. It could vibrate a vehicle to pieces at any speed faster than a crawl. But still he was in a hurry. One of the sets should produce. They were just off a well-used game trail and baited with freshly killed chickens. Harmon, putting himself in the predator's place, could not resist them.

He had to leave the pickup at the bottom of the hill, but he took his rifle from the window rack before he started up the grade on foot. The first set was back of a washout that had dried already, and the dirt was soft and dusty. The trap was buried under fine sand, and the chicken was buried, though not fully covered, between the trap and the crumbly bank. Harmon looked at it carefully from thirty feet away. He could see no tracks, nothing seemed disturbed. The next traps were set under small bushes, and the bait was hung from branches. Nothing had bothered them either. The fine sand covering the traps was exactly as he had left it the day before. It was impossible to tell it from any of the other soil within a hundred yards. The sets were good and would have worked if they had been in the right place.

The last set was made like the first, in a washout with the bait partially covered, and from the time Harmon had set it, he had felt something special about it. He was superstitious about things like that and had purposely arranged it so that he would check that set last. As he approached, he caught a strange odor on the breeze coming up the washout. It was a smell he could not categorize. It made Haron feel odd, and had his nose been as good as the animal he was pitted against, he would have smelled the odor bursting from his own pores.

The earth around the set was no longer smooth where he had buried the trap, and the chicken had been partially pulled from the ground. He did not go too close but could see the exposed chain that held the trap secure to the stake he had driven into the ground. His eyes followed the three-foot chain to where it disappeared into the tangle of sagebrush to the right of the set. Checking the magazine of his rifle, he brought the stock halfway to his shoulder. He moved toward where the animal lay hidden in the brush. It would not be dead. It would be hiding, hoping that he would pass by, and ready to fight if it had to. He approached head-on, walked into the opening and directly toward where the animal waited. He was still six feet away when the sagebrush exploded. Harmon leaped back, bringing the rifle to his shoulder at the same time. The chain snapped tight, and Harmon, the odor thick now, stood sighting down the snarling, lunging throat of a medium-sized red fox. It pounded against the chain trying to get at him.

Harmon didn't shoot, but stood frozen by the savageness of the normally timid animal now forced to fight. The eyes were insane, and from between the needle-sharp white teeth came guttural sounds drowned in saliva. The lunging was convulsive and jerked the heavy chain taut with a rhythmic crack. This was not a coyote, certainly not a wolf. It was not the killer of his father's sheep. It was a wild animal no bigger than a good-size tomcat, and standing over its fury, hearing and smelling it, Harmon Knutson was terrified.

From the top of the washout, where the wheat grass grew tall, the boy could be seen to step back from the fox. Now the smells were mingled. It was no longer simply the smell of a wounded fox. Now it was the smell of fear and the smell of man. The smell of an easy meal was gone, and the one smell to be feared was thick in the air that rolled gently from the washout. The boy brought the rifle up to his shoulder again and found the fox in the sights. In the wheat grass at the top of the washout the wet, heavy breathing stopped. The moment seemed to last forever. And in the silence, after the shot had sounded and the fox had died, the boy thought he heard a noise behind him. He turned toward the sound of what might have been a bird passing behind him, or an independent gust of wind, or a large mammal slipping away through the wheat grass at the top of the washout.

Rapid City is a small town on the edge of the Black Hills. There is very little industry there. The only two industries, in fact, are agriculture and tourism. The agricultural industry feeds off the prairies that lie to the north, east, and south of Rapid City. The tourist industry feeds off the Hills. Built into them are tourist attractions. The wildlife, streams, trees, and pristine beauty have never been enough to hold the tourists. So the people have built dude ranches, animal parks, taffy shops, antique car museums, simulated Indian villages, and imitation gold mines along the highways that wind through the Hills. There is even a complete replica of the Flintstones' city of Bedrock. People can park their trailer homes and Winnebagos there for the night. There are people dressed up like Barney and Fred and Dino to amuse the children. At the height of the tourist season the cars are literally bumper to bumper along the highways in the Hills.

And Rapid City supplies it all. The interstate highway that connects Rapid City with the eastern part of the country is lined with carloads of tourists in the summertime, and thousands of semi-trucks bring the supplies down that highway to keep it all running. Almost everyone who comes to Rapid City and to the Hills stays only a week or so. There are the people who work in and around the town whose ancestors came from the countries of northern Europe. And then there are those whose families have always been there. There are people in the Black Hills who believe that it is the center of the world, that it is a holy place, and that the evil that now takes place there is only temporary. These people see the Black Hills as a good place. It is only in the last one hundred years that the good has slipped away. They mark the beginning of this change to about the time Custer discovered gold in the Hills, about the time the treaties that gave the Hills to them forever were broken.

James Lebeaux was one of those people. Yet he was not angry. He didn't hate the white men the way some of the Sioux did. He was a patient man, believed that time would straighten things out, and that violence was not the way of the Hills. But he also believed that pressure must be applied when possible. Now he was driving up Highway 44 from the Pine Ridge Reservation toward Rapid City. This was one of the cases where pressure was necessary, a peaceful takeover of a campground in the Black Hills. The object was to reiterate their rightful claim to the Hills and point to the injustice of the broken treaty. As always, Lebeaux's hope was that cool heads and education would prevail, but he was aware of the danger. Many were more angry than he; many lacked his patience and wanted the Hills returned immediately. And there were those who were only interested in the violence that these situations could foster. There was always a risk.

He passed the airport and noticed a jet airplane landing. Only a few miles north was a U.S. Air Force base. The plan was to station B-1 bombers there in the next few years. Lebeaux shook his head. B-1 bombers in the holy land of the Sioux? It was not right, he thought. Then he reminded himself, Be patient. What is a hundred years to the Hills?

The Hills. They rose up ahead of him, underlining the western sky with their blackness. A haze hung over Rapid City and Lebeaux watched his hills through it. A hundred years ago Rapid City did not exist. The creek that the town is named after was a favorite camping site for his ancestors. But there hadn't been a camp there for a long time. Lebeaux wondered what his ancestors would think of taking over a campground in the National Forest. He looked past the town, up into the Black Hills, and tried to figure out where the camp would be. But his perspective was off. He was disoriented and could not tell one peak from the others. It was best to concentrate on his driving. He pushed the accelerator down and sped along Highway 44, past the convenience stores and gas stations, the hamburger joints and the junkyards, toward Rapid City and the Hills beyond.

Lindon County had a board of commissioners but it seemed to Junior Bailey that he was the only county official who ever did anything. He knew for a fact that he was the only one who was responsible for anything. Everybody else was either on civil service or just donating their time. Nobody else took it on the chin like he did. It was as if his office had a one-way valve on it; the buck could come in, but there was no way to send it on its way. Junior Bailey didn't care about that, didn't mind covering for all the county business—it was all in the job of sheriff. What he did mind was being the state and federal errand boy. The people of Lindon County could get along fine without the state and federal governments, and if the big boys in the capital and Washington thought it was so important that they be represented out here, why didn't they get someone on their payroll out here to handle things? There was no state or federal official for eighty miles. No district attorney, no patrolman, not even a game warden. Bailey wore all those hats. And he wore them for nothing.

He was not a big man, but if you were to ask one of the local drunks how tall he was, they might say six four. They might say he weighed two forty, but he was five ten and weighed one ninety-five. He just seemed bigger sometimes—like when he'd stand at the door of the Oasis bar and call out someone's name, or when he took you by the arm and led you down the street. He was maybe a little overweight, but nobody teased him to see if he could run them down. It was assumed that if Bailey ever started to run after someone, they would never get away; it was assumed that he would always get his man, even if it killed him. He had a voice that could stop a bank robber cold. It was directional. He could point it at an individual and make him shudder. It was not that the voice was so loud; it was the quality of the voice. It penetrated. It came from somewhere in his thick chest and out through his heavy neck and jowls, creating shock waves. Bailey could turn it off and on according to his mood. When something made him angry, he could whisper it through the telephone, which is exactly what he did when he got the call from the Forest Service asking him to see that Bill Egan was made to feel at home. There was no possible way that Junior Bailey could make a federal trapper feel at home in his county, and he told them that, but he did say that he could get him a room. After listening to the way that Bailey said it, the voice on the other end of the line seemed grateful for the room.

The old-timers said that the Oasis was once a fancy place. They said that when the railroad was still running from Rapid City there were a lot of people who stayed there. The rooms were usually all occupied, they said, and the medicine baths were full. But the whole town was bigger then. Now there were never more than one or two guests staying at the Oasis at a time; the baths were run down and only used occasionally. The bar and the hotel were the only things that were still functioning. The lobby was dusty, and the portraits on the walls were so faded, no one knew who they were anymore. It was dark in the lobby, and the three old men who were permanent residents of the hotel watched television from musty old chairs set back in the shadows. It was the only place left in town that rented rooms.

Bailey tapped on the service bell. Finally Johnny came out from behind a curtain that hid a tiny kitchen where he was having his dinner. He nodded to Bailey. "Sheriff," he said.

"Hi, Johnny," Bailey said. "I want to rent a room for a few days, starting tomorrow."

"Wife throw you out?" The old man's eyes sparkled, and his face stretched into a toothless smile.

"No, Johnny, it isn't for me. It's for a fellow working for the Forest Service," Bailey said.

"Going to try a little trapping, huh?"

"Guess so, Johnny."

"He'll never catch him," the old man said.

Bailey didn't want to talk about it. He grunted in a sort of agreement with Johnny.

"Now what's the name?" Johnny asked.

Bailey dug into his pocket and came up with the note that he had scribbled down. "Egan," he said.

The old man looked up from the register.

"Bill Egan?" he asked. Bailey looked back down at the paper.

"Yea," he said. "Who's Bill Egan?"

"Bill Egan is still kickin'?" Johnny said. "By God, I take it back."

"What?"

"Egan just might catch that son of a bitch."

"Who's Egan?" Bailey asked again. But the old man wasn't listening. He was thinking. Bailey leaned over the desk and made sure that Johnny was looking at him. "Who's Egan?"

"You don't know?" Johnny said. Bailey shook his head. "Bill Egan is an ace-high wolf trapper." The old man nodded sharply to show that it was a fact. "Maybe the best ever," he said.

Bailey nodded back. He wanted to get out of this conversation. He waved toward the register to hurry Johnny up.

Johnny was mumbling. "Wolf trappin' son of a bitch," he was saying.

"Johnny," Bailey said, "that thing out there ain't no wolf, and you know it. All the wolves are dead. There haven't been any for years. Now you're going to stir people up with your stories about wolves and wolf trappers."

"You'll see, Sheriff. Things are poppin' around here. People coming from all over. Place will be full in a week. You watch. They'll be coming here for the action. I'll bet the word's spreading already."

"That's great," Bailey said. "Just great." He stared past Johnny and out the picture window. The sky was darkening, the wind was coming up.

"And think of it," Johnny said. "Bill Egan is coming in tomorrow."

"Shit, Johnny," Bailey said.

Johnny showed his gums in a smile. "He's a wolf trapper, I'm telling you. You young guys don't know nothing," he said, and glanced to where the sheriff had been. But Bailey was gone. He was out on the street watching the sky boiling into thunderheads over the prairie. It was going to rain.

Bailey pulled his hat down lower and hunched his shoulders, pushing his fur collar farther up his neck. The lights of Medicine Springs were slowly popping on. Should have been home an hour ago, he thought, as he walked slowly up the street toward his car. A pickup was coming from the other direction. Bailey had seen it before. It was an old green Chevy with a dented rear quarter panel. In the cab rode three young Indians. They stared at him coldly as they passed, and Bailey stared back. He had nothing against Indians personally, but he didn't like to see them in Medicine Springs. These were the new breed of Indian—Sioux, he suspected. They were nothing more than political activists. They were young and frightening to Bailey. They were angry at the government and at white men in general. Bailey watched the pickup pull up to the Oasis. Angry for good reasons, Bailey thought, but they still frightened him. They claimed the Hills were theirs and had set up an illegal camp in there somewhere to protest. The FBI was watching it, and Bailey had heard that there were some rough characters involved. But that was in the Hills. He stayed out of them, there was plenty to do out on the flats. He watched the three disappear into the Oasis, then, feeling a sudden urge to get into his car, hunched his shoulders higher against the building wind and continued down the street.

Once behind the wheel, he felt suddenly comfortable. He turned the ignition on. Deliberately, he pulled the eight-track tape, Faron

Young, from the player mounted below the dash and put it back in the black plastic case on the seat beside him. A quick look over his shoulder and Bailey reached into the glove compartment. He pulled out a tape that was still in the cardboard package it came in. It could have been a new tape except that the printing on the package was worn off from fingers taking it out of and returning it to the glove compartment. Bailey took one more look around and slipped the tape from the package. He slid it into the player and put the car in drive at the same time. The interior of the car burst into sound and a drowsy smile came to Bailey's face.

This was Bailey's secret. Maybe his only secret. It was not a secret so much because Bailey was ashamed of this soft spot of his, but more because he knew the embarrassment that would be generated should he be found out. His friends and neighbors would suspect the manliness of any man who would listen to that sort of music; there would be jokes and catcalls from regulars at the Oasis; and, generally, Bailey's image would suffer. That part would be bad enough, but Bailey could handle that sort of ribbing. Then there would be the embarrassment of explaining why he enjoyed this tape so much. As he drove in the car that night, he could not think of a single thing to say in its defense. He could not think of anything to say about it, period. The truth was, Bailey wasn't even sure he could pronounce the name of the man who composed it. *Chopin*. It looked easy to pronounce, but Bailey was leery of foreign words. It was much easier to just listen to it and not mention the tape to anyone.

The car cruised at an even, soundless seventy miles per hour. Bailey's eyes were half-closed, his head swayed nearly imperceivably. Opus Twenty-five, he thought. My favorite.

Most of the Black Hills belong to the U.S. Government. They are public land, administered by the Forest Service. They are laced with asphalt roads for tourists and mud roads for loggers. There is a winding asphalt road that climbs south from the edge of the town of Medicine Springs for seven miles. It changes to gravel then, in the trees, and another road crosses it. This road is mud and takes off toward the southwest. This is the part of the Hills where the trees grow thickest. There were tire tracks on the mud road, and they led to a cold-water stream and a clearing where six automobiles were parked. Sitting on the cars and standing around the small clearing were a dozen men and women, mostly Sioux. They were talking about the Black Hills, but they did not call them the Black Hills. They used the Indian name, *Paha Sapa*, and reminded each other that they belonged to them.

One of the women was Katie Running. She had just returned from Minneapolis and was joking with some of the men she had grown up with on the reservation. It was a surprise for her to find people that she had known because it had been nearly ten years since she had left South Dakota. When she went, she had said that she would not be back, but she had been eighteen then, and reservation life had seemed unbearable. She had always been a beautiful girl and had thought that would take her places. But after ten years in Minneapolis, she learned that life was hard everywhere. The dull depression that had always been there grew worse, and in the last few years she found herself thinking about going home. The camp in the Black Hills had seemed a perfect excuse. Though she thought the camp was important, the truth was that she had begun to slide in Minneapolis. It was a rough crowd, and she found herself drinking too much. She lost a couple of jobs and was broke. There was action in the Black Hills, so she hitched a ride with another Indian and came to have a look.

Katie joked with one of the men, who was struggling to put up a tent beside the others. "You really going to sleep out here?"

"Damn right," the man said and turned his full attention to the tent.

"You guys will last about three days," she said. "You aren't Sitting Bull, you know."

The man did not look at her, and she realized that she had hurt his feelings. She began to say something more but was stopped by the sound of a car coming down the road. They all stopped what they were doing. There was some fear of the police. But the car was an old white Chevy Impala with a smashed front fender. One of the men ran out to meet it, his braids flopped wildly. "James," he cried.

The car came to a stop, and James Lebeaux stepped out. Katie was amazed. Another familiar face. It had been a long time, but Katie remembered James as a friend of her family's. She had heard him and her father talking late many nights at the kitchen table in the old house on the reservation. Her father was dead now, but James Lebeaux, though older, seemed quite lively. He hugged several of the younger men and threw his head back in a big laugh.

Then he saw Katie. When he walked over to her, she felt embarrassed. He reminded her of her father, and had he known the way that she had been living since they last saw each other, she would have expected a lecture like one her father would have delivered. But James Lebeaux smiled broadly.

"Little Katie Running," he said. "All grown up."

Katie could only manage a hello. It was strange that he made her feel shy. She was not a shy woman.

"I didn't expect to see you here," he said. "You here for good?"

Katie shook her head. "No, I'm not much of a camper." And it struck her that what she meant was that she would not feel comfortable without a house. Maybe she needed a town too, bright lights. Maybe she needed a bar.

"It won't be camping for long," Lebeaux said. He looked around at the others. "We're here to stay."

Everyone nodded and the jokes began again. Katie nodded too, but she felt very uncomfortable. Suddenly she wanted to get away. Find a place to stay, a way to make some money. This camp made her nervous. It was as if these people wanted something from her.

The drive up through Nebraska and the corner of South Dakota had been something different for McVay. He'd never seen the prairie before. He tried to ignore the feeling he'd gotten, even laughed at himself for the nervousness, and told himself that this was the heart of America. But still he felt exposed. He drove for hours without seeing any trees except those scattered along some intermittent streambeds that wound themselves across the sea of grass.

He had very little to go on, just the name P.J. Billion. The fact that Billion grew and dealt in marijuana would do no good. McVay did not know what he was getting into, but he was sure that Billion's business would be kept secret from inhabitants of Medicine Springs. And as he got closer to the town and the Black Hills, he realized he would have to create an excuse for being there. According to his map, Medicine Springs was tiny, and he was sure that his presence would not go unnoticed. He didn't want Billion to know there was a stranger in town before he found him. He wanted Billion to be the one who was surprised. McVay felt a tenseness, and he knew it was because he was in a new country. He was unfamiliar with the land and the people, and that meant he could not plan and would have to play it by ear.

It was late afternoon when the Black Hills came into sight. They were still fifty miles off, but true to their name, they rose on the northwestern horizon absolutely black. It was not until the road jogged close to them that McVay realized the blackness came from the fact that the Hills were covered with tall dark pine trees. He was traveling along their eastern side then. There were still a couple of hours of light left in the sky, and McVay studied the map. There was a way to get to Medicine Springs by going through the Hills. It didn't look much farther, and unless the roads were worse, it shouldn't take more time. McVay turned to the west before he got to Rapid City and headed up into the Hills.

The road climbed, began to twist, and McVay realized that he had made a mistake. It would be impossible to make good time on roads like this. But he was committed by that time and drove on, letting himself fall back into thought. He thought about growing up in Ohio and how different it was from this country. He thought about high school and his one year of college. And he tried to think about that four-year period after he'd flunked out. But it was hard for him to focus on anything concrete that happened during those years. He remembered boot camp as if it were a dream. Like so much of that time, nothing seemed real. He remembered in colors. Yellow for the feeling that filled his nights, red for the pain in his head and the shame, and green for sickness and confusion. And then there was pride—it didn't have a color. He remembered that clearly. "If you're going to do it, you might as well be good at it," someone had said, but now he couldn't remember who. The road wound on, and McVay realized that he hadn't been paying any attention, and now he didn't know where he was.

Pride. It was a matter of making yourself proud, of being the best. And he'd found himself in places where it had paid off. Or, at least, it had kept him alive. But now the memories closed the lids on themselves, and all McVay could feel were the colors again. The road made a few more twists as it climbed, and he could see that there was something up ahead. He had been passsing more and more cars, and there was some kind of parking lot to his right. It was half-filled with cars and trucks. Maybe a couple hundred vehicles in all. He was behind a line of cars now and, as if of its own accord, his truck followed them into the parking lot.

There were men in uniforms standing along the walkway where the people crowded, coming and going. And flags. Flags, he supposed, of every nation in the world. It was getting dark now, and from the tone of the crowd McVay got the impression that something was about to happen. They funneled up the walkway and onto a huge observation deck. The sign on the building that stood along the entire length of the deck read VISITORS CENTER.

McVay had been in a kind of daze, from the drive and from trying to think about those four lost years, but now he was awake and decided he had gone far enough without knowing where he was. He walked up to one of the uniformed men. Before he got a chance to ask his question, the night burst into light, and the crowd sighed. The public address system squealed with the sounds of a partriotic song that McVay had heard before but could not place now. When he turned, the entire mountain was lit up. His mouth actually came open. He stared at the giant, ghostly white heads carved into the granite mountain. It was Mount Rushmore. McVay recognized the faces, but just then he could not remember who they were.

The road fell and twisted on its way toward Medicine Springs from the monument, and now the pavement was poor and the pot holes were frequent. McVay could see that Medicine Springs was on the back side of the Hills, out of the crush of tourist traffic. The first indication that the town was ahead was a sign at the side of the road.

THE OASIS
MEDICINAL BATHING
SOOTHING TO THE AILMENTS OF THE BODY
BAR, CAFÉ, LODGING, PUBLIC BATHS
MEDICINE SPRINGS, S.D. 7 MILES.

The sign was small, falling down, and very old, but McVay was interested. He'd wondered if there would be a place to stay in Medicine Springs. The road was bad. It began to fall and weave, and then it leveled off. Just before McVay saw the lights of the town, the road turned to crushed stone, then to poor asphalt, and for the first time, McVay noticed that the ground was wet, as if there had been a good rain there that day. The road he was traveling was obviously the main street of the town. He could see lights, but not a glow of lights. No friendly municipal halo like regular towns. Each individual light stood out clear and stark. Six of them. McVay could count them. When he saw the Oasis, he smiled and shook his head. It was a big enough building, the main part was three stories, and behind, sticking out into the prairie somewhere, there was another section, only one level, long, windowless, and dark. One of the town's six lights turned out to be a sign: BUDWEISER—plain and simple as the country. He pulled the pickup to the hitching rail beside the other automobiles, two Fords and a GMC, all pickups and all with sporting rifles in the rear windows.

Three cowboys and a bartender swung their heads to watch McVay come through the door. An elk head hung over the bar. Stuffed birds and animals of every description covered the walls; above the two doors marked BUCKS and DOES were twin stuffed eagles. The jukebox blinked dully as it wailed something foreign to McVay; above the pool table the light was pushing Dr. Pepper. McVay's smile came as he nodded to the cowboys who refused to look away.

A pleasant-looking young man with short black hair stood behind the bar. He looked at McVay and smiled. "What can I get you?"

"Just a beer. Whatever you have." McVay swung up onto a bar stool.

When the beer came, it was a brand he'd never heard of. He poured it slowly into the small glass the bartender slid toward him.

"The sign down the road said lodging," McVay said as he watched the head build in the small glass.

"Yea," the bartender said, "there's a couple rooms above the main building that they still rent out. You'll have to talk to Johnny. He takes care of that end of it." He nodded toward a door off the bar. "Probably find him through there."

"Thanks," McVay said. Then, "What about the medicinal baths?"

"You're about twenty years too late." The bartender smiled. "The baths are still here, in the back." He motioned with his head and right hand. "Johnny might give you a key. They aren't really open, though."

"Did they really soothe the ailments of the body?"

The bartender laughed. "Don't know about that. I'm sort of new around here. They haven't been open since I've been here." McVay liked the bartender. He seemed to be a little different from the others, who sat around the small tables in cowboy hats and boots. The jukebox started up again; the lights on the pinball machine twinkled, and McVay ordered another beer.

Two hours later McVay stepped into the lobby of the Oasis. The first thing that came to his mind was oldness, then a little touch of grandeur as he scanned the office, and finally neglect. The couches and chairs were leather, but worn. The woodwork was oak and looked rich, but it, too, had seen a lot of use. There was a fine gray dust over everything. Probably from the prairie to the north of town. McVay tried to imagine the town when the wind blew. He stepped up to the old desk and tapped the bell, waited for a minute, then tapped again. Finally, from behind a curtain, he heard a noise. He tapped the bell again, and an old man's head popped out from behind the curtain.

"I thought I heard that bell," the old man said as he stepped out, adjusting his suspenders. "What can I do for you?"

"I'd like a room."

"You would?"

"Yea."

"What are you doing here in town?"

The question stopped McVay cold. It was the one thing he'd hoped no one would ask until he'd had time to look around. The old man was pushing a registration card at him. He took the card casually and tried to think. "Just business," he said.

"Business, huh?" The old man looked hard at him, as if he might know what the business was, then raised a finger and pointed at him. McVay tightened but kept on filling out the card.

"Say," the old man said. "I'll bet I know." McVay did not look up but pushed the completed card toward the old man. He was trying to think of something that would be believed. "I was in the *Recorder* office the other day. I'll bet you're a reporter from the East." He snapped his finger. "Come to write about our wolf." He chuckled at his own perception. "You from the *New York Times?*" He looked right at McVay. He wanted an answer.

McVay gazed calmly back. "No," he said. "I work for the *Toledo Blade*."

"The what?"

"The *Toledo Blade*." McVay didn't know anything about the *New York Times*. If he was going to be a reporter, he decided it should be for a newspaper he'd at least read. "One of America's really great papers," he said and picked the key from the old man's hand.

"Room three?" he asked, looking at the key.

"Yes, sir, room three. Top of stairs, then left."

McVay couldn't help smiling to himself as he climbed the old, dusty stairs. He could feel the old man's stare of amazement on his back and knew that he was elated to have a reporter staying at his hotel. But as McVay opened the door, he wondered if he could pull it off. It was a great excuse as long as nobody questioned it. And what was that about a wolf? The ramifications of what he'd done began to sink in as he swung the door open.

The room was amazingly clean. There was a sink in the corner, a straight-backed wood chair, and a cheap veneered dresser. The ceiling was ten feet high, and in the center hung a light bulb on a cord with a plastic shade. While the whole thing could have been the set for a Hollywood western, it was not unlike an R-and-R room in Tokyo. He walked to the sink and read the sign hung over it: NO COLD WATER IN MEDICINE SPRINGS. There was only one spigot.

McVay flopped onto the bed. The mattress was soft, but he'd be able to sleep on it. He rolled onto his back and immediately Jimmy came into his mind. He wished he were back in Toledo, wished he'd never gotten into this. Then he glanced at his watch. Eight-fifteen—ten-fifteen back in Ohio—and he began to wonder what he was doing here. It occurred to him that he might be crazy.

Billion came into his mind then, and he began to plan just how he'd find him, and what he'd do when he did. He could be down in the bar right now, he thought. Maybe Billion was a regular. Maybe he could get this over with in a couple of days. But maybe it would take longer. And if it did, he'd have to use his newfound cover as reporter. Immediately he became troubled. He didn't even know what he was supposed to be reporting. He'd have to find a way to get caught up on this story without making a fool of himself.

As if thinking about it had made it happen, there was a knock on the door. Out of instinct he was on his feet moving toward the door before the knocking had stopped. "Mr. McVay? It's Johnny. The fella that checked you in."

The old man smiled toothlessly as McVay opened the door. In his arms was a stack of books and newspapers. He nodded to McVay, and McVay stepped aside, letting him come in.

"I know your editor probably made you read all the articles in the *Recorder*, but I brought them up anyway. I had a couple old books, too. See, I'm kinda interested in the old prairie wolves." He hesitated. "I'm pretty sure that's what we got here. You know, I might not look it, but I'm old enough to remember when there was lots of them." McVay reached out and took the stack of books and newspapers from the old man. "Heck, I remember chasing Old Lefty on horseback in the 1920s." McVay was looking at the books. They were just what he needed. "That was when old Bill Egan was trapping in Montana, just before he went South."

McVay looked up at Johnny. The intensity of the green eyes made him stop talking. "Thank you, Johnny," McVay said. "This will make it easier for me." Johnny smiled. "Are you an expert on wolves?" McVay asked.

"Well"—Johnny looked away grinning—"maybe not an expert."

He straightened up and tapped the stack of books in McVay's hands. "But I read all them books."

"Good. If I have any questions, maybe I could ask you?"

"Sure."

"And maybe I'll be quoting you in my article as an expert." McVay looked calm, but inside he could hardly believe he was talking like he was.

"Great," Johnny said. The grin was even wider now, and he stood awkwardly for a moment. "Well, you probably want to dig into that stuff." McVay nodded. "I'll leave you alone," Johnny said as he backed out the door. McVay continued to nod until the door shut on Johnny. He walked back to the bed and laid the books down. He shook his head as he thought of the old man and looked at the pile of books and newspapers, then he walked to the window. The wind was whipping the trees across the street. He could see a few people in the café.

The trees were just budding. Back in Toledo the trees had their leaves already. A woman came out of the café. She stood for an instant, letting the dusty wind wash her face, then moved to the largest of the cottonwood trees and, using its trunk to stop the wind, lit a cigarette. Her hair was very long and very black. It tossed in the wind. The woman was gone before McVay could see much more, but he saw that she was young, good-looking. He supposed she was Indian. He thought about going to the bar again, going down to talk to that bartender, maybe finding out something about Billion, but the books lured him to the bed. He sat down and opened one of them. There was a photograph of a wolf. McVay was impressed. It was impossible to tell how large the animal was by the photograph, but his chest looked much wider than McVay had imagined a wolf's would be. He had always thought that wolves were like large mangy dogs. This picture was of a sleek, long-coated, friendly-looking animal, with hair around its neck that made him look like he was wearing a collar. Above that collar was a much more intelligent face than McVay had imagined. It was a very old picture and reminded McVay of an old tintype, but the picture was good. He could see that the eyes of the animal were light. McVay was sure that it had been a tame wolf, that a wild wolf would never stand for such a picture. But the animal was standing with one leg toed in, and when McVay looked close, he could see that the leg was twisted. A steel trap clung to the leg below the twist. The caption read simply, "Lobo."

McVay's curiosity had been aroused. He flipped through the book and found a glossary. The term *Lobo* was a catchall. It meant wolf, but more specifically, the gray wolf, which was also called the buffalo wolf or prairie wolf. At the end of the explanation was a short sentence, "Now extinct." McVay thumbed back to the beginning of the book. The copyright was 1944. He lay down on the bed and started from the beginning. Outside his window, the wind tumbled the prairie air.

By the time Tom McVay had finished the first chapter, he knew that the lobo wolf had fed mostly on buffalo for eons, that they were large wolves, and that originally they had no fear of man. He stopped reading for a moment and listened. The wind had blown into a gale, and he felt slightly disoriented.

The trees along the Grand River bent at a forty-five degree angle in the gusts, and along the south bank one of Boyd Knutson's heifers was standing out of the wind. She had pushed through a fence that afternoon, and her instinct had brought her to the south bank of the Grand. In that country, the breaks, which are dry most of the year but fill to overflowing for a few days in the spring, form ridges, and when the wind is just right, the moist air funnels up them between the ridges and spreads out as the country flattens. The air flows in the opposite direction from the run-off in the spring. A few miles from the river, on the grasslands, the wet air disperses in the wind and comes across the prairie several feet thick. That night the air carried the smell of the heifer and had just reached the grassland when Tom McVay turned the page that explained that when the buffalo started disappearing, the wolves turned to the domestic livestock that was taking their place on the prairie.

Knutson's cows and heifers were up close to the buildings because it was calving time. The next four weeks would be hard work for the Knutsons. They would check the cattle five times a day. If the animals had trouble calving, the men would help. If they were careful and had a little luck, 90 percent of the cows would have good healthy calves. If they had bad luck, they might only get 80 percent. Much lower than that and they would be in for a rough year. They were waiting for the calving to start. But nothing had happened up to this evening.

The heifer was the first to feel the contractions in her womb and, driven by something in her that was primeval, she had forced her way out of the fence and gone in search of solitude. She found what she needed beside the river. But her scent and the scent of her coming calf had fanned out, and to some on the prairie it was strong, pungent, the smell of life itself.

McVay read about the local attempts to control the wolves by ill-equipped settlers and finally by a bureau of the federal government. It was in that section of the book, under the heading "U.S. Bureau of Biological Survey," that McVay saw a name that he had heard before. It was in a caption, under a picture of a serious man in baggy pants and a tall cowboy hat. But it was not until the heifer's magnetic scent had been sorted out from all the other smells coming across the flat lands that McVay remembered where he'd heard the name. Johnny had said it. "Bill Egan," the caption read, "Last of the great wolfers." McVay threw back his head, smiled, let out a chuckle at the ceiling, and from the top of one of the breaks that led upwind toward the river, where the heifer had started having her calf, came a tortured sound that has made man, from the beginning, hold tight to his weapons, move closer to the fire, and stare wide-eyed into the night.

Harmon Knutson heard it, though he wasn't sure. He was checking the cattle for the last time that night, and what he heard, he told himself, could have been the wind that was blowing then with a hint of rain. He did not notice that the heifer was gone, moved toward the house, and did not switch off his flashlight until he reached the porch. He turned back and faced the night from the porch, listened, but heard nothing more.

The heifer raised her head from the pains of birth. The calf was nearly born. She stood slobbering and exhausted but held her head up, facing where the gully rose gradually toward the prairie. The rain was coming now. It felt good there out of the wind, and suddenly the pain was gone. The calf was born, but the heifer still was not at ease. She turned immediately and licked at the afterbirth. She cleaned the calf and nosed it to its feet. She wanted it to move. She tried to keep it on its feet, but the calf wobbled, wanting only to lie down. Finally she gave up, stood over her resting calf, and watched the blackness around them.

McVay had finished leafing through the book about the lobo wolf. It had interested him, but now he stood at the window of his room watching the cottonwoods again. It was raining. He wondered where the woman had gone. Without the light from the café the street would have been perfectly black. The rain clouds covered up any stars that might have shown. The wind roared.

The heifer did not hear the movement the way she should have, but she sensed it. The rush came from the rear, and she spun too slowly to stop it. The calf bellowed, and instantly the heifer could smell fresh blood. She wheeled to where she thought the danger was coming from. She lowered her head, wide-eyed, and charged a few feet into the darkness. But the bellow came again from the calf. When she pivoted, she knew that the calf had been injured severely. She snorted and bawled, made a few more short attacks into the darkness, and finally stood still over her dying calf. The whimpering of her calf below her made the mother frantic, but she could not know where the danger was. She stood ready, her head down, breathing the blood smell of her newborn calf. The wind blew, the rain continued, and for a long time nothing happened. Then, from the side, the heifer was hit. It struck with the force of an automobile. She was bowled to the ground. She bellowed and righted herself. The hot pain hit her again and stuck. There was a low rumbling close to her ear. She flung her head, and the weight was gone, but the pain hit her in the flank, and she began to run. Then there was no more pain. She stopped just out of the gully where her calf had been born and had died. There were no trees to shelter her. The rain seemed cold. It mixed with the warm blood that ran from her neck and thigh, and her bellowing was lost in the wind.

Tom McVay spread his arms out in the clean sheets of the bed in the upstairs of the Oasis and listened to the storm. The feeling of being off balance came to him again. The rain was pounding against the window. Powerful, unfamiliar forces moved outside. Now it was raining hard. It reminded him of the ten months he had spent in Vietnam. The storm surprised him. He hadn't expected rain.

To Bill Egan, only the small things had changed. The highways were paved now. There were more cars, more buildings, less sage-brush. But the big things were all the same. The land still pitched and rolled; there were still ridges and washouts; and it breathed, pumping the air from one part to the other. He saw it all. It was like he'd never been away. The night before, camped along the highway, he had got-ten wet, but like the prairie, he was dry by nine o'clock. He looked at the sky as he drove. There was more rain coming.

Egan thought of all the rain and clouds that he had seen coming across the prairie. He thought about his daughter and how she had never understood any of it. Then he thought of how he had never been able to explain, even to himself, what it was about. A clutching feeling came to Egan. It was like something was pushing on his chest, telling him to forget it, to go home. But Egan had no home. He had never had a home, never had anything that mattered—or if it mattered, it had never lasted. It was always disappearing, like Egan's dreams of walking toward something that he doesn't recognize but wants and needs, only to have it move out of reach as he tries to touch it. The feeling in his chest worried him, and he thought of taking one of the pills the doctor had given him. But in a while it moved up from Egan's chest and forced against his throat. For the first time since he had started out, the thought occurred to him that there might really be a wolf. Through some slipup in civilization, one wolf, a strange, intelli-gent individual, might have lived through it all, might have found enough solitude to survive, and Egan would come face to face with him. He looked around again. The little things had changed. He won-dered if the existence of wolves would be considered a little thing.

Medicine Springs was familiar to Egan. He'd never been there, but still it was familiar. There was one main street and several dead-end streets that branched off it. He drove slowly, taking in everything he could. The town was very small. Had it not been for the rain, the streets would have been dusty. At the end of the main street, in the distance, the Black Hills rose high and dark. Egan studied them. The Hills had a reputation for magic, holiness, and evil. Egan nodded his head. It didn't surprise him really. Yes, he thought, this could be the place.

He had spent the previous afternoon with Mel Simmons, and Mel had told him what to expect. He talked about Medicine Springs as if he had forgotten that Egan had spent half his life in towns like that. Simmons was getting fat. He smiled most of the time. But when he talked about Medicine Springs and the kills that had taken place there, he shook his head and looked hard at Egan. It embarrassed Egan to know that Simmons was thinking how old he was. Egan wanted to tell him that he felt good, that he felt up to doing a day's work like he used to. But he didn't say anything. He listened.

"Now, Bill," Simmons said, "this job is as much public relations as it is fieldwork. People want us to do something about those kills, and they won't be happy until we send a wolfer out." Simmons waved Egan toward a chair, and they sat down. "What's important is that the people out there in that country think that we're doing our best to take care of them, which we are."

Egan nodded. He had never really liked Simmons. But years ago he had only been another kid working for the U.S. Biological Survey. He'd had no power then, and so Egan had never thought much about him. Now, behind a desk and in charge of an entire national forest, it was different.

"I know that you understand this kind of situation, Bill. All you have to do is go out and look at the kills they've got and tell the people that there isn't anything to worry about." Simmons leaned over the desk at Egan. "What do you figure, Bill, coyotes?" He said it as if he was sure himself, but Egan could see that Simmons wanted him to say the impossible. He wanted him to say it could be a wolf.

"Hard to tell," Egan said, and was going to leave it at that, but Simmons looked at him, waiting for more. Egan went on. "Could be bobcats," he said. "Or, in this day and age, even a dog gone wild."

Simmons's smile came back. "Well," he said, "you'll know if you see a couple of kills."

Egan nodded. "Yes," he said, and that seemed to make Simmons feel good.

When he was talking to Simmons, it didn't seem real. But now, as

Egan drove down the main street of Medicine Springs, it was very real. These were the people whom he had worked and lived with most of his life. He had almost forgotten how a stranger stuck out to them. There was a lady walking down the sidewalk who stopped completely and stared at him. He could see a face appear at the window of the bar. Once again Egan got the feeling that only the small things were different. He had the feeling that it had all happened to him before.

He pulled close to the curb in front of the sheriff's office. Simmons had told him that the sheriff was cooperating with the Forest Service and that he should start there. Egan stepped from the pickup and into a puddle left from the night's rain.

The sheriff's door was locked. Egan checked his watch. It was nine-thirty. The sun was bright in the sky now, but clouds ringed the horizon. Egan climbed back in the pickup, careful this time to miss the puddle, and went down the street to the Oasis.

There was a little man waiting behind the desk. When he saw Egan, he came around to meet him. "You Bill Egan?" he said.

Egan nodded.

"Got your room all ready, Mr. Egan. The sheriff checked you in." Johnny took his bag.

"Where is the sheriff?" Egan asked.

"Office right up the street," Johnny said.

"He's not there."

Johnny looked at the clock above the desk and shrugged his shoulders. "Must be trouble somewhere," he said.

At seven o'clock that morning a stocky, tough-looking character was at McVay's door. McVay, wide-awake from when he heard the footsteps on the stairs, peered carefully over the chain lock on the door, the .45 in his hand out of sight of the man standing outside.

"You Tom McVay?" the stranger said.

"Yes."

"Newspaper reporter?"

"Yes. Who are you?"

"Sheriff Bailey, Lindon County." The .45 came up. "May I come in?"

McVay saw that Bailey was friendly. "Sure." He shut the door, hid the pistol, put on his pants, and opened the door.

Bailey walked past him, took off his hat. "I figured I'd come and get you and save us both the trouble of you trying to find Knutson's and getting lost and me having to go find you. Not to mention the fact that I don't want you out stirring people up." McVay was staring at the sheriff, trying to follow.

"Look, McVay, you seem like a nice guy. Let's get things off on the right foot. I know you got a job to do, so do I. We'll be better off if we work things out together. Now I can't figure out why people in Toledo, Ohio, would care about anything out here, but you newspaper people don't always make sense. I've had some experience with you press people, and I don't like some of the shit that you pull off."

"You talked with Johnny?"

The sheriff nodded. "Get your clothes on. You got a story to write. I'm going to see that you get the facts straight."

"What facts?"

"The attack. If you'd get out of bed at a reasonable time, you'd find these things out."

"The wolf."

"No wolf, McVay. Get your clothes on, and I'll show you."

McVay started putting the rest of his clothes on. The sheriff paced. McVay wanted to stop the masquerade. It could easily go too far. He wanted to find Billion and didn't particularly want the sheriff to find out who he really was. But the book that he'd read the night before was still vivid in his mind, and curiosity began to work on him. "What happened?" he asked.

"Coyotes killed a calf," Bailey said.

And curiosity killed the cat, McVay thought as he buttoned the last button of his shirt. Bailey flopped his hat on his head and pulled it down over his eyes. "Come on," he said.

The ride out to Knutson's ranch took forty minutes. They went north out of town on the asphalt highway and turned west onto gravel. They followed that road for twenty miles, then turned south again. "Now we're on Knutson's ranch," Bailey said. But it was still ten minutes before the outbuildings came into sight. They were tucked down behind a solitary butte that rose from the prairie like a fist and protected the buildings from the north wind. There were some trees around the house, but short and gnarled. They looked like ash trees to McVay, but they were dwarfed, so he could not be sure. The house was red, wooden shingles, and the buildings were all metal.

Three men came from the largest building. "The old one with bushy hair and mustache is Boyd Knutson," the sheriff said. "The young one is his son, Harmon, and the other is Doc Sheen, vet out of Bell." McVay nodded. They parked beside the pickup trucks in the yard.

"Morning, Junior," Boyd Knutson said.

"Good morning, Boyd," the sheriff said. Then, "Doc, Harmon." McVay stepped up but wasn't introduced.

"We got it again last night," Knutson said. "Son of a bitch, Junior, if we lose cattle, this thing's going to get rough."

"What happened, Boyd?" Bailey asked.

Knutson motioned for him to follow, and all five men went inside the building. It was dark inside, with only four sections of green plastic letting in light from the roof. Knutson pointed into a wooden stall. "Whatever it was," Knutson said, "had a pretty good hold on her." Bailey looked into the stall, then back at Knutson. "Doc here says she must have had the calf about the same time."

McVay eased over to the stall and looked in. His eyes were adjusting to the light. "No sign of the calf, though?" Bailey said. Knutson shook his head. McVay could see the heifer standing in the stall. She was pacing, very nervous. "Where'd it happen?" the sheriff said. McVay kept watching the heifer and listening to the men. He could see nothing wrong.

"Don't know for sure," Harmon said. "I found her standing outside the fence this morning, but no sign of nothing." Just then, the heifer turned her other side to McVay. He could see well now. A large flap of skin had been sewn back in place on her neck. Her whole left side was stained with blood, and fluid oozed from the hole where her eye had been. "I backtracked her, but ran out of tracks 'cause of the rain," Harmon said. McVay looked at the boy who was speaking, then back at the heifer. But she had turned again and looked perfectly normal.

"Well, hell," Bailey said. "I don't know what to tell you."

"When is that trapper supposed to be in?" Harmon asked.

"Any time," Bailey said.

"Well, get him out here as fast as you can," Boyd said. The sheriff nodded. "And make out some kind of report, Junior. I'm going to try my insurance out on predator kills."

"Shit," Junior said. And they started back out into the sunlight. McVay took one last look at the heifer in the stall. She was standing still now, staring at the men, one good eye and the raw fleshy cavern on the left side of her head.

McVay stepped into the Oasis bar, and the bartender raised his hand to greet him.

"How's it going?"

McVay nodded. "Strange place," he said. "I'll have one of those beers I was drinking last night." He moved in between two bar stools and reached into his back pocket for his billfold. As he did that, he turned slightly and noticed that the clouds were building again to the west.

"Does it rain every night here this time of year?"

"Guess so. This is my first spring in the country, but last fall she dried out pretty good." The bartender rolled his eyes. "I mean she really dried out—dust so thick you couldn't breathe."

McVay looked out the window again. He could see the Black Hills in the distance. They held his attention. Looming over the prairie and the town, they looked unnaturally dark, ominous. The bartender's voice brought him back.

"Johnny tells me you're a reporter."

McVay's head snapped back. "Yea, Tom McVay from Toledo, Ohio." He held out his hand.

"Traverse Best. I guess I'm from here, now."

They took each other's hand, and the grip pulsed back and forth, testing a little, subconsciously assessing each other, recognizing and filing it in the part of the mind that does not speak.

"Old Johnny really gets around, doesn't he?" McVay said.

"Yea, talks a lot, but harmless."

McVay felt that this man might know Billion, might be able to tell him something valuable. But before he could begin to question him, the door swung open, and Jerry Stockton came into the bar. He walked right over to McVay and held out his hand. McVay's hand pulsed as before, but the pulse came back weak, and the information was not recorded.

"Jerry Stockton, *Medicine Springs Recorder.*"

"Tom McVay."

"*Toledo Blade*, right?"

McVay looked at Traverse Best.

"Johnny strikes again," Best said.

"Understand you're going to write a story."

McVay nodded, feeling trapped and wanting at least to go slowly.

"Well, I've done a lot of research and, of course, written several articles in the *Recorder.* I might be able to help you out." He paused, obviously wanting some response.

"Yes," McVay said, "I planned to get over to see you today, but the sheriff took me out to a cow that had been attacked."

"A heifer," Stockton said.

"Yes, a heifer."

"Out at the Knutson place."

"Yes."

"I heard about it and marked it down. The sheriff and I don't see eye to eye, so I don't get special treatment. But I know about everything you'll need for your story. You can ask me anything. I'm willing to talk about anything. I think this story needs national attention."

McVay could feel Traverse Best looking at him, waiting for him to ask Stockton some questions.

"Ask me anything," Stockton said.

"Well, why don't we start with what you know about the wolf."

"Oh, you must not have talked to the sheriff. There is no wolf."

"Well, what do you know about whatever it is that's killing livestock around here?" McVay said.

"Well, I know what it's killed so far." Stockton reached into his coat pocket and came up with a copy of the story he had written. He handed it to McVay. It was one that Johnny had given him the night before. "And I know how it kills them, and I know that he's a smart one." McVay was nodding his head.

"Twenty-one head by my count. Of course, that could be inflated by some natural mortality." And Stockton started into an explanation of just how a lamb is killed, and how it would be when cattle started to be killed. It all had a familiar ring to it. "And he'll make a mistake someday," Stockton said, "and someone will catch him, and then we'll put him right out there in the street on display."

"In the street?" McVay asked.

"You always hang the bad ones up and display them in the street," Stockton said as if everyone knew that.

McVay's interest was up. "Why?"

Stockton looked at Best and shrugged. "Tradition, I guess. Just always have."

"Did you ever see one hung up in a street?"

"Well, no. There haven't been any around for a long time."

"Yes," McVay said, "about forty-five years."

Stockton smiled. "You've been doing homework."

The two men looked at each other until Traverse Best stepped up and asked if they needed another drink.

"Not for me, Traverse," Stockton said. "But let me buy Tom one." He laid a dollar on the bar and turned to McVay. "Stop by the office. I'll give you a look at my statistics sheet."

McVay nodded. "Yes, I'd be interested."

When McVay turned back from the door shutting behind Stockton, Best was setting a new beer in front of him. Best shrugged. "He came from California," he said.

McVay poured a little beer into the glass. "What about you? What do you think about this wolf business?"

Best shrugged his shoulders. "Beats me. Some people have had some stock killed this spring." He shrugged again. "Could be lots of things."

McVay wondered what he meant. "Like what?"

"Oh, I don't know. There's all kinds of bad stuff out there." He motioned toward the Hills, then turned his attention toward cleaning the bar in front of McVay.

"I've got the name of a man here in town," McVay said. "You ever hear of a guy named Billion?"

Best's bar rag hesitated, then went on mopping the bar. He picked up McVay's beer and made a pass under it. "Yea," he said. "He's one of those bad things out there in the Hills. Where'd you get his name?"

McVay never hesitated. "My editor dug it up. Somebody said he knew these Hills and might be able to help."

"He knows the Hills alright, but I don't think Billion would help you much. He's pretty private," Best said, and moved down the bar to serve two men who had just come in.

McVay swung around on his stool and looked the room over. Like his room upstairs, it could have been a set for a movie. Even the patrons, three cowboys playing pool and the two Indians that Best was serving, looked like they'd been made up for the parts. He wondered why he was there, why Billion didn't live in Dallas or L.A. There was a feeling in this place—the bar, the town, the hills, and prairie, with their violent churning sky—that made him nervous; fear was part of it, but fear with a sense of wonder and expectation. He was excited, enjoying his charade, wondering what would happen next. One time he'd told a friend that nothing was any fun unless there was a chance you might get killed. But he'd said that as a joke. He didn't really feel that way. It was just that things happened that called for action. People came to him for all kinds of things. Friends asked for money, advice, and occasionally help. Like now, in a way, he was helping his brother. Jimmy could never take care of his own life; he had always needed help.

Suddenly McVay wanted to go home. He wanted to go back to his job in the tire plant, the apartment he had just moved into. There was a big furniture sale coming up, and he had planned to buy a new couch and maybe a reclining chair. Once he had the place fixed up nice, he thought he might start looking around for a steady girl. In a way he longed for that kind of life. But this thing with Jimmy had come up. Maybe he wasn't intended to be the stable homebody that from time to time he wished he was. At least that is the way that it had worked out so far. He had never been able to stay away from crises, in Vietnam, as a bouncer at a local club, and with stock-car racing. A woman had told him once that he was selfish, that he only thought about himself. She told him that he'd never have any peace and quiet until he could learn to see a point of view that was not his own. McVay did not understand that. All he knew was that he was tired of the situations he found himself in. Right now, he wanted to forget the whole thing, but he knew he couldn't. He swiveled on the chair again and held up his empty glass.

Best had been talking with the cowboys playing pool. When he brought the beer to McVay, he refused money. "Guess we'll find out what's killing that livestock," he said.

McVay tilted his head in a question.

"We got us the meanest, toughest, smartest, wolf-catching son of a bitch that ever came down the pike staying right upstairs."

Somehow McVay knew who it was. "Egan?"

Best's expression contorted. "How'd you know? I never heard of him."

Before McVay could answer, the front door swung open, and along with a gust of cold air came a woman and two men. McVay guessed them to be part Indian. They were hanging on each other and laughing. The woman, McVay saw instantly, was beautiful. He was almost sure it was the one he'd seen from his window the night before. He turned back to Best, hoping he wouldn't press him about Egan.

"They're having a good time," he said. "Is this it for nightlife in Medicine Springs?"

Best shook his head as he reached for a bottle to pour the three their regulars. "Some guys watch the paint peel, count horse flies, try to wear out the Conway Twitty records. 'Course they're not too imaginative." He grinned. "Me, I got a few patented moves."

"Like what?"

"You forget," he said, gathering up the three drinks in his big hands, "this place was once a mecca of extravagance and pleasure. Still is if you got the keys."

Then he was off to the table where the two men sat with the woman. As McVay's eyes followed Best he caught her watching him. There was something about the way she turned her attention back to the table that made it imposible for McVay to believe she did not want him to catch her. It crossed his mind that he should go over and talk with her, but he decided against it. It was late and, besides, he wasn't exactly on vacation.

McVay walked out of the bar. He wanted to get a little fresh air before he went to sleep. The wind was blowing in great gusts of force, first from one direction, and then from the other. He stood on the sidewalk outside the Oasis and watched an old gray cat come out from between the two buildings across the street. The cat sat and stared into the street much as McVay was doing from his side of the street. The first sign of human life was the lights of a pickup truck coming from McVay's left. The lights approached slowly, and the pickup moved close to the curb in front of the Oasis and stopped. The bed of the pickup was filled and covered with a tarp. McVay noticed that the license plate was from Illinois.

When the old man got out of the truck, he looked tired and weak. McVay watched him go to the back of the vehicle and pull an old leather satchel from under the tarp. The bag was heavy, and the old man struggled to get it out. McVay came out from the shadows of the building as the old man moved from behind the pickup. The weight of the satchel made him stagger, and McVay moved close and caught the handle. The old man did not let go of it, and for an instant they stood inches apart, both with one hand on the satchel handle and staring into each other's eyes. McVay was several inches taller and looked down at the frail, yet leathery, old face. When he had moved away from the building, it had been to help—he had felt sorry for the old man. But now, looking into the pale blue eyes, he was not sure that the old man needed help. The eyes were neither grateful nor defiant. "Thanks," he said.

McVay released the handle but could not turn his eyes away. Finally the old eyes seemed to release him, and McVay nodded. The old man straightened himself and turned toward the door of the Oasis. Egan was nearly inside when McVay realized who he was. He watched Egan go through the door, and as it closed, McVay stood alone again on the windy street. He felt an urge to go after Egan, to introduce himself, to ask questions. Instead, he stood in the dark and wondered if the old man who had just walked past him had really been the hero that he had heard about. He looked to be on his last legs, and McVay wondered what Egan thought he was doing. Did he really have one last hunt left in him? What would make an old man like that even care?

When McVay went inside, Egan was gone, and there was no sign of Johnny. Fatigued, McVay went upstairs to bed early, but he slept badly. He dreamed of St. Louis, his dead brother, and unreal things. There were black-haired women, some crying, some smiling. He recognized the woman from the bar. Then the women all turned Vietnamese. They watched him with dark eyes, and he reached out to touch the smooth skin of their faces. They walked past him in their tight blue jeans and smiled over their shoulders. But then he was in a cheap hotel room, making love to one of the women on her quick-change sheets. There was shouting in the street, and a one-eyed cow drank soapy water from a dishpan in the corner.

Downstairs in the bar, Traverse Best wondered how a reporter from Toledo, Ohio, had got P.J. Billion's name. He saw the look that Katie Running had given the stranger—a look that Billion would have given anything to receive from her. Then, as if thinking of him made it happen, P.J. Billion stepped through the door.

Best did not pull a beer from the cooler; he could see that Billion had already had plenty to drink. Billion sat down on a bar stool and fumbled for a cigarette. No sooner had he got it in his mouth and lit than it fell to the floor. Billion smiled, more of a snarl, and looked toward the floor. He did not see the cigarette though everyone else in the bar could. No one offered to help him. He lit another one, told Best to bring a beer. Then he began to talk about the Mekong River.

Billion shook his head while he talked. His eyes did not focus, but they gave the impression that he could see the things he was talking about. "You'd never know what it was like 'less you'd been here. We swam up and down that river three times in one night." He looked at the floor and paused as if he had forgotten what he wanted to say. Most of the people in the bar had heard it before. But he went on. "Towin' sea lockers, every one of us. Packed with a hundred pounds of C-4 and extra tanks. Little fuckin' bars of the stuff, pound apiece. One bar, blow your head off."

Then he dropped his cigarette again and knelt to look for it. Best noticed the bulk of his shoulders; he could see that the arms had been hard once and that they were still solid, a permanent souvenir of the times that Billion was talking about.

Billion lit another cigarette. "Did you ever . . ." he said, then thought how best to finish what he wanted to say. He pushed his hand against his cheek and jaw, letting skin and jaw slide to the side. "Did you ever get to feel it?" he asked. He saw that Best was not following. "I mean feel how bones give way when you hit someone just right?" He held a big hard fist up, more for himself to look at than for Best. "I mean when it's really right?" he said softly to himself.

He drank from the beer, and Best thought he might be done talking. "I love to fight," he went on. "And I ain't scared, and that's what makes me tough." He stared at Best, and for an instant Best thought that there was some kind of challenge in the slurred words. But Billion smiled. "*Pow!*" he shouted, hitting his hand with his fist. "*Pow! Pow!* 'Cause it's always the one that ain't afraid that wins. Right?" Best remembered that from his own boot camp days.

"Yea," he said.

"God," Billion shouted again. "You know," he said, smiling, "bones are really soft. It don't take much. I just love it." Tightening both hands into fists again, he put his head down and shivered as if he was remembering the taste of something sweet. Then he looked up. "That," he said, "and fuckin'." He put his hands out in front of him then, as if they were holding hips, and moved his pelvis back and forth and side to side.

Then he pointed to Katie Running, who'd been sitting in a booth with two men, trying to ignore what Billion was saying. "I'd love to fuck that squaw," he said.

All the Indians in the bar looked at him. The whites moved nervously in their chairs. But no one said anything except Katie. She got up and walked slowly to where Billion stood. Best watched Billion, and although he sneered and laughed, the eyes changed. When the slap came, he thought that Billion might cry. "You're a pig," Katie said, and Best moved between them. They both seemed relieved to have him intervene, and that was the end of it.

When Bailey first saw Egan at the hotel, he thought that there had been a mistake. The man who faced him didn't look like he would know a wolf if it was in the hotel room with him. He was thin, maybe five ten and one hundred fifty pounds. His eyes were blue and sunken in. But when they shook hands, Egan's felt somehow big and bony, with a hint of strength. Bailey said his last name and Egan said his. They stood in the doorway looking at each other, then Egan invited him in.

The room was filled with luggage. There were traps spread out on the bed, and a can of oil stood on the dresser. "Looks like you came prepared," Bailey said.

"Ready for anything." Egan smiled.

"Well, I don't know what we got," Bailey said. "I just came from the Knutson ranch, and something got a newborn calf and chewed on the heifer a little."

"When'd it happen?"

"Last night. But the rain washed away the signs. Knutson's kid looked for them. He couldn't tell nothing."

Egan went to the dresser and took a notebook from the top drawer. He jotted something down. "I'll go out there first thing tomorrow," he said. "How do I get there?"

"Well, it's a hell of a way," Bailey said. "You eat dinner yet?"

"No."

"I'll tell you how to get there over a sandwich. In fact, I'll run it all down for you. Then it's all yours. I quit," Bailey said.

Egan nodded. "Fine, Sheriff," he said, "but I'd appreciate it if you'd stand by."

"Stand by?" Bailey said.

"Just in case," said Egan.

"In case of what?"

Egan drew back. "I might need a little help, that's all."

Bailey looked at the old man, trying to see what he had meant. "Sure," he said, "I'm always around. That's my job."

"Good," said Egan. And the two men looked at each other trying to decide what the other thought.

"How about that sandwich?" Bailey said.

"Sure. You got a good place in this town to eat? I can't eat just anything anymore," Egan said.

Bailey smiled. "The café can fix up anything you want," he said. Now Bailey was confused: Egan was certainly an old man, but Bailey had the feeling that he could eat anything that was put in front of him.

The grayness was back in the sky when the sun appeared in the east. It wasn't cloudy; it wasn't that simple. In fact it looked like it might be a bright day. It was more of a feeling in Egan's body. It came from the crispness just before sunrise. But there wasn't a real sunrise that morning. There was nothing breathtaking. The sun was just there, tired, a dull yellow hole burned into the sky. In the west there were clouds, but wispy things, not like the rolling black thunderheads that Egan had seen the night before. It wouldn't rain now until afternoon, but there was dew. It lay like liquid skin on everything. The grasses, the sagebrush, the bare rocks, and the tiny cactus were covered with the dew. It was very thin and temporary.

Egan watched as he drove up the driveway to the Knutson ranch. He wanted to stop the pickup and move out slowly across the prairie making no sound. But he needed to talk to the Knutsons. They could save him a lot of time. He'd never been in this country before, and even though he felt at ease, he knew better than to start off looking for a kill without getting all the information that he could.

The lights were on in the house, and when he pulled into the yard, Egan saw someone glance out the window. Before he was out of the pickup, a young man was standing on the porch. He let Egan walk to the porch without saying a word. When they stood facing each other, the young man nodded to Egan and waited.

Egan pushed out his hand. "I'm Bill Egan," he said. "I'm part-time with the Forest Service. I came to look at your kill."

Harmon Knutson took his hand. "Good morning. We got a fresh pot of coffee on," he said, and motioned for Egan to lead the way into the house.

Boyd Knutson stood up from the table.

"This is Mr. Egan, Dad," said Harmon. "He's a trapper."

Knutson looked at his watch. "By God, you're on time," he said. They shook hands and sat down.

Egan had forgotten that there was coffee like that. It was black and almost thick, but by design. "Well," said Boyd, "I guess the sheriff filled you in. We've lost seven head of sheep, and now a calf, and had a heifer hurt pretty bad." Knutson paused for a sip of coffee. "Whatever it is is starting to piss me off."

Egan nodded. He liked these people. "I'll want to look at that heifer," he said.

Knutson nodded. "Harmon here will show you anything you want to see. As long as you're on our place, he's yours. You might as well take him. I can't get any work out of him while there's something out there to trap." He looked at his son and shook his head. "Hell," he said, "I'd be out with you if I weren't so old." Egan looked down at the table. Boyd Knutson was twenty years his junior.

The heifer didn't tell Egan very much. Whatever it was, it wasn't a cat, and he was already pretty sure that there weren't any mountain lions around. He knew that a bobcat wouldn't take grown cattle. So if it wasn't a cat, that meant that it was a canine. Everybody in the county knew that. "Where'd it happen, Harmon?" Egan asked.

"Don't know for sure. The heifers were penned up there by the barn, and she must have gotten out and had her calf somewhere else. I found her the next morning trying to get back into the pen."

"What night was that?"

"The night it rained."

Egan nodded, thinking back. "Which way was the wind blowing that night?"

Harmon thought for a minute. He turned, facing the pen, remembered the wind in his face when he came in from checking the cattle. "South," he said.

Egan looked out across the ranch. "What's the name of that river?" he asked, pointing to the line of trees in the distance.

"That's the Grand," Harmon said.

Egan squinted toward the river and sucked his cheek. "I think that's the place to start," he said.

"That was a pretty good rain. There won't be any signs left," Harmon said.

"Let's take a look anyway," Egan said.

Harmon never thought about walking to the river. He expected that the old man would want to ride in the four-wheel drive, but he didn't. He wanted to walk. And he walked very slowly.

At first Harmon thought that it was just that he was old, but as he watched him, he saw that Egan was moving slowly for a reason. He never talked, so Harmon held back on his questions and walked just behind him. They moved slowly across the prairie, soundlessly. Egan's blue eyes did not jump from obstacle to obstacle, they swept across the country rhythmically. Twice mule deer moved beside them, and when Harmon turned to point them out to Egan, the old man had already seen them and was looking farther ahead. They saw fox pups playing at the mouth of their den. They kept playing until the men were out of sight. It was as if, moving like that, they were invisible.

Before they left the buildings, Egan had gone to his pickup and taken out a rifle. Harmon had noticed it because he'd never seen one like it. In that country no one carried a scoped rifle. Scopes were for shooting prairie dogs from the pickup. The real shooting was done with iron sights. Scopes were too slow for a quick shot. But Bill Egan's rifle was mounted with a scope. It was a bolt action with a clip. There was a crescent moon inlaid on the cheek piece. Harmon had asked if he could see the rifle. It was light. It felt nice, but when he looked at the muzzle he was astonished. "It's a twenty-two," he said.

Egan took the gun back. "A twenty-two express," he said. "Bud Dalrymple made it for me. It's a seven-millimeter case, necked down to take a seventy-grain bullet." He handed Harmon one of the cartridges.

The case was bigger than Harmon's .30-30, but it was still a .22. "I'll stick with a little bigger caliber," Harmon said.

The .22 express swung with Egan's stride like it was part of his arm. The scope didn't seem to get in the way. Harmon had decided that he used a scope because his eyes probably weren't that good, but Egan didn't miss anything on the prairie. It was like being with a horse; when Harmon heard a sound, he would look up and find that Egan was already looking. He was a good old man.

They stopped on a rise above the river. The wind had been blowing from behind them, toward the river, on the night that the heifer had calved. "Is there a place to cross the river? Where a cow could cross?" Egan asked.

"There's a crossing right over there." Harmon pointed downstream a quarter mile. Without a word Egan headed toward where he had indicated.

The crossing was high but still less than a foot deep. Egan slowed even more when they got to the trees that lined the river. He stared at the muddy ground around the crossing. Then he pointed to a tiny dent in the mud. Harmon looked at it. It was only a dent. Egan walked down the river and found a broken limb. He dragged it back and laid it across the stream. He made his way to the other side. Harmon waded it.

"There," Egan said, and pointed to a track in the mud.

It was a cow track. "But that can't be the heifer. It rained hard that night," Harmon said.

"She would have crossed back in the morning," Egan said.

They were in the breaks now. It was warming up, and the wind was starting to blow. Egan watched the ground and kept going. Sometimes he would stop and make several circles around the point where he had stopped. Harmon stared at the ground. He saw nothing. It took an hour to travel a hundred yards upstream. They stayed right along the edge of the grass, and finally, from the top of one of the breaks, Egan pointed. "There," he said. And tucked down in the break, close to the river, on the south side of a thick stand of juniper were the remains of the calf.

Everything had been eaten except the head and feet. Egan did not stay long with the carcass. He saw that there were no good tracks, then faced north, where the wind would have been coming from that night. He turned one hundred and eighty degrees and looked over the country, then started up the break. Harmon scrambled behind him. It was clear that he wasn't supposed to talk, but he couldn't help it. "You're a hell of a tracker," he said.

Egan smiled. "There weren't any tracks the last hundred yards. You were right. The rain washed them away."

"You trackin' now?"

"No. Just going to go up there and look around. Why don't you get on that other ridge, and we'll just walk them out to the prairie? They'll probably come together out there."

"Right," Harmon said.

"Keep looking ahead of you. Something might turn up."

Egan stood and watched him go. Not a hell of a lot different, he thought, than Bill Egan fifty years ago.

Egan and Harmon Knutson had been split up almost an hour. They saw each other once in a while but most of the time worked alone. Egan stopped on a high spot to look the country over. The land fell away in sagebrush. A hundred yards ahead there was a stock dam, bulldozed out of the land, glimmering in the afternoon sun and wind. Beyond the dam were the Black Hills. Egan reached into the large pocket of his hunting coat and brought out a pair of binoculars. He scanned the countryside in all directions. As he looked south, over the ridges that marked the beginning of the Hills, he caught a reflection along the first line of pine trees. He focused the binoculars on a pickup. It looked like a white Chevrolet. The reflection had come off the chrome wheels. There was a man beside the pickup, and though it was too far to tell for sure, Egan thought the man was doing exactly what Egan was doing: surveying the land, looking for something.

Egan swung the binoculars around again, taking in the panorama. He put them back into his pocket and raised his head to breathe the air coming up at him from the dam. Beginning a circle toward the open prairie, he quickened his pace. There would be nothing to see in this area, and he wanted to intercept Harmon.

They met midway between, where the two ridges became prairie. Harmon held up his hands. He had seen nothing. They moved more quickly then, back down the draw from where they'd come, in the opposite direction from which the heifer's scent had moved that night, and crossed the river at the same spot they had crossed that morning. They were back at the ranch before the rain began.

They drank more coffee, and Harmon asked all the questions he had been thinking as they walked that day. He asked how Egan could do it. How he could see those signs and how he could keep going. Harmon admitted that he was tired. Egan said only that it took a lot of wandering around on the prairie, that he had fifty years experience.

Then Harmon asked him what was killing their stock. Egan told him that he didn't know. He said that to be sure, he needed a better sign than they'd found that day. "But you have an idea?" Harmon said.

"No, it would be a mistake even to make a guess," Egan said.

Harmon looked at him. "I think it's a wolf," he said.

Egan did not smile. "It's not likely," he said.

"Oh, I know all that." Harmon jumped up and went to the cupboard. He pulled out a stack of books. "They're extinct," he said and put a book down in front of Egan. "That's what the book says. But this book says it's possible, and this one tells how wolves act, and that's the way this thing is acting." Harmon looked embarrassed. "I told Mr. Stockton all about it. He printed it."

"I saw that," Egan said.

"Well, it's possible, isn't it?" Harmon said. Egan looked into his coffee cup. "Mr. Egan, this is a big country. It's as big as the ocean, and they're always finding extinct things in the ocean. So it has to be possible, doesn't it?"

Egan swirled the coffee in the cup. "Yes, Harmon, it's possible."

"Damn right," said Harmon, "and I'm going to get him."

Egan was forced to smile. Harmon was a rare young man, and Egan liked that kind.

Above the Indian camp to the south, deeper into *Paha Sapa,* there is a very gradual slope that burned a hundred years ago. It is a place where lightning hit a giant ponderosa pine one night in August when the forest was tinder dry. The old tree did not burn right away. But its smoldering branches tumbled into the dead, dry needles on the forest floor. There the fire began and burned wildly until rains that followed the lightning reduced the fire to isolated piles of smoldering undergrowth. All this happened a year before the white man's army scoured the Hills looking for the gold that they found. It was before the settlers arrived in violation of treaties, before the Forest Service began its policy of controlling fires, before the meadows began being overtaken by the forest growing out of control, before the habitat for wildlife began to diminish because of the homogeneous tree growth. The fire, one of hundreds that year, happened at the close of a million-year history of natural growth in the forest, at the close of the times when there were great numbers of animals using the forest, when birds that needed mature trees to nest in could find them, when the rabbits that need the edges of open fields with grass and brush had a home in *Paha Sapa*, when the deer could find both food and shelter, and when even the creatures who dwelt in rotten wood could thrive.

Now the forest was all the same; fire was not allowed, because *Paha Sapa* was a tree farm for the white man. It was all second growth, uniform trees, a sterile environment. The forest floor grew nothing; the canopy of trees held out the light. The rest of the forest was all like the gradual slope above the Indian camp where the four men were walking. The men were led by Robert Lance and were almost an hour out of camp, deep in the remotest part of the forest. They came within sight of a group of buildings set deep in the forest. The men knew the spot and did not step out into the clearing. Instead they continued to walk under cover of the trees for a quarter mile. They passed an area in a valley where the trees were thinned, and they smiled. They walked a while longer, then Robert Lance pointed to a flat place, clear of trees, and the men began to gather stones. They aligned the stones and piled them, using tree branches where they were needed. They labored for two hours, then stood back and looked at what they had made. Robert Lance nodded at the structure, and the others smiled. "It will work," he said. "Our Rushmore Arsenal."

McVay was up early. It had been his second night in the hotel, and he felt time slipping away from him. It was still too early to do anything in Medicine Springs. He stood at the window and watched the sun coming up at the edge of the Black Hills.

Sometime in the night it had come to him that today he must begin his search for Billion. He would use his reporter identity as cover. But the clock beside the bed told him it was six-fifteen, hours before he could do anything about Billion.

He walked back across the room to his bed, switched on the overhead light, and the bulb snapped harshly brilliant. One of Johnny's books was on the bedstand. He had skimmed through all the books and newspapers except this one, and so he sat on the bed and opened it. He leafed through, looking at the pictures: panoramas of mountains; a man surrounded by dead wolves and coyotes; and finally, jumping off the page at McVay, a picture of a man in a ten-gallon hat and old western clothes. It was taken on the main street of a western town. And hanging head down from a storefront behind the man was a wolf. McVay looked at the wolf's head. The tongue was out, and though the picture was poor, it looked like there was blood in the mouth. He looked at the caption under the picture. "Old Bobtail," it said, "and Bill Egan." McVay looked at Egan's face. It was somber, the jaw set in steel determination. But the eyes, and McVay squinted his own eyes to see, were not sure. The eyes were uneasy, confused, a little sad.

Five minutes later Tom McVay was standing on the street of Medicine Springs. Wanting breakfast, he headed toward the Top Café across the street. He was eager to find Billion, but he could feel curiosity building inside him and wanted to know more about whatever it was that was killing livestock around Medicine Springs. He wanted to talk to Bill Egan.

McVay hadn't had a breakfast like that since he was a kid. Bacon, six slices. Eggs, toast, coffee, and a short stack of blueberry pancakes. He sat enjoying another cup of coffee and looking out the window. Although he wasn't any closer to finding Billion than he was two days ago, he did not want to seem anxious. He ordered another cup of coffee. When the waitress came with the pot, she also carried a dice cup. "Things are a little quiet," she said. "I'll roll you for the jukebox." McVay turned in the direction she indicated. He hadn't noticed it before, but in the corner, beside the coffee machine, stood an ancient jukebox.

"Sure, why not," he said.

Two hours later McVay was still sitting at the table drinking coffee.

The jukebox played unfamiliar western songs which his money had paid for. He watched out the window as the little town went about its daily routine. Ranchers came and went from the hardware store, a few Indians sat on the curb in front of the Oasis. The sheriff, looking very busy, came out of his office and got into his car. McVay wondered if any of the people were Billion. And he tried to think of ways to locate him without drawing attention to himself. Traverse Best knew where to find him, but there was something about Best that made McVay not want to ask him many questions. The sheriff would know, but he wanted to stay as far from the law as he could. Maybe the post office. They'd certainly know. It was just a question of whether he could get it out of them without arousing their suspicion.

McVay forced himself to get up. He took his check just as he noticed Egan's old pickup stop in front of the Oasis. The bed of the pickup was full of metal and wooden boxes. Egan got out, and McVay watched the way he moved—easy, a touch of stiffness, but easy. He went to the back of the truck. Egan checked his equipment, tested the locks on the boxes, and McVay knew he had to talk to him. He reached in his pocket for money to pay the check as Egan turned toward the Oasis. He fumbled; wrong change. The waitress smiled, took his money, and made change. When McVay stepped out onto the street, Egan was gone.

At the same time, Katie Running was waking up in a ranch house just at the edge of the Hills. Her head hurt from drinking too much the night before, but not badly. She went to the kitchen and put the coffee on. Jake was asleep in the chair beside the stove, and his breathing whined a little like the perking coffee. The door to Pete's room was shut, so she assumed he'd made it to bed after she'd chased him out of her room for the third time. She laughed as she poured the coffee. Jake and Peter were brothers. Neither of them must have believed what she had said when she moved in. They had both tried the bed-creeping trick more than once. But they were good-natured about it, sometimes claiming they must have been too drunk to know, and so she didn't mind.

She took the coffeepot into her room and then came back out into the hall to get the telephone. With a little difficulty, she ran the cord around the corner and shut her door on it. Then she sat down on the floor with her back against the door and dialed a number.

"This is Katie," she said when the call was answered. "No, nothing happening."

She nodded her head as she listened. "Sure, there's a couple new guys around." She nodded again. "Yea, there's a creep who calls himself Robert Lance, and that white guy in the bar."

"I don't know," she said, and forced a tone of indifference into her voice. "I didn't pay much attention to him."

Then she held the phone with her shoulder and looked at her fingernails. "Yea. Yea. Look, I'm not going to do this forever. I'm just broke. You keep the checks coming." She nodded again. "Sure. Yea, I'll be in touch." She clicked the receiver down too hard. The night before had given her a headache. Her stomach felt tight. Maybe she should go back to bed, she thought. But the bed was a mess and just looking at it depressed her even more.

When she went to the kitchen to put the coffeepot back, she looked out the window over the sink. Behind the house the land rose gradually, and the trees of the Black Hills began. She had walked to the top of that hill the first day she moved in. The air had made her feel better. It would help her today, she thought. A little walk in the crisp air would clear her head. It was something she had been deprived of for a long time, one of the reasons she had returned to the Hills.

The *Recorder* came out on Thursday. Stockton set the type late on Wednesday afternoon. Sometimes it took until early Thursday morning to get a thousand copies run off. This Wednesday he got a late start. He'd been working on his editorial all day.

It started with a quote from the first governor of the territory: "The prairie cannot be settled while there are still wolves at large." This time Stockton didn't refer to the possibility of a wolf. He stated flatly that there was a wolf. It was strictly an editorial. There were few references to material that supported Stockton's views, and he knew that the sheriff would be in his office as soon as he read the paper. But Stockton was ready for him. He had proof.

Old Joe Standing Elk had come into his office Tuesday afternoon just before closing time. Had Stockton seen him coming, he would have closed early, pretended that he was not there. Old Joe was a sheepherder. Not a sheep rancher, an old-time sheepherder. He was full-blood Sioux, a rarity now, very dark-skinned and quiet. Unlike the new Indians, he was not rebellious. He stayed to himself, practiced the old ways, spoke the old language, and believed in magic. His home was a tent, and he moved his boss's flock across the prairie from April to October. He was reputed to have every vice of a sheepherder, and though Stockton had never really talked to him much, Joe was not the kind of man that he wanted visiting him. But there was one good thing about old Joe that was widely believed—being a full-blood, he did not lie.

The first thing that Stockton asked was who was watching his sheep. Joe told him that he had left them alone to come and talk; he could not stay long. Stockton knew then that there was something important on Joe's mind. He had never known him to leave his sheep.

"Two weeks ago," Joe said, "I read your article in the paper." He talked slowly, trying hard to get the English right. "I remember when there were wolves here and, Mr. Stockton, it was not funny." Stockton could see that Joe was serious. He seemed almost frightened. "I was mad at you for writing lies in your paper," Joe said. Stockton drew in his breath, ready to defend himself. "Now I am sorry," said Joe.

"Sorry?" said Stockton.

"You were right." Joe looked at the floor. "There is a wolf." Stockton looked hard at Joe, trying his best to see into the old man's eyes. For the first time he realized what it was that he had been writing about. Joe was frightened. "The biggest I have ever seen," Joe said.

Stockton believed him from that moment. But as if Joe had come expecting not to be believed, he reached into a big canvas pocket on his coat and took from it a skull that he held in both hands. Stockton pulled back. It was not a dried, sun-bleached skull. It was fresh. Hair and flesh still clung to it. The lower jaw hung twisted from torn white and red tendons. It was long, definitely not human. "This is my dog," Joe said. "The best dog I have ever had for sheep." He placed the skull between them. "He was protecting the sheep."

Stockton looked closer at the head. It must have been a huge dog.

He guessed eighty pounds. A hundred questions came to his mind, but before he could ask, Joe turned the skull over. Stockton had to look even more closely to recognize what he was being shown. Finally it came to him. Lodged tight in a hole just behind the eye cavity on the left side was an enormous canine tooth, broken off at the root. The tooth was embedded an inch and a half into the skull.

"There was time for one shot," Joe said. "When he pulled away, he left the tooth." The old man brought a handkerchief from his pocket, unwrapped it, and showed Stockton a dozen bloody strands of hair. "I hit him," Joe said.

Stockton leaned forward in his chair. He looked at the skull and the hair. He tapped his cheek with his index finger, thinking. "Did you bring those for me, Joe?"

The old man nodded. "I want you to do something," he said. "I'm alone out there." Stockton nodded. He handed Joe an envelope for the hair and found a box to put the skull in.

"I'll do what I can," Stockton told him, and that evening he started his editorial. He kept it all secret. He didn't tell Bailey, avoided the trapper. They would howl when they saw the editorial, and they would burst into his office, but he would have the hair and the skull to back up what he had said. Stockton was proud of the editorial when it was finished. It was solid. It would make anyone listen who read it—and maybe someone would do something. To Stockton it was all academic. He was not afraid of wolves; he would never have to deal with one. Something in him was sure that they were like most other wild animals, scared and responding to a changing world. As Stockton worked that night, Joe's old face kept appearing in the corners of the office. The face was scared. To Joe Standing Elk, wolves were more than academic.

Katie Running was frying some potatoes for Jake and Pete. That was part of the deal: she'd cook. They had been out the night before with some of the men from the camp in the Hills, and she'd been with Traverse Best. She was up by nine o'clock, but Jake and Pete had stayed in bed until three. Now it was after five and time for some food, fuel to start it all over again.

The house they lived in used to belong to Jake and Pete's grandmother. Mother Hermany-horses, they called her. It was on deeded ground, and along with the house and the seventy acres around it went a Forest Service grazing permit. They were allowed to graze fifty head of cattle for the summer in the trees along Whitewood Creek. While the cows grazed, Jake and Pete put up what hay they could on the deeded land to feed the cattle when they came off the summer range. After they sold the calves in the fall, there wasn't much money, but there was always beef to eat and, with the government checks, they got by.

Katie had met Jake and Pete only a couple of weeks before. But like most Sioux, their families had known each other. They were like cousins. They had partied for a couple of days, and all ended up at the house. She just never moved out. Things were working all right; it was better than Minneapolis, but not that different. The cooking and a little picking up had fallen to her, but she was looking for a real job. Sometimes she asked herself why she'd come back to the Hills. It seemed strange; she was just there. It was as if she was waiting for something.

Jake and Pete took care of their cattle and worked for some of the other ranchers when they needed help. Pete was actually a sheep man and had always hired out to help big outfits with their lambing. The lambing season started in late January and lasted until June. But this year Pete had not taken a job. Both Pete and Jake had been too busy with the men at the camp to work for any other ranchers. Besides, they had begun to resent the white ranchers, the government, the Forest Service.

They sat silently at the table, nursing hangovers, and looked at the plates Katie had set in front of them. There was a lot of grease on the potatoes, and the onions that she'd sliced and fried along with them lay limp and yellow in tangled masses at the edge of the plates. She put a bottle of catsup on the table between them. They moved slowly, each taking the catsup in turn and smothering the potatoes. As they ate, they began to revive. Jake asked for a glass of milk. Katie brought it and laughed.

"You guys are real cheery today."

"Big time last night," Pete said. He was a pure-blood, darker than Jake, and his speech was thicker.

"Drank about a case of beer apiece," Jake said.

"Who all was there?"

"Louie and Pattie," Pete began.

"Can't really tell you everybody that was there," Jake said, causing Pete to look up from his plate.

"Christ, Jake, you think you're James Bond or something? Lebeaux, a guy from New Mexico, and a couple from Denver."

"What were their names?" Katie asked.

Jake shook his head. "Christ," he said, "everybody wants to know everything. Now you want names."

Pete waved him silent. "Little Eagle, Big Eagle, Eagle Wing, something like that. Don't remember the Denver guys." Pete shook his head. "Then there's Robert Lance. You know him. Phony as a three-dollar bill."

Jake shrugged. "He's all right."

"Bull, didn't you hear Lebeaux laying it on him? Lance isn't even his real name. It's Lancaster. Lebeaux says he's from Virginia." Pete laughed. "He's just a little guy trying to be tough."

Jake shrugged. "He's tough enough."

"You going out again tonight?" Katie asked. The two men didn't answer. They weren't sure. "When you go out to the camp again, I'd like to go."

"Sure," Pete said. He took a pack of cigarettes from his shirt pocket and, without even looking at Jake, took one out and tossed it across the table to him. He lit his own and skidded the book of matches to Jake. They were still sitting silently at the table smoking cigarettes when Katie finished washing the dishes. By the time she'd gotten ready to go to town, they had moved to the living room. The blue light from the television flickered on their shapes as she said good-bye. Pete was asleep on the couch.

Jake lay on the floor watching the television and finishing a cigarette. "Yea," he said, "have a good time."

Bill Egan came into the bar about six-thirty, and McVay fought an urge to walk over immediately and introduce himself. Instead, he sat at the bar talking with Traverse Best and listening to the jukebox. Egan ordered a whiskey and soda, and Best took it to where he sat in one of the booths, against the wall. McVay glanced that way a couple of times and tried to see what this Egan really looked like. But Egan sensed the glances each time, and McVay had to look away to keep from getting caught. When Best came back, he pointed Egan out. McVay nodded, to say he knew who the old man was, and seized the opportunity to excuse himself from the bar, telling Best that he needed to talk with Egar for the story he was writing.

When he touched Egan's hand, it seemed harder than it had when he had brushed it on the satchel handle. He could feel the strength in the old hand, could feel the long, sinewy fingers wrapped around his own, and knew that, years before, there had been a pad of muscle at the base of the thumb. The feel of the hand shocked McVay. He looked down at the old hand in his own and knew that there was no difference in their hands, save age and the waxy, transparent skin that stretched tight over Egan's scarred knuckles. The old blue eyes pulled his back, and Egan said, "Nice to meet you again."

McVay nodded, caught for an instant without his power of speech. "I've read about you," he finally said, and that seemed to ease the pressure. The hands released, and the two men sat down.

Now McVay could see Egan's whole face, and while they made small talk about the town and the hotel, McVay scanned the face and upper body. The hair was white and close-cut, receding above his temples, and thin toward the top. The face was porous as sandstone, burned dark with sun and wind. The wrinkles around the mouth suggested both smiles and frowns, but those at the edge of the eyes, by far the most pronounced, told McVay of endless hours of squinting into the sun, squinting east at first light and west in the late afternoons. He could see Egan squinting as the sun bounced into his face from snowdrifts blown hard by the same wind that helped sculpt the face. The neck was thin now, veined, and the Adam's apple moved as Egan spoke softly. The shoulders and chest, like the rest of him, were thin now but they had once been strong. It seemed that Egan had been the kind of man who was understated, capable of feats that seemed beyond him. But it was the old blue eyes that drew McVay to Egan and made him listen to what he was saying. He could hear Best and another man, the only others in the bar, talking behind him, but the eyes held him, and Egan's gentle words came in answer to the questions he was asking mechanically.

"Nineteen ten," Egan said, "in a little town in Nebraska."

"And when'd you start trappin' wolves?"

Egan showed no expression. "Don't really remember. Just after the war sometime."

"The First World War?"

"Of course."

"I was in a war."

"Of course," Egan said again.

Then Best was there to ask if they needed another drink. McVay ordered beer, but Egan refused. "One's about my limit these days."

McVay looked at him as he swallowed the last of his drink. "You must have been out looking for the wolf today."

Egan smiled. "I was out. Did some walking. But not sure I was really looking for a wolf."

"You don't think there is a wolf, do you?"

For the first time the eyes looked away. "No," he said, "don't 'spose there is."

But McVay wasn't satisfied. "Could there be?" The bar door opened and several people came in. There was a lot of noise. Egan stood up and looked down at McVay.

"Sure," he said. "There's still a chance."

Then McVay was standing up, looking into the eyes again. He heard himself ask if he could go out with him sometime, and he saw Egan's head nodding. Then he heard himself say he wanted to hear more. And Egan said, "There's a lot more to tell," and turned toward the door.

The people behind him were singing to the jukebox. He watched Egan go out. Just before the door closed behind Egan, McVay noticed that the trees were bent with the wind. When he turned back to the bar, he nearly ran into a woman. It was she. She smiled up at him, round face, big eyes framed in straight black hair.

"Hi," she said. "My name is Katie."

Bailey had watched the wind come up. It started low along the ground, moving just the old prairie grass. Then it began to work on the sagebrush, and finally, just before dark, it had started whipping the cottonwoods. Now it was night. Bailey was in his own backyard, walking and thinking. He walked farther away from the house, even though he was not the kind of man who needed to walk. But it seemed right, that night, to walk in the dark, the wind whistling the beginning of a storm. Above him the stars and moon shone bright. The prairie was light. But to the west the stars stopped, and a bank of blackness began. A front was moving in.

Bailey had felt uneasy all day long. He had the feeling something was beginning. Things had been going well so far that spring. There had been a small incident that day—nothing really big. Ordinarily it would have meant nothing to Bailey; he would have forgotten it, but his senses were sharp. Bailey didn't believe in omens—he wasn't superstitious. The fact that David Olson's boy had been shot at by mistake didn't mean anything. It had just been another kid out on the prairie. The Olson boy was riding a bicycle down a back road. It had been an honest mistake, Bailey was sure of that. No one had gotten hurt, but still it bothered him. He had the feeling that the rifleman would not have been out on the prairie if it weren't for this wolf business. The bullet missing the kid on a bicycle wasn't the cause of Bailey's uneasiness. It was more of a symptom. Bailey didn't know why he was standing out in his backyard being whipped by the wind. The real problem hadn't surfaced yet. It was nothing that he could pin down. The lights from the house spread across his weedy backyard at the edge of town. The prairie began a hundred yards off the end of his property. It was black out there. The few lights were sparkling clear, and he could see them for miles. The melody from a Chopin tape came to Bailey, and he wondered what it would be like to play the piano.

Harmon Knutson was looking over the same prairie. It was endless, full of places vision couldn't penetrate. He had stopped his pickup along the gravel road that led from town to the ranch. The pickup box was full of bags of mineral for the cattle. He had been in town most of the afternoon. But now, in the half-light, he was parked, looking out over the prairie. He thought that he'd seen something move on a distant ridge, but the light was poor and he could not be sure. He put the truck back into gear and turned off the gravel toward the ridge. The moon was coming up high.

Hours later, Tom McVay stepped from the Oasis bar, around the corner and into the lobby. He moved to the window that overlooked the street and saw the sky. It was blacker now; the moon was full and round and still bright, but the clouds would have it all soon. He'd go out looking for Billion the next day, he said to himself. He was sure that Katie could help. She seemed very interested in him, and she said she knew P.J. Billion.

As he climbed the hotel stairs, he thought of the people he had met in Medicine Springs. He could not help but think that they were strange, very different, somehow special people assembled in this place for a reason. He had drunk too many beers, he knew, but the faces of Best and Katie and finally Egan kept coming up in his mind. It was the old times again, sneaking into his soggy mind. He did not know these people, but must know people who reminded him of them—he must know their type. Now even the hallway looked familiar, like the hallways in the hotels in Saigon. He stopped and looked up at a door. The number was two; he was sure it was Egan's room. He imagined the old man sleeping ghostlike on the bed, lying on his back, his mouth agape, trying for all the air he could. McVay rubbed his head and moved on.

But Egan was not asleep. He was not gasping for air. He was staring at the clouds taking over the sky. There was something in the night that wouldn't let him sleep, so he sat in the hard-backed chair in his white underwear, his neck too thin, and watched the sky. He imagined that he could move endlessly and silently over the land.

Harmon was right. There had been something on the ridge. As he approached, he had seen it again. The daylight was gone, it was starlight and moonlight now, but he had seen something. It didn't seem to be afraid of him, didn't run wildly; it had let itself be seen again. Harmon bounced slowly across the top of the ridge in the pickup, feeling foolish for driving across the prairie in the night. He would go to the top of the next ridge and look. The land flattened out from there, so he would be able to see nearly a mile.

The ridge rolled up into the darkness. It was not a high ridge, more of a rise, but on its top were small trees. The moonlight broke the shadows of the trees into stripes across the pickup hood. The trees were close together, and he had to be sure that he could squeeze the truck past them. Finally he was through and focused his eyes out across the grasslands that fell off gradually. The light was bad, and whatever it was that he had seen was not in sight now. He decided to give it up and turned to back the truck through the trees. Harmon's eyes reflected the moonlight as he faced behind him, then his eyes widened. Something moved out of the trees to his left and started across the flatland. Harmon reached for the rifle in the rack behind the seat as he accelerated backward. By the time he had the pickup straightened out, the rifle was across his lap. Now the truck was pointed down the hill. For an instant, Harmon hesitated. The hill was steep. But then he saw the movement again, far out on the flat below. He pushed the accelerator hard to the floor, and the truck leapt forward.

There was a tearing sound as Jerry Stockton pulled the first copy of the *Recorder* from the press. He smiled and turned it until his editorial was upright in front of him. "Killer Wolf," it said. Stockton smiled again. He had proof.

Part Three

Bill Egan opened his eyes and rolled them across the ceiling of his room. He was still in the chair. It was a gray morning, and a light rain was coming down outside. But something else had awakened him.

Bailey's fist crashed three more times on the door. "Wake up, Egan. There's been an accident."

Egan came out of the chair rubbing his face. His legs were stiff, and he was forced to slow down halfway to the door. When he opened the door, the sheriff didn't look at him. He came in. "Hell of an accident," Bailey said. "Get your pants on." Then they looked at each other. "Harmon Knutson," Bailey said. Egan nodded. He went to get his pants.

The clock behind the desk said five-thirty when the two came down the stairs. Johnny stood beside the desk in his pajamas. "Is he dead, Sheriff?"

"Shut up, Johnny," the sheriff said.

Johnny nodded. "Yes, sir," he said.

The two men said nothing for the first five miles. Egan had gotten up too fast. He felt a little sick to his stomach, and his legs were very sore. Bailey began to talk.

"Boyd found him," he said. "He's been looking since midnight." Egan didn't answer. "Boyd says he's dead for sure." Bailey wiped his mouth. "Said the truck rolled right over him." Egan nodded but didn't speak for a long time.

"Why me?" he said finally. The brightness was back in his eyes.

Bailey glanced at him, then back at the road. "I don't know, Egan. It just seemed like you should come along."

"It's not my job," Egan said.

"I know."

"You think there's something funny about this accident, don't you?"

"I don't know, Egan. Things are screwed up around here," Bailey said. He wouldn't look at the old man. He watched the road. "Harmon Knutson wasn't a hot-rodder kid, Egan."

Boyd Knutson was sitting in his pickup truck on the gravel road. His face was tight, like he was mad, but they could see that he'd been crying.

"He's about a mile and a half off the road," Knutson said, pointing.

"The ambulance should be here in a few minutes from Rapid City," Bailey said.

"He don't need an ambulance. He's dead, Junior."

"You stay here so they know where to go when they come. We'll go have a look," Bailey said. Knutson nodded and walked back to sit down in his truck.

Bailey was cussing to himself. "Goddamn," he said, "goddamn," and pulled his car off the road in the direction that Boyd had pointed. Then, louder, "Goddamn, Egan. That kid knew better."

"When'd it happen?" Egan asked.

"Last night," Bailey said. The older man nodded.

Bailey drove through the same trees that Harmon had driven through. They looked over the same grassland that he had looked over in the moonlight. Three hundred yards down the grade the pickup lay on its side, its cargo of mineral bags scattered over the prairie. As they started toward it, Egan began to watch the ground.

"He rolled it," Bailey said. "He rolled the goddamn pickup." Egan nodded. The ground was very rough, and they moved toward the truck slowly.

Harmon had been crushed under the cab of the pickup. He was dead. Bailey kicked the ground. "Something stinks," Bailey said. "He must have been going fifty miles an hour to roll this outfit, loaded like that. Harmon didn't drive that way." They heard the engine of the ambulance. It came over the hill with Boyd Knutson following. Bailey walked out to meet them, and Egan began to circle the pickup.

They hooked a chain to the truck and righted it with Boyd's four-wheel drive. It took some time. Once they had the pickup almost on its wheels, and the chain slipped. The truck came down hard on Harmon's body, and Boyd slammed his fist into the door. Finally Harmon's body lay free from the crushing weight, and the ambulance men loaded it and drove away. All that time Egan had been circling the pickup. He was now a hundred yards down the hill from the wreck. When Bailey called to him and he came back toward the sheriff and Boyd Knutson, Egan was carrying a rifle.

As he got close, he heard Bailey ask Knutson if he had any idea what Harmon was doing out there. Knutson shook his head, then forced a little smile when Egan came up. "Found his rifle," Egan said. "Must have gotten thrown from the cab." Bailey reached out and took it from Egan. "He was a good boy," Egan said. Boyd nodded and, in the awkward moment that followed, Bailey nervously flipped the lever on the .30-30. An empty shell somersaulted out, and Bailey's eyes snapped up to meet Egan's. Egan wasn't surprised. He had checked the rifle when he found it in the sagebrush. Bailey glanced at Boyd Knutson, who had not seen it, so Bailey closed the rifle's chamber and eased the hammer to safe.

Suddenly P.J. Billion realized how dirty the house was. He looked around the room where he had been sitting for he did not know how long. He saw the dust on the shelves and the lint under the furniture. There were magazines scattered on the floor and unopened mail piled on the table beside the telephone. He kept his hands perfectly still on the arms of the chair and tried not to move his head. He let his eyes travel around the room. It was morning. Had he been asleep? No. Just resting. He didn't like to sleep.

Now it was morning, and it was all right to move, but he must be quiet. He wondered if the room was bugged. He let his eyes roll again. This time he looked at the undersurfaces of the tables and chairs and at the back of the furniture that was pushed against the walls. It's morning, he thought again. Morning, time to make the coffee. He breathed deeply, trying not to let the expansion of his chest show beyond the white cotton of his undershirt. The coffeepot was in the kitchen. The dishes would be unwashed. Unless, he thought, someone has done them in the night. But he knew that no one had been in his house. Unless it was the Feds. The agents, he thought, might have done the dishes when they wired the house.

Suddenly he brought his hands up hard against his face. Christ. He rubbed his face. It was morning, he thought. Christ. He needed a cup of coffee. Pushing the dishes aside, he looked for the insides of the coffeepot. There was a stemlike thing and a little basket that you put the coffee in, he thought. How could it get separated from the pot itself? He held the pot in his right hand and shook it. There was still coffee in it. Old, cold coffee. He pulled the lid off and poured the coffee into the sink. The stem and basket clattered against the white enamel, and he jumped back. He slammed the pot down and brought his hands up behind his neck. When the tension had left his arms, he began to massage his neck, then he heard his dog whining and turned to see the big German shepherd sitting alert in the kitchen doorway. Billion did not smile.

"Come," he said sharply. The dog sprinted to his side, faced the same direction as Billion, and sat. They both stared straight ahead. "Heel," and they walked together, out of the kitchen. They crossed the living room, and Billion turned quickly into the bedroom. The dog stayed right with him. When they got to the dresser in the bedroom, they stopped. Billion expelled a deep breath. "All right," he said, and the dog slumped to the floor, his head flat between his front legs.

Billion thought about the Feds as he slid open the dresser drawer.

He would have to find out when they were coming. He lifted a small jewelry box from the top drawer and put it lightly on the dresser top. The box was covered with velvet, and the rim of the lid was brass. Billion stared at it for a long time before he raised the lid. Inside were two Purple Hearts and a Navy Cross. He closed his eyes and let his fingers touch them lightly. He felt the features of the face on the Purple Hearts and told himself that his wounds were better. He took the bronze cross out of the box and held it between his hands. Then he put it back and closed the lid to the box. He held the box to his chest, his eyes still closed, and rocked back and forth. They'll never get these, he thought. The Feds would never get these.

"What was he chasing?" Bailey asked as they pulled back onto the graveled road.

"I don't know," Egan said.

"You mean you walked around out there for an hour and didn't see a track?"

"No."

"No what?" Bailey said. "No tracks?"

"There were some tracks," Egan said.

Bailey slowed the car down. "Give it to me easy," he said. "Is there a wolf running around here?"

Egan looked at him. "I don't know, Sheriff. There was a little rain last night. But Harmon Knutson was chasing something when he rolled his pickup."

"What? A coyote? Harmon wouldn't kill himself for a coyote."

"Don't know," Egan said. "I'd say it was a canine, though."

The sheriff nodded to himself. He speeded up the car. "Right," he said. "One unidentified, running son of a bitch. I'll put that on the report."

Bailey dropped Egan off at the hotel and went down the street to his office. The *Recorder* was waiting for him. He didn't even sit down. He put both hands on the desk and leaned over to read it. When he finished, he grabbed the paper up with his right hand, wrinkling it, and walked back out the door.

Stockton had been expecting him since eight o'clock. It was almost noon. "Before you say anything, Junior, I want to tell you that I got proof," Stockton said.

"Proof?" Bailey held up the paper. "Proof of a 'Killer Wolf?" He slammed the paper down on Stockton's desk. "I got my own proof, Stockton. I got proof that there's been a killing, and it's this kind of shit that's responsible." He picked the paper back up and tore it in half.

"You fucking worm," Bailey said. "Harmon Knutson killed himself this morning chasing a goddamn spook that you put into his head. He wound his truck up to about fifty miles an hour across the prairie and ended up with the whole damn thing on top of him." Bailey's face was shaking. "His chest was about two inches thick when we found him, Jerry."

Bailey turned and went to the front door. He locked it, pulled down the blind, and swung the OPEN sign over to OUT TO LUNCH. "Now," Bailey said, holding up the newspaper. "It says here that there is a wolf." Stockton was still thinking about Harmon Knutson and didn't answer.

"I told you two weeks ago not to write any more shit like this, or someone would get hurt. You didn't listen. A kid got shot at yesterday and Harmon Knutson's dead, so now I'm telling you again."

Stockton cleared his throat. "Junior?" he said.

Bailey turned to him and glared. "Don't say a fucking word," he said.

"I have to, Junior. There really is a wolf." Bailey blew out a deep breath. "I tried to say that I got proof," Stockton said. He opened the bottom drawer of his desk and took out the envelope and the box. He opened the envelope and shook the hair out onto a piece of paper, then opened the box. Bailey moved close to the desk. He stared down at what Stockton was showing him. It took a moment, but he understood. Then without another word to Stockton, he reached for the telephone and dialed a number

"Johnny," he said, "get ahold of Bill Egan. Tell him to get his ass down to the *Recorder* office on the double."

Simmons was getting more pressure. More calls about the "wolf" in the Black Hills. He'd said it a thousand times, "Can't be a wolf, hasn't been a wolf in the forest for decades, closest ones are in Canada, and they're timber wolves." He said it as nicely as he could. He told the three ranchers who called him directly; he told the state senators who called on the special state telephone; and he told his boss when he called from Denver, "Damn near impossible, longest shot in the world." And besides, he was doing all he could. He already had the only real wolf trapper left in the United States out looking for answers. What more could he do?

There was nothing more that Mel Simmons could do, but it still bothered him. There was something special about a wolf, or just the thought of a wolf. Scared the pee out of people. Could be, he thought, being scared of wolves was genetic. People have been scared of wolves since the ice age, but they are not just scared that wolves will do damage or even that they'll kill people. People are scared because somewhere, way back in their Pleistocene consciousness, they remember or sense that, when the ice descended from the north and man was forced to learn to prey on the large mammals of the snow cap, man at this latitude was rivaled for dominance by the wolf. The truth of the matter, as Mel Simmons saw it, was that people panicked when they heard the word "wolf," because they are not truly convinced that the struggle for dominance is over. In man's primordial mind he is still not certain that his brains have beaten the wolf's brawn, that he is truly the most ruthless predator ever to roam the earth. People, Simmons thought, must still be afraid that the wolf is in the running. Why else make them the villain they are not? Vicious killers they are not. Ghoulish eaters of human flesh they are not. They're just animals making a living the same way they've made a living for millions of years. Besides all that, there were no wolves in his state, certainly not in his forest. Simmons said it once more, this time to himself.

But, as certain as the nonexistence of wolves in his state was the definite existence of politics. Who did these people think they were to put pressure on him to catch a wolf that didn't exist? They'd have to pass a law creating a wolf before he could catch it. But Simmons knew politics. A person didn't get a job like his by being ignorant of the workings of government. He knew that if this wolf notion continued, he'd be called upon for answers to some pretty silly questions. He might even have to make a trip to Medicine Springs to lend the whole thing a bit of officialism, make it look good. With a little luck, old Egan would clear it up in a week or so. In the meantime, Simmons dug out a bibliography of wolf literature and had his secretary see what the state library had that was current.

"Can you say definitely that that is a wolf's tooth?" Bailey said to Egan.

Egan took the dog's head in his hands and held it up to the light. He looked at the tooth from every possible angle, stared at it a long time. "No," Egan said, "I can't say for sure."

"How about the hair?" Stockton said.

"I'm asking the questions," Bailey said. "How about the hair, Egan?" Again Egan looked closely. He rolled the strands between his fingers.

"Can't say for sure," he said.

"That's wolf hair, gray buffalo wolf," said Stockton.

"Shut up," Bailey said, turning on Stockton. "Just keep quiet."

"Could this be a wolf's tooth and this wolf's hair?" Bailey said.

"Yes," Egan said.

"Okay." Bailey was trying to be thorough. "Is it possible that the story that old Joe told Jerry is true?"

"Forty years ago it would have been," Egan said. "Wolves killed domestic dogs every chance they got."

"So you're saying that it's possible that there really is a wolf?" Stockton said.

Bailey waved him quiet. "There's been too damn much jumping to conclusions already," he said. "Joe could have had that stuff since he was a boy."

"It's a fresh skull," Egan said.

"Joe doesn't lie," Stockton said.

"You can't tell, Jerry." Bailey looked back at Egan. He picked up the skull. "Could a wolf, or anything else, do that?" He pointed to the tooth jammed through the skull behind the eye socket of the dog. "That was a hell of a big dog," he added and hefted the skull.

Egan looked at the skull again. "A big wolf could have done that," Egan said. He took the skull from Bailey. "A damn big wolf," he said.

An hour later the three men were bouncing down a dirt path that led to Joe Standing Elk's sheep camp. Neither Stockton nor Bailey were sure that they could find it, but they knew about where to look. It was hot, and Bailey noticed that Egan looked uncomfortable. He turned on the air conditioner, which blew dust at first. When the cold air came, Bailey sat even farther back in his seat and let the coolness hit him square in the face. Outside, tiny mirages, the first of the year, wiggled in the draws and tested their elasticity on the sides of the hills.

Joe's tent was right on the edge of the Hills. The pine trees rolled up behind the camp to the ridge that marked the beginning of the mountains and the end of the prairie. It was a neat camp. The tent was an old military-style hexagonal with a single ridge pole and three-foot side walls roped out to rails that Joe had lashed to dwarf pine trees. The stove wood was stacked beside the tent flap which was tied shut, and on the rocks around the camp and hung from the closest trees were tools and equipment. A bucksaw, wash pan and towel, lead rope and hobbles, an ax, even small lengths of rope were coiled and hung in the trees safe from pack rats. Fifty feet from the tent the old Indian had built a shade house. It was entirely pine and all freshly cut. It had not been warm enough to need it yet, but apparently Joe was getting ready for hot days they all knew were coming. The uprights of the shade house were four trees. He had cut the tops off and used the thick pine branches to lay across the rails he'd lashed to the trees. It was twenty feet square and shut out all direct sunlight from above. In the center of the shadow created by the roof of pine boughs was an old kitchen chair. Joe had evidently established his summer resting place.

The three men stood in the middle of Joe's camp. Egan felt uncomfortable at being in another man's camp with the other man gone. Stockton was fascinated and moved from place to place looking closely at Joe's possessions, picking them up occasionally and rotating them in his hands. Bailey showed no emotion. He simply scanned the horizon for some sign of where the old Indian could be.

They had been in camp for only a half-hour when Bailey called to them that he saw Joe. By this time Egan had found a comfortable place to sit, on a rock, at the edge and above the camp. He had seen the old Indian five minutes before, letting his horse pick his own way home through the sage and yucca, but there had been no reason to call to the others. Led by two sheep dogs, old Joe was coming; there was nothing that could, or should, be done to hurry him. When Bailey called back to them, Stockton was untying the canvas strings that held the tent flap shut. There were three strings, and Stockton had unfastened them all. Hearing that Joe was coming, he hurriedly began to tie the strings back together. He was looking over his shoulder in the wrong direction as he tied and managed to tie the bottom string on the left to the top string on the right. Egan watched him from his rock. When Stockton noticed what he'd done, he quickly began untying them again. But instead of calmly untying the knot, he jerked at it until it was tight, then began to struggle with it. Joe was still several minutes away, but now Stockton panicked. He looked over his shoulder again, then turned and stared for an instant. When he turned back to the tent flaps, he had evidently given up on untying the knot. With jerking movements and an air of finality he tied the bottom string on the right to the top string on the left. His hands flew away from the knot like a calf roper shooting for a ten-second time. As Stockton walked away, Egan looked at the strings tied in an X across Joe Standing Elk's doorway and shook his head. Then he climbed down off his rock to meet the Indian whose dogs had begun barking and circling Bailey.

Joe Standing Elk was indeed the old kind of Indian, like the Indians Egan had known in his youth. Joe was full-blood, Egan guessed, or very close. The color of his skin was much darker than the average Indian, and his hair, except for a touch of white at the temples, was very black and straight. He rode a short stocky horse that was as woolly as one of his sheep—it had not yet begun to lose its winter coat. His bridle was woven leather. Egan guessed that Joe had made it himself, and over the saddle was thrown a wool blanket. The saddle was invisible except for the wooden stirrups that hung below the red woven border of the blanket. Joe spoke softly to the dogs from his horse, and they both scurried to their place beside the tent and curled up, laying their heads on their tails but watching the strangers with solid black eyes.

Joe dismounted, tied his horse, and loosened the cinch before he turned to the men. He nodded Bailey a hello while Stockton jabbered. Once on the ground he looked older, the deep-cut lines in the face showing years, but giving no hint of how many.

Bailey and Stockton began to quiz him. It started out orderly, with Bailey asking the questions in an official, precise way. But Stockton insisted on interrupting the questions. "You said you saw it," Stockton said.

"Yes."

"Now hold on," Bailey said. "Let me get some background."

"Phoo on background. The man says he saw a wolf."

"It's easy to make mistakes. I just want to be sure."

"It killed his dog," Stockton said, and turned to the two curled beside the tent.

"Jerry." Stockton turned to look at Bailey. "Shut up, okay? Just for a minute?"

Joe was looking away from the two men, toward his tent. "Now, Joe, I know you told Jerry you saw a wolf, and I'm not saying you didn't. I just want you to describe what you saw to Mr. Egan here." Bailey pointed to Egan, who had been standing thirty feet away.

"Christ, Junior, he's an Indian. You think he doesn't know a wolf when he sees one?"

"Shut up, Jerry."

"You have no reason or right to tell me to shut up."

Bailey's face began to turn red. "I'm the goddamned sheriff of this county, and I'm trying to get to the bottom of this deal, and you're only making it worse." Bailey and Stockton were nose to nose now. Bailey's face was red, and Stockton was obviously shaken. "Now," Bailey said, "if you don't mind, I'm going to ask a few questions of Mr. Standing Elk."

His voice had calmed, but when he turned, Joe had moved away. Joe Standing Elk and Bill Egan stood under the shade house, the kitchen chair between them, looking directly into each other's faces. The old men talked. They nodded and held their hands up to subtly express themselves. Outside the shade house the sun had begun to get hot. Bailey and Stockton began to sweat but didn't join the two under the pine boughs.

When they finished talking, they nodded to each other, and Egan came toward the other men. Without a word they followed him as he passed and got into Bailey's car. On the way back to town Stockton asked Egan what Joe had said. Egan was facing front, sitting beside Bailey, who was driving.

"He said a lot of things," Egan said, and went on before Stockton had a chance to push him. "He said there is evil in the Hills and more coming every day. He's afraid there won't be enough good men to fight it."

"Is that all? Just superstition?"

"No," Egan said. "He said he wanted me to catch the wolf. And he wanted to know who had been in his tent."

McVay had been sitting in the Oasis bar since six-thirty trying, subtly, to get Traverse Best to tell him something about P.J. Billion. But Best wasn't talking, and that bothered McVay. What did Best have going with Billion? Why should he care if McVay found out exactly where Billion lived? McVay had been in town too long the way it was. Everyone in town knew him, even if they didn't know who he really was, and he wasn't any closer to P.J. Billion. The woman, Katie, might help if she ever showed up again, but if something didn't start happening, he'd have to use this reporter deal to get some answers.

He'd been drinking beer again. Not much, because he wanted to stay sharp, but enough to make everyone believe he was just out enjoying himself. Best was a good bartender. When one was empty, it disappeared and another showed up. He never asked or pushed; at least he never pushed McVay. But at the other end of the bar there were two Indians whom McVay was sure Best was trying to get drunk. Sometimes he'd put new beers in front of them before they were done with the last ones, and more than once McVay didn't see any money change hands. If Best was trying to get their government checks away from them, he was going about it in a very strange way.

There was little else going on in the bar, and so McVay, while trying to act wrapped up in the music he'd played, watched the two Indians and Best. At first Best talked with McVay and only went to the other end of the bar when he felt the Indians needed a drink, but each time he hesitated a moment and talked with the pair. With each drink Best seemed to stay a little longer. He joked with them and slapped them on the back. The men seemed to be having a good time, but with each drink they slouched into their bar stools more and McVay could hear that their speech was becoming slurred.

When Best returned with another drink for him, McVay asked him who the men were.

"Pete and Jake. They're just a couple of Indians that do a little ranching outside of town."

McVay watched Best as he talked. There was something not right about the matter-of-factness in his voice and the casual way Best glanced at him as he soaked up a beer spill on the bar in front of him. McVay slid a quarter from the pile of change in front of him. "Flip you for the jukebox," he said.

Best seemed relieved. "Sure," he said and reached into his pocket for his own quarter. As he did, McVay heard the door open. He looked at the mirror behind the bar and saw Katie standing in back of him. Best made a low whistle, intended for only McVay. It was obvious what he was whistling at. Katie looked good. Her long black hair hung symmetrically in two thick braids that touched the tops of the button-down pockets on her western shirt. Her skin seemed tanned to McVay, and her blue jeans and boots looked almost brand-new. Pete and Jake looked up and yelled for her to come down and sit with them. She looked at McVay, who had turned to look at her. She smiled at him, nodded to Best, and went to sit with Pete and Jake.

"I'll match you," Best said.

McVay, turning back and reaching for his quarter, said, "Right." He picked the quarter up and flipped it into the air. As he watched it fly, his eyes met Katie's in the mirror.

"Heads," he said.

"Me too," Best said uncovering his coin. "Play B-12, would you?"

McVay heard Best ask her what she was drinking. More beer. And then she was there beside him. "Need some help?"

"Sure."

McVay and Katie went about selecting the songs on the jukebox as if it were very serious business. Behind them they heard Pete and Jake calling to Katie to come back and sit down, but they ignored them. Then came the sound of more people coming into the bar. Pete and Jake were drowned out.

"I need to talk to you," McVay said.

Katie looked up at him. "Okay, let's get a booth."

McVay took his beer to a booth, and Katie went to get hers. Best had left it on the bar beside the two other Indians. McVay watched; there was no real trouble. When Katie picked up her beer, Pete took her by the arm, but gently. There were a few words, then Katie turned away from them and came to the booth. She smiled at McVay, showing him a line of perfectly white, straight teeth. She was holding her beer in one hand and her purse in the other. When she sat down, McVay could smell her perfume. It was not sweet but musty, and it sent a chill down McVay's neck. More people came into the bar, but McVay did not look. He watched Katie as she dug into her purse and came out with a cigarette. McVay hated cigarettes, but as she brought the lighter up, he reached out and took it gently from her hand. He lit her cigarette for her, and she smiled the round-faced smile that bunched her dimples tightly at the edge of her mouth. She showed the perfect teeth again. McVay had to smile back. She is beautiful, he thought.

Someone had asked Traverse Best if they could turn the jukebox up, and after a token argument, Best had said yes. There were more people now, and the tempo of the evening was picking up. Katie and McVay tried to talk. Mostly small talk. There was too much activity for McVay to ask her about P.J. Billion. He glanced around the room trying to gauge when things might slow down.

Best was running now. People were calling off drinks at both ends of the bar, and there was no time for him to talk to the two Indians who still sat on their bar stools. McVay watched them closely over Katie's shoulder. Occasionally they glanced his way, and McVay was sure that they were talking about him when they turned back and slouched over their drinks. McVay wondered if one of the men in the room was P.J. Billion. Finally he leaned over and whispered into Katie's ear. The musty smell caught him off guard, and he lingered there with his cheek against the raven braid and nostrils taking in the smell. "Billion," he said at last. "I need to talk to you about P.J. Billion." Katie looked at McVay, questioning. Then she nodded and took his hand. As they rose and headed toward the door, McVay saw the two Indians turn to watch them.

They moved slowly across the dance floor, where three couples were dancing. Before they reached the door, another couple stopped Katie to talk. McVay looked back and saw that the two at the bar were swiveled in their seats now, and he suspected that they were trying to gather their courage to say something to him before he and Katie made it to the door. McVay did not want trouble. He took Katie gently by the arm, smiled at the couple, and headed Katie outside. Best was filling three orders at the same time, but when McVay looked back, he was still able to shake his head and wave as if to wish them good luck. The last thing that McVay saw before the door shut was the two Indians slide off their bar stools onto wobbly legs.

"Whew," Katie said as the fresh air hit them. "What a rat race."

McVay nodded and took in some of the air. It was warm and seemed very clean. A spring night, he thought, but not humid like back in Toledo—dry, and bigger somehow. He looked down at Katie, and they smiled again. Without a word they moved away from the front of the building and under the old cottonwood that stood just twenty feet away, toward the corner of the building.

McVay had no intention of kissing her. He wanted her to tell him how to find P.J. Billion, and then had to convince her not to warn Billion that someone was looking for him. But when she looked up at him, with the light from the bar window making her skin look olive, he could not talk. She reminded him just then of another woman, a woman in Saigon whose name McVay could not remember, but who had seemed to know more about what he'd needed on that R and R than he himself had known. The woman in Saigon could not speak English, so they had not talked. Maybe that was why it seemed perfectly natural for him and Katie to stare at each other without a word as their faces drew closer, then focusing on the lips, closer until they touched. Then pressure at his lips and her breasts against his chest and more pressure and the lips opening. It all seemed exactly as it should be until McVay heard the bar door open. He snapped his head away from Katie's, still holding her closely, to see the two Indians stagger from the bar.

"It's Pete and Jake," Katie whispered. She did not know why she was still holding McVay, but she was. "Be still," she said. She'd hoped they would stagger off and be gone without seeing them. She could feel McVay's muscles tighten, and she felt herself run her hands over them.

But the two did not stagger away. They were not going anywhere. They were looking for Katie and McVay, and as their eyes adjusted to the darkness and found the couple standing under the cottonwood tree, Katie let loose of McVay, who had already stopped holding her and now stood calm but alert beside her. They came forward slowly, talking to themselves, still trying to screw up their courage, McVay observed, but filled with drunken menace. Katie met them twenty feet from where McVay stood rigid.

"What the hell are you two doing?" she said. Her voice sounded different to McVay, and he could not place the difference until the men spoke.

"Just wondering what you were doing with the *Wasicu*," Jake said. And McVay knew that she had made herself sound more Indian when she spoke to them.

"None of your business," she said.

Pete was very drunk. "He's an asshole," he said.

"Shut up," she said.

"Asshole!"

They came past Katie. "Go on home and sleep it off," she said.

McVay felt behind him to be sure he knew where the tree was. "What you doing, white man?" Pete said.

"You come out here for more land?"

"Cars?"

"You fucked it all up, white man."

McVay said nothing.

"Okay," Katie said. "You guys have had your fun."

"This guy's a fuckin' asshole," Jake said. He, too, was slurring his words and weaving.

"Don't pay any attention to them," Katie said to McVay. "They're so drunk they don't know what they're doing."

"What's wrong, white man? Cat got your tongue?"

"They don't know what they're doing," she said again. "They'll never remember it in the morning." She turned to McVay and smiled, but she could see that he was breathing hard, and she wondered if he was afraid.

"This fuckin' asshole won't talk, Jake."

The men were very close to McVay now, and she watched him, trying to see what was happening in his mind.

"Maybe we should loosen his tongue a little."

"Like the fuckin' asshole white man loosened the buffalo's tongue," Jake said. "With a knife!"

Katie saw the flash of the blade the same instant she felt McVay move. At first she thought he was running away—that is what she expected. But McVay was not running away. He had covered the five feet between himself and Jake so fast that Katie had lost track of him. She saw a boot come around five and a half feet off the ground, catch Jake just above the ear, and follow through to grind the hand that had held the knife into the gravel of the side street. It was dark, and it all happened too fast. She could hear McVay breathing rhythmically, a half snarl coming from him as the blows lashed out from his hands and feet. He had the two Indians down, and they kicked and punched up at him ineffectually. McVay continued to deliver the snarling blows, and Katie could hear them when they hit. There was blood on McVay's fists, and she had heard at least one bone break.

"Stop it!" Katie cried. She went to McVay and from behind tried to grab one of the arms. But McVay could not feel her.

"Stop!"

And then she saw McVay reach to his boot, without breaking rhythm. When the arm came up this time, there was a knife in it.

"Stop!" This time she flung herself in front of McVay.

His eyes terrified her. "Stop!" she said. His breathing came lustily, and she could smell his insides. "Stop, they're only two drunken Indians." The knife hovered, but the breathing did not slow. They looked into each other's eyes again, and they both took in the smells of the fight: the sweat and blood, the fear and excitement. She could smell his breath coming out in billows.

The knife came down, and he enveloped her in a viselike embrace. They pressed their lips tight against each other's now, his tongue penetrated her mouth, and he bit at her. Then they were running. McVay did not know where, but the air felt good against his sweating body. He ran harder, faster, dragging her with him, and he could hear her laughing.

When they came to the pine trees, they collapsed, both laughing now and sweating and breathing hard. They tore at each other's clothes impatiently. But they waited until both were completely naked. Now the laughing had stopped. McVay knelt between her legs and looked down at her. Her breasts were hard and erect. McVay was large, and she was ready. When he entered her, they shuddered together and expelled a moan that was heard across the prairie.

The smell of sex is strong, and on the prairie, even now in early summer, it was rare. It lays calm and thick in the low areas on still nights. It is an essence that confuses some, frightens some, and interests others.

Katie Running lay on the slightly damp but soft pine needles which had fallen for years from the trees that partially obscured her view of the moon, threatened, now, by clouds rolling in from the west. Her eyes were open wide; she was letting herself flow with the clouds. The sound of Tom McVay's breathing beside her mixed with the breeze that moved the pine boughs above her. What was she doing here? she asked herself. She let her hands run lightly over McVay's chest and knew that was part of it. She shook her head; the biology factor, she thought. But a mistake. Almost always a mistake. McVay was what Lebeaux would call the evil in these hills. But it wasn't McVay's fault, she thought. He just didn't belong. He had been drawn here for some reason. It was different for her—she belonged here but didn't want to admit it. She also didn't want to admit that men had always been a diversion for her. Men were bad enough, but men like McVay, the demon wrestlers, should be left alone. She knew better, knew they weren't any kind of answer, knew they would never fill the hollowness inside. But what would? she thought. What was missing, what would make her feel glad she was who she was? She ran her hand over McVay's chest again and listened to his breathing, knowing that his was a world of unruly forces and, of course, that was part of the attraction. Then she looked southward, toward the black peaks, and asked herself again what she was doing.

The smell of sex mingled now with human voices, and drifted almost unnoticed from the small stand of pine trees behind the town of Medicine Springs. The smell blended with the scent of sagebrush, and the voices with the tiny breeze that was beginning to stir.

"Come on, get your clothes on." Voices in the wind. It was a kind of puzzle at night. Smell and sound, unlike sight, form a sort of elongated circle according to the wind. They radiate from the center of the circle, but the land and wind, even a small wind like tonight, distorts the picture and makes the center hard to find.

"Where are we going?" The game was to know what the wind and land were doing to the circle and where they were hiding the center.

"How about a bath?" There, over the ridge. Perhaps in the pine trees in the shallow draw above the spring.

"What are you talking about?" McVay said as he pulled on his shirt.

She was sitting in front of him, cross-legged, pulling her own shirt on. Her blue jeans were still wadded on the pine needles beside her. "Have a little faith," she said.

Once inside the circle the smell is pervasive. It is rich and thick and becomes nondirectional. Once inside the circle the key is sound. The trick is to be still and listen.

She smiled her wide smile and rocked up on her knees. Now McVay and Katie were face to face, both on their knees, half-dressed. "Okay," McVay said. "I trust you."

Yes. There. The pine trees.

They stood up together and struggled into their pants. Katie pulled her boots on and stuffed her socks and panties into her back pocket. "Won't need those."

They moved quickly away from the pine trees, toward town, out of the circle, tripping over the sagebrush and dodging the pointed shapes of the cactus. McVay wondered how they had run across this stretch only an hour before. Then he thought of the two Indians, Pete and Jake, and hoped that he had not hurt them too badly. It would only make things more difficult if they remembered what had happened.

McVay and Katie found their way back to town directly behind the Oasis. The building was larger than it looked from the front, and McVay wondered at its construction. They moved down the wall to the single door, and Katie held a finger to her lips. She produced a key from her jeans pocket. "A present from our friendly bartender," she said as she slipped it into the lock and opened the door. They stepped inside, and Katie flipped on the lights.

McVay was blinded by the glitter. There were lights everywhere, brilliant, heat-producing lights, and McVay leaped for the light switch.

"Everybody in town will see."

Katie held him back. She smiled. "No windows," she said, and pointed to the area behind McVay. "Look."

McVay turned and saw, for the first time, the inside of the building. It was a hundred feet long, no windows to let light out, a swimming pool the entire length, and along one side, benches with sunlamps hanging from the ceiling. Along the other side of the pool was a row of doors, some shut, some standing partly open. They were booths, dressing rooms of some sort. It was all in poor repair—pieces of the concrete around the pool were chipped off; over half the sunlights were not working; some of the slats in the benches were broken—but it was obvious that it was once a showplace.

"What the hell is this?" McVay whispered.

"The Oasis," Katie whispered back. "Medicinal bathing. People used to come from all over to swim here."

McVay moved closer to the water. "It's moving."

"Medicine Springs," Katie said. "Starts right here, eighty-three degrees. It goes underground then, for half a mile. Outside of town it becomes the Medicine River." She began to unbutton her shirt.

"What are you doing?" McVay said.

"Going for a swim," she said. "Aren't you going to join me?"

McVay stood for a minute looking at her. Katie spread her arms and turned slowly in the bright lights. "Do you like me like this?" she said, and smiled. "Don't look so worried, no one knows we're in here. This place is lighttight." She took one step forward and arched neatly into the warm water.

But the pool room of the Oasis was not lighttight. There was a tiny crack along the back wall where the mortar had fallen away from the cement block. It was nearly impossible to see, visible only from the prairie. It had gone unnoticed for years. But tonight it was reflected from yellow eyes, set above moist nostrils that methodically investigated the pine needles where Tom McVay and Katie Running had made love.

Simmons's office was swamped. A few tourists had started to dribble into the Hills. They were complaining that the campsites weren't clean, and that there was still snow up high. Simmons would see that the campsites were clean, but he couldn't do anything about the snow. There were complaints from the loggers that there weren't enough trees being sold, and from private persons that too many were being sold. There was the standing complaint that the Forest Service tree-cutting policy was altering the environment, but that was from the same people who disapproved of uranium mining, and Simmons had long since stopped listening to them. There were coyotes killing lambs all over the Hills, but the trappers were out there working, so there wasn't much for Simmons to do.

All of it, Simmons knew, was as natural as the geese flying back up north. But the Medicine Springs thing was different. He'd received the report of the calf killed on the Knutson place. Egan himself had said that the mother had been attacked too. A two-year-old heifer was a little large for coyotes. Simmons knew that, and Egan knew that, though neither of them said anything over the phone. But what could it have been? Egan would have been able to tell in an instant if it was some sort of big cat. Could have been dogs, of course, but dogs usually aren't sneaky enough to keep from getting caught for very long. That left a wolf. Egan hadn't said it wasn't a wolf. Simmons knew as much as anyone about wolves, at least in theory, and he knew that there couldn't be a gray buffalo wolf still alive. Simmons let his mind wander. Could be a timber wolf drifted down from Canada. He shook his head; that would be one thousand miles across farmland—impossible. It was the gray buffalo wolves' habitat, the prairie, the open plains, the edge of the Hills.

Simmons gave in to a little daydream. They were, after all, the most attractive of all the wolves; clearly, to a lover of the plains, the most admirable of all the many subspecies of wolves. It was true that the arctic wolves closely resembled the grays in behavior, were even slightly larger, but the arctic wolves followed the caribou, the grays had been followers of the buffalo. The fact that the gray wolves had been capable of dragging down animals the size and strength of a buffalo made them the most formidable of all the wolves. The disappearance of the buffalo and the subsequent disappearance of the wolves made them mysterious and even more attractive. Simmons was not devoid of romantic spirit and saw the gray wolf as something of a tragic hero, a sort of canine Hamlet gone mad in an unjust world.

Like Hamlet, their fates had been sealed, a collision course with destiny and extinction. Still, Simmons reflected, there's always a chance. If there weren't, there could be no tragedy. And wouldn't it be something if the Medicine Springs killer did indeed turn out to be a gray buffalo wolf? And what if Egan would catch it in such a way as to keep it alive? It would be like getting ahold of a dinosaur. It would mean a lot of recognition and notoriety for the Service, Simmons thought. And a lot of recognition for him. Simmons thumbed through the pages of his appointment book. He had a couple of days. A little fieldwork might do him good; it had been a long time since he'd been on the prairie. He really only had one thing to take care of that couldn't be handled by an assistant. Larry Mullens with the Park Service had called, wanting to meet with him to talk about security. Simmons rolled his eyes at the thought. The National Park Service and the Forest Service didn't get along so well. There were three national parks within the Forest: Wind Cave, Jewel Cave, and, of course, Mount Rushmore. Larry Mullens was the park ranger in charge of security at Mount Rushmore. He had a typical law enforcement mentality, fancying himself a weapons specialist. He wore reflector sunglasses.

Simmons knew what the meeting would be about. Mullens had several contingency plans for protecting Mount Rushmore in case it was attacked by what he called terrorists. That had seemed funny until the seventies when militant Indians had occupied the foot of the mountain with gallons of paint and acid, ready to deface the heads. It was one of Mullens's plans that the federal marshals had used to keep the Indians from gaining the summit. Simmons had been called in on that one; deposited on top by a helicopter, he personally inspected the rock fortifications built by Mullens and the federal marshals. Simmons had seen concertina wire and automatic weapons guarding the narrow stone valley that led to the plateau above the heads. Each marshal had carried, in addition to a rifle and side arm, grenades and walkie-talkies. It had seemed a little overdone, but later the reports came in that some of the Indians were armed the same way. It had been quite a stink over four granite heads, but Simmons knew they were symbolic for both sides, and so a likely place for an incident.

Mullens had gained his reputation the week of the siege. No one had taken him very seriously until then. But now, after Mullens himself had retold the story a thousand times, he was a bit of a legend at the Park Service. Just another reason why Simmons, Chief Forest Ranger, didn't want even to talk with him. He knew Mullens would have some cockamamie story about Indian forces massing somewhere in Simmons's forest to attack Mullens's monument. The prospect of spending an afternoon listening to his paranoid suspicions and looking at his reflector sunglasses did not excite Simmons. He'd rather take a look at the Medicine Springs situation. But federal agencies had at least to appear to work together, so he'd have to meet with Mullens before he went into the field. Reluctantly he picked up the phone. Mullens would be full of wild talk about the threat posed by the Indian camp. He'd be insane with fear for Mount Rushmore and probably have a list of the felons who were using the camp for refuge. Simmons wanted to treat this situation seriously, but for him, it was difficult.

Bailey had been thinking. For a reporter, McVay didn't ask many questions. He'd done some checking and found McVay hadn't interviewed anybody. He hadn't asked questions of any substance. Something didn't seem quite right. Maybe Bailey had frightened him with his gruffness. People had told him he did that to strangers sometimes. But McVay didn't seem to be the kind that would be intimidated by a little growling. McVay didn't appear to be intimidated by much of anything. In fact, he didn't act like a reporter. Bailey had never liked reporters—take Jerry Stockton, for example. But McVay was all right, probably because he didn't ask any questions. But reporters always asked questions. Bailey decided to pay more attention to McVay—maybe he was shy. That sort of thing was hard to tell about a man, especially a stranger.

Strangers. That was another thing. Nobody ever came to Medicine Springs or Lindon County, but lately they were everywhere. There was McVay and Egan in the last week. Traverse Best had come in about a year ago. And that Indian gal who was living out at Jake's. Bailey winced a little when he thought of the other strangers, those agitators from outside. The ones up at the illegal Indian camp on the Forest Service land. He was glad they were right there, on the Forest Service land, out of his jurisdiction, up there with the other big troublemaker of the country, P.J. Billion. Just the thought of those outside, radical Indians camped alongside P.J. Billion's little ranch gave Bailey the creeps.

He was thinking about the troubles in the Hills when Egan came into the office. All of the problems closer to home came back to him like the recall of a bad dream. He was glad Egan had come. He wanted to talk the whole thing over, wanted to make some sense out of it and get some kind of plan. Egan moved slowly to the desk, dragging a wooden chair behind him. To Bailey he looked as old as he ever had. His wrinkled eyes were partially closed, and the crow's-feet at the edges of them disappeared under the narrow brim of his hat.

"Good morning, Sheriff," he said.

The sheriff took off his own hat and tossed it onto the cluttered filing cabinet behind him. He started to tell Egan to pull up a chair, but Egan was already sitting down. "So where are we now, Egan?" Bailey said.

"Not much closer," Egan said softly.

"Where do we go from here?"

"We don't go anywhere," Egan said.

"I mean, should we get some men together and look that country over, between old Joe's place and the Hills?"

"I think what you're looking for will be in the Hills themselves," Egan said.

Bailey shook his head. "I was afraid you were going to say that. I do my best to stay out of the Hills. Nothing good ever came out of that country."

"Do what you like," Egan said. "I'm going home."

"Home? What do you mean, home?" Bailey distorted his face. Egan slid the note he had received from Simmons across the desk. "What is this, Egan?" Egan looked at the note. Bailey picked it up and read it. "Who the hell does this guy think he is?"

"The man who hired me. Chief Forest Ranger. He's taking over. I'm going home."

"Bullshit." Bailey was reading the note again. "This guy just wants to help you." Egan didn't answer. "Really, Egan, you got it wrong." Bailey waved the note.

"See what he's got in mind?" Egan said.

Bailey looked again at the note. He shook his head.

"Wants to catch it alive," Egan said.

"So?"

"I won't do it." Egan's old jaw was tight.

"So screw him," Bailey said. "I mean you can do what you want. Hell, you're free, white, and twenty-one."

"Work on my own?"

"Damn it, Egan, I want you to stay. This Simmons can't do nothing. I need you."

Egan nodded his head. "Simmons can't catch a wolf," he said. "If there is a wolf."

Egan's comment did not go unnoticed. Bailey watched him, trying to gauge its weight. "You've seen what's been happening around here," he said slowly. "Something's funny and you know it. I got a feeling I'm going to need a person who knows what he's doing." Bailey was talking seriously now. "I want you to stay."

"To tell the truth, Sheriff, I'd like to stay. But this Simmons is the fellow that hired me, and I guess he can fire me if I don't do what he says."

"So, you're fired. That don't mean you can't stick around a few days. You broke?"

Egan looked at him quickly, then realized that Bailey was prepared to lend him money. "No, I got some money."

"Then stay. You can't leave me with all this shit and a guy coming that could easily be an idiot." Egan was looking down at the floor. "Just a couple of days?" Bailey said. "You got a stake in this, Egan."

Egan began to nod. "Okay," he said. "I'll stay awhile just to see what happens."

Bailey reached across and gave Egan a little punch on the shoulder. "That's it," he said. He winked and smiled.

The air came still for the first time since early morning, and the crumbling edges of the stony buttes seemed to grow more grotesque in the shadows of varying darkness. And at the westernmost end of an oblong butte, silhouetted starkly against an eternity of pink sky, a figure, eerie in the evening light, struggled to put the last stone in its place at the top of a perfect tower, now the tallest point on the horizon. The tower was round, six feet at its base and tapered toward the top where a single stone, eighteen inches square, finished the conical shape, now seven feet tall. The figure climbed down and stepped back. A monument, he thought, for loneliness, boredom, and fear.

Joe Standing Elk, like all shepherds, had built a thousand Stone-Johnnies in his life, for no reason except to stay busy. As a boy he had marveled at them, standing rigid in a country where men, he had thought, had never been. He began building them when he became a shepherd, because shepherds always built them. At first not knowing why, then, after years, seeing them as the monuments that they are. And from then on his Stone-Johnnies became more perfect. They became more like the towers he had seen when he was young, towers that had made him wonder at the creators who had come before, the ones who never returned, who had no reason to believe that anyone would ever see what they had done. Lately, Joe's own towers had become indistinguishable from those ancient ones.

And so, thinking, he stepped back and looked at what he had done. Now the light was coming from the buttes, lighting the tower from beneath. The base rocks were huge and had been within rolling distance of the site that Joe had chosen. Then each tier contained rocks slightly smaller than the last, chosen from the countryside, sometimes miles away, and finally this last stone, balanced seven feet from the top of the butte. It was good. Joe felt somehow it would bring him the peace that the men from town hadn't. They would laugh at the Stone-Johnny, except, perhaps, the old one, the one called Egan.

Joe's eyes swung from the tower to the last of the setting sun. He took his rifle from a boulder where he had leaned it while he worked. It would be dark soon. But there would be no sleep again that night. No sleep for old Joe Standing Elk. He would be watching tonight again. The tower had filled his day. Guarding his sheep would keep boredom away at night.

At one-thirty in the morning Traverse Best walked over to the corner booth and collected three empty beer bottles. He woke up the man who had been in the booth since eleven o'clock. "Time to go, Buddy." Buddy's eyes popped open, and he looked fully awake. He was still drunk, of course, but he sprang to his feet, nervous and a little embarrassed.

"Huh," he said, "must have dozed off. Boy, don't know what happened to me. Must be that getting up early, been working like the devil, you know." Best nodded. "Spring's my busy time."

"I know," said Best, trying to head him toward the door.

"Thanks, Traverse," Buddy said as the door shut on him.

Best turned then, bar rag in hand, and began giving each table a onceover on his way back to the bar. As he worked he thought about McVay. He liked the man, it was too bad that he was mixed up with P.J. Billion somehow. Best had taken note of the fact that McVay was not asking questions about the wolf. The only thing he seemed to be interested in was Billion, and there was no way he could have known about Billion unless he was mixed up with him somehow. Probably drugs, Best thought. Too bad, but if he was dealing with Billion, the chances were great that, when it all came down, they'd be on opposite sides. Too bad, Best thought.

The night air was cool. It felt good to Best after hours of the bar room. He leaned against his pickup and lit a cigarette. The moon was up, but the clouds were starting to billow and roll again. There were several spots of mud on the fender and absently Best rubbed them off. He polished the chrome with his shirt sleeve until it shone like the rest of the truck. Then he got into the driver's seat. But he didn't close the door. He sat for a moment looking out over the prairie behind the Oasis. Finally he slid his legs in and shut the door. His headlights spilled out across the prairie, and he started toward the old ranch house he'd been renting. The prairie came alive as he passed along the highway. Like actors waiting in the wings for the floodlights to reveal them, the jackrabbits and mule deer held their heads high and began to move only when the lights reflected in their eyes. Best took only a vague interest in them. He was thinking about McVay and Billion, then about Katie Running, and he wondered what her game was.

From time to time they'd seen each other, at the bar, parties at different places, and though Best had always known better, they'd ended up talking together, late a couple nights. There was something about her that at once attracted and frightened him. He was convinced she was acting most of the time. That was nothing strange—a lot of people act. What bothered him was the way he'd been attracted to her. No woman had ever affected him in quite that way, and he knew that he'd gone too far in talking about himself. He'd told her too much, and he had the feeling she could do that to any man. He'd never even made love to her, yet he'd babbled to her as if she was his best friend. He'd disappointed himself but knew it was not such an odd reaction. Best knew that he was vulnerable. He'd been living alone for too long, hated this job, hated the ranch house he was living in. The end was in sight, but he was still lonely. He'd be glad when it was all over. There was something about this place that made him act funny.

There are, in fact, few on the prairie who can stand to be alone. To a large extent it is a place of the herd mentality. The power that drives animals together, deranges them when they are separated, makes it easier for those who wait. The deer, the antelope, the sheep, the cattle, the buffalo, the humans—they are all herd animals. Very few of them can think when they are alone. Without others of their own kind they are easily frightened, make mistakes, run in the wrong direction, corner themselves, fail to see the obvious, the ambushes, the shadows where the loners wait.

It was dark now. The moon was completely covered by the clouds as he turned into the long lane that followed the fence line for a quarter of a mile and finally became his driveway. Best flipped his lights to bright. A little more of the blackness disappeared, a few more rabbit eyes flashed back at him. The road jerked him in the seat, and he became aware of the empty pickup box in the rearview mirror. There was a halo of red light from his taillights.

His house was flat, one story, with shingle siding, and it came into sight like a huge prehistoric reptile. There were trees in the yard. In the winter the wind blew right through the walls of the house. Best stopped the pickup in front of the house, then thought again and pulled it into the shed beside the grainery. The interior of the shed lit up, and for an instant Best felt warm. But the feeling didn't last. He turned the engine off first, then fumbled in the glove compartment for his flashlight. When he found it, he switched it on, opened the truck door, and flipped off the headlights. The flashlight beam was old and weak. It shone dully on the wall of the shed. Best moved quickly to the rear of the truck and pulled down the door. It closed with a squeal. Then he turned for the house, and the yellow beam fell on deep tire tracks at his feet. The tracks did not turn into the shed where he had parked his truck. They went on past it and disappeared into the darkness. Best shook the flashlight for more light. It flickered as if to go out, but it did not. It burned on dimly, and Best raised it toward his house. The beam faded before it reached the back door, was lost in the deep shadows of the bushes between him and the house. Best's heart was pounding like a frightened antelope. He thought of getting back in the pickup, waiting for daylight, maybe even going back to town. He swung the light to each side, peered into the dark. Then he took a deep breath, shone the light toward the house, and hurried after it.

It's all in the waiting. If one waits long enough, they will come. And when they come, they come blindly. Then the hiding place and patience have served their purposes. When they come, without thinking, the time of waiting is over, the shadows are no longer necessary. Now, it is automatic.

The next morning the air was very still. The clouds that had come up late the night before had not yet spilled their contents on the prairie. There was a chance that they would not. The rain was almost through for the year. The clouds might disperse and not gather again until sometime in the late fall when they would bring snow. But that morning they were there and hanging, mildly threatening, around the town of Medicine Springs. They did not move. There was no wind. The grayness was stationary.

McVay was on a hillside, far from the town, in the shadow of the pine trees. He was wearing his combat boots and fatigues and studying the buildings and small clearings below him through binoculars. Katie had told him where to find Billion. McVay was convinced that she had not wanted him to know. "You and P.J. Billion won't mix too well," she'd said. And he'd understood that she wanted to know what he had to do with Billion, but she didn't ask.

McVay had left his truck two miles away, at a deserted campground, and cut through the forest. He'd traveled in the dark. The clouds had hidden the stars, and so he'd had to do some dead reckoning, taking his check points from the geological survey map that he'd picked up at Mount Rushmore the day he'd come in. He'd had to use the compass that was on the end of his map light twice, but twenty minutes before light he'd arrived at the spot where he now sat watching the country below. He was not surprised when the rising sun revealed that he was on exactly the hill he'd marked on his map. What did surprise him was the remoteness of the spot. According to his map the only road into Billion's place was one that left the county road not far from where he'd left his truck. He could see it winding into the buildings. But his map gave no real indication of the view that appeared slowly out of the grayness. The hill he was on was very high relative to everything in the immediate vicinity. To his right was the deeper forest, and McVay noted again that the Hills were indeed black. To his left was the prairie. When the light got better, he could see buttes in the distance. He guessed them to be fifty miles away. Directly in front of him, however, was what he'd come to look at.

P.J. Billion's place was situated in the valley at the foot of the hill. There was a little live water in the drainage, but McVay guessed it was just because it was spring. Farther up the valley other small meadows opened, and through his binoculars he could see a few cattle grazing. He studied the hills and draws around the house, making mental notes of any features that he might need when he went in after Billion. It was still very early, and McVay took his time. He noticed that the far hillside, unlike the one he was sitting on, was rocky and the trees seemed poorer. Where he sat, the trees were tall and straight, all a uniform size, and they shaded the ground so that no grass grew. It seemed strange to McVay. He looked around and realized that nothing grew where he was. No grass, no bushes, no berries, only the tall, thin pine trees. And there was one other thing that was strange. McVay had heard no birds. The hour of dawn in every other place he had ever been was filled with bird sounds. In Asia it had been deafening, terrifying at times, and even in Toledo, Ohio, in the city, the birds began before light and by this time were singing and flying everywhere. But here there was nothing—only a few cows in the distance.

McVay looked at the cows again. They were black with white heads, and some had calves by their sides. They chewed at the grass of the meadow. With the binoculars McVay could see that they gathered whole clumps of grass in their mouths as they moved slowly across the meadow. With a jerk of their big heads they tore the grass off and went on to the next clump. McVay looked farther up the valley to see if there were more cattle. He found no more, but his binoculars picked up a splotch of color. It was green, like the forest, but a different shade, too green really to be pine trees and certainly not the clump grass that the cattle were chewing. The splotch of color lay in a branch of the main valley. McVay checked his watch. It was still very early. He stood up and swung his day pack onto his back. He was just slipping the binoculars into his breast pocket, preparing to swing around to the patch of green, when there was a movement at the door of the house below. McVay raised the binoculars and saw a large German shepherd come out of the house, go to the edge of the yard to urinate. At the same time Billion came out onto the porch.

McVay studied the man. From the way he walked it had to be Billion. He was not a large man; McVay guessed one hundred seventy pounds and five foot eight inches tall. He could see him clearly in the binoculars. He seemed well built and wore a beard, but scraggly and not trimmed. His hair was also unkempt. Billion went to the porch rail and, like his dog, relieved himself. When he was finished, he whistled once, and the dog returned immediately. McVay made another mental note of the way the dog responded and the stiff, cocksure way that both of them moved back into the house.

McVay was suddenly possessed with the idea of going in, getting it over with. The .45 caliber automatic was in the pack. It might be a snap, but that wasn't his original plan. It was always best to stick to the plan. Impulse kills—those were words he'd lived by in Vietnam. He knew that half the game was staying cool. And so he pushed the idea out of his head and began making the wide circle through the trees that would take him past the curious green valley and then back, eventually, to his truck. He'd return to town, check out of the hotel, maybe go see Katie again, then come back out here, spend the night, and gather his energy and thoughts for what he'd have to do. He took one last look at the buildings below, memorizing their relative positions. It could be, he thought, that he'd go in at night.

Simmons came into town about ten-thirty. Bailey was there, waiting. Bailey stood with his hands on his hips, watching Simmons as he got out of his car. He was a tall man. In different clothes he could have been a farmer, but he wore a Forest Service uniform, and Bailey never trusted grown men who wore uniforms—especially those who seemed to like wearing them. Simmons was that kind of man. Right away, Bailey didn't like Simmons. He had made up his mind.

"Nice to meet you, Sheriff," Simmons said, offering his hand. Bailey nodded. He had an impulse to squeeze the other's hand as hard as he could, but he didn't. He said that he was glad that Simmons had made it. Simmons had a way of turning his head when he was listening, like he was deaf in one ear. He was wearing sunglasses, so Bailey wasn't sure if he was listening when he turned his head, or maybe looking the other way. They stood for a moment talking about small things. They looked at the sky, decided that the rain was over until fall. They never mentioned what Simmons had come for. Finally Bailey said that he'd like to talk to Simmons as soon as he got settled in.

"Could you come down to my office after supper?" Bailey said. "I'd like to get a few things figured out."

Simmons tilted his head and smiled. "Sure, Sheriff, I'd like to pick your brain"—he nodded his head quickly—"and anybody else who might know something."

Bailey thought that that was a strange thing to say. "Right," he said. "Egan will be in by then." Johnny had come out of the hotel and stood waiting to help Simmons.

"Yes, I'll have to talk to Bill," Simmons said.

"Come around about six," Bailey said.

They watched Bailey go into the café. "I'm Johnny," the old man said.

Simmons pushed his glasses down on his nose and looked over the tops of them. "So that's the sheriff of Lindon County," he said mostly to himself.

"That's him," Johnny said. He picked up the last of the suitcases. "Is this it? No traps or guns or anything like that?"

"No. I'm not an exterminator. My interest is pretty much academic."

"But what about the wolf?"

Simmons smiled. "There's no wolf, my good man. I think we know that."

"Well, I'm not so sure," Johnny said. "But either way, the people around here are going to be upset when they find out that you didn't bring any traps."

"There are four live traps coming in from St. Louis in the next couple of days. If it is a wolf, which it isn't, it's worth more alive than dead."

It was almost eleven o'clock. The sheriff had lost at dice again. They were playing for coffee. There were seven hours before they all would come together. Egan was somewhere out on the prairie thinking about leaving the next day. Bailey tossed seventy-five cents on the counter and took three toothpicks from the dispenser. The reporter was out of sight, but he'd find him for the meeting, and maybe even Stockton. Get it all out in the open, Bailey thought. He sucked at his teeth as he used a pick, then stepped from the café and looked at the thermometer nailed to the wall. Eighty degrees. Spring was over. It was a lot like summer.

Egan wished that he could keep on walking. He wanted somehow to break the bonds that tied him to roads and highways and pickup trucks and towns and people. He hated being human. It was like being condemned to a lifetime of looking on. The best he could hope for was to be unnoticed for a while, and that was very difficult. He was working on it as he walked. He'd been working on it for fifty years, and he felt like a beginner.

But today it was working well. He was moving unnoticed. He had that invisible feeling that was as close as he had ever come to fitting in. He was trying as hard as he could. He had the feeling that he might never get the chance to move through the prairie again. All that day Egan had been thinking that he might be going to die soon.

The thought had been in his mind since before the sun had come up that morning. He had awakened with it. It flooded in through the window as he stared out at the blackness before the sun, and it pecked at him as he ate his eggs silently in the café. He wanted to spend this day on the prairie, and so he had come out to where two sheep had been killed. Now he was four miles on the other side of the water tank. He had crossed two roads, gravel, untraveled, and he had come to only three fences. The country pitched and rolled, and as Egan walked steadily, it made him think of the sand hills of Nebraska, thirty years before. The symmetry came back to him, the timelessness, the rhythm. His strides were as long as ever. It was effortless, like floating. No. It was like sailing, moving ahead of something invisible toward something unseen. Bill Egan threw his head back and pushed a wail out of his lungs, long and solitary, toward the sky.

Over the hill, where the mule deer grazed with her fawn, there was no sound. She sheared off the native buffalo grass with the scissoring of teeth, chewed slowly in the warming sun, and blinked her round eyes.

He tried to be content with being part of it, but he knew what he was there for. He was looking for a wolf he was almost certain wasn't there. There was no reason why there should be a wolf. He, and others like him, had killed them. All of them. But more, they had humiliated them. The images of wolves hanging from lampposts and displayed in the back of pickup trucks came to him. Their dull, sunken eyes and the dried blood at their mouths were vivid. He remembered how the men had changed the way they'd walked when they approached the dead wolves, remembered the women going faint and the children poking the carcasses with sticks. He'd never noticed the humiliation then, never realized how both he and the wolf were being used. It was the onlookers and the gawkers who needed him, said they did, fed off what he could do, and at the same time took all dignity away from the wolf. He was ashamed of his part in it. It wasn't the killing that bothered him. He was sure the wolves accepted that. It was what happened afterward, the humiliation, the loss of dignity. Now that Egan was getting old he thought much more about dignity, and he cursed the power he had had to take it away. There was no way, he thought as he walked, to restore the dignity he'd taken from those wolves. It had been destroyed, and he had played a major part in it. The animals were lost, and his own dignity had gone with theirs. He had no right to expect a chance to restore some of that grandeur. He had no right even to hope that there was a wolf walking the same prairie he was walking.

The green valley was what McVay had expected it to be: young marijuana plants. He stood in the trees and tried to estimate how many plants there were and how much marijuana there would be at harvest time. Billion had been clever. The field was much bigger than it had seemed. He had cleared some trees, enough to let some light down to the ground yet leaving enough to hide the plants from aircraft. The portion of the field that McVay had seen was very little, and as he lined it up, from the field to the hillside where he'd been sitting, he realized that even what he'd seen would be invisible to an aircraft unless it was very low and moving very slowly.

McVay estimated six tons. He'd seen marijuana growing before, in Vietnam, but never so much. He had no idea what Billion would be wholesaling it for, but there was potentially millions of dollars' worth in the field in front of him. It was not much good now, but with the weather warming up it would triple its size in a short time. McVay hoped that somewhere, in one of Billion's buildings perhaps, there was some of last year's crop. He knew there was a good chance that Billion wouldn't keep any cash around.

Again McVay took a minute to study the lay of the land before he set out to complete the circle to his truck. He looked closely at the forest and realized what had seemed wrong to him from the hillside across the valley. There had been too many trees. They restricted the light to the ground. Billion had used that to make the marijuana field work—grow well, yet still be hidden. McVay took one last look, glanced at his compass, and slipped back into the thick trees.

Now McVay began to move quickly through the trees. He moved silently, and he watched ahead of him, all the time keeping his mental compass tuned to the distorting curves of the earth. His subconscious mind distinguished the rock and log structure from the forest before his conscious mind, and he stopped, instinctively sinking lower. He eased behind a tree, somehow expecting whoever built the structure to still be around. He watched, scanned the forest, for nearly a full minute. But he saw no one, only the small stone and log building standing among the trees, looking very out of place.

An old habit made him stand perfectly quiet behind his tree, watching for several more minutes. Fighting the knee-jerk feelings of fear and distrust, he told himself that this was the center of America, that there was no ambush waiting for him at the stone and log building, there were no trip wires or booby traps between him and the structure. But still he moved slowly, staying involuntarily behind trees, zigzagging his way toward the structure, and always watching openings between the trees ahead of him for movement. The familiar tension crushed in on him, and as he moved, he realized what it was. As on the hillside, there were no bird sounds, only a deadly calm. In the Delta this would have told him all he needed to know, but here it meant nothing. In this sterile place the void of bird songs meant nothing.

The structure was simple: four walls and a flat roof, with a rough door on leather hinges. It was too small for anyone to use as shelter for long. The roof was only three feet high, and the walls formed a square perhaps five feet on each side. The walls were thick though, built out of stones that had been gathered from the immediate area. McVay could see the fresh craters from where they had been gathered. It looked like an old trapper's cache, but it was obviously newly built. McVay looked inside. It was absolutely empty. A lot of work just for the fun of it, he thought as he looked the cache over. He glanced at his watch; the morning was half gone, and he wanted to see Katie that afternoon. As he started away from the building, he noticed something white in the dry pine needles. It was a cigarette butt. He bent down and picked it up. The filter tip was brown from being smoked, but the cigarette itself was still very white. It had not lain there long enough to yellow.

Larry Mullens and two other park rangers had walked the steep three-quarter-mile path from the visitors' center to the area above and behind the carved heads on Mount Rushmore. Mullens took pride in being able to make the walk without stopping to rest. The other two men had fallen behind, but finally they had joined him at the top. Being ahead of them had given him a chance to catch his breath so that when they arrived, panting and sweating, Mullens could talk normally, as if the climb had not bothered him at all.

The area where they now stood was strewn with the remnants of the construction of the monument. They were not too far from the vault that Gutzon Borglum, the sculptor of the mountain, had never had a chance to finish. Borglum had invisioned it as a place to keep special documents, a kind of shrine within a shrine. But the money had run out. They'd been lucky, Mullens thought, to finish the heads after Borglum died. The government had come through with the money to finish the heads, but the vault was still not done. Once in a while Mullens would hear that there was a bill in the House or Senate to fund the completion, but it never seemed to pass. It was a shame, Mullens thought, that the government didn't get squarely behind the monument. After all, it was a national treasure. Even the monument budget was too small, he thought, looking at the array of junk that had been left when Borglum abandoned work. There were small broken mining cars still on narrow-gauge track, wheelbarrows, several winches they'd used to lower themselves over the edge. It should all be in a museum. And then there was security—just himself and a little help on a part-time basis from the two rangers he had with him today. A long way from enough in a crisis. He remembered the siege of the seventies. Could have been a bad deal, he thought; we were lucky. But the terrorists had gotten onto the mountain then, strictly off limits to any but authorized personnel. They could do it again if the authorities weren't careful.

That was why they had climbed up behind the heads—to patrol it, look for anything strange. Mullens glanced around the perimeter where he and the federal marshals had been encamped those days of the siege. He noted the signs of the siege and some of the original construction, but nothing out of the ordinary. He walked farther up the rocky draw to the winches they now used to clean and patch the heads. He could see the badlands of South Dakota seventy miles away and the distinct edge of the Black Hills only fifteen miles east. It was strictly against policy, but Mullens walked to the edge of Washington's head and looked down at the visitors' center. He thought how insignificant it looked now, wondered if anyone down there at the pay telescopes was watching him, right there on Washington's head.

As he looked down, he became aware of a buzzing sound. His first impulse was to look back at the other rangers. They stood leaning against a huge rock, waiting for Mullens. He looked around, hearing the sound getting louder, then scanned the sky and finally saw a light aircraft coming toward the mountain. Mullens turned to the other men. "Get the Center on the walkie-talkie, there's an airplane coming." He stared at the airplane. Yes, it was coming their way. "Christ," he yelled, "this is a controlled airspace." Then back at the other rangers: "Get this guy's numbers. Christ, this is a controlled area." It occurred to Mullens that the Indians from the camp could be making a survey of the monument. He couldn't help himself. "Get down," he shouted as he drew his pistol. He tried to wave the airplane away. Now the plane began a slow bank along the front of the faces. "Get away," he shouted, taking cover behind a rock. He flung his arms violently. "Get out," he screamed and sighted down the pistol's barrel. As the plane passed him, a small child at a rear window smiled and waved at him. "Get away," he screamed. He stood up, realizing that it was not Indian. "Get their numbers," he said. His voice was official now, a little embarrassed. "They're just tourists," he said. But he did not put his pistol back into its holster until the airplane was nearly out of sight.

Tom McVay slid his arms out of the straps on his backpack, swung the pack onto the hood of his truck, and took out the .45 automatic. Then he threw the pack behind the seat and put the .45 in the glove compartment. He got behind the wheel and took a deep breath. The hike had felt good. He looked back toward where he'd been and started the engine. He thought through the whole route again as the truck warmed up, so he'd be sure and would not have to hesitate in the dark. If he had checked out of the hotel, if he had all his gear, he would have just stayed. But he hadn't, and he did want to see Katie again. He eased the truck into gear and headed down the road toward the prairie.

Egan had just finished a circle and come back into sight of his own truck. His second circle would go out to a kill the land owner had told him about. It was a mile or so away, and he'd decided, even though there was no sign in the area, to take some traps in case. He was heading back to his truck for his equipment and was nearly there when he saw another truck coming out of the hills.

McVay saw the truck and the old man and recognized them immediately. McVay had been wondering what Egan was up to. The memory of the old man had stayed with him since they'd met in the Oasis.

By the time McVay stopped beside Egan's pickup, the old man was pulling a gray canvas bag from the back. "Good morning," McVay said.

"Morning," Egan said and leaned into the pickup for another small bag.

"Let me give you a hand with that," McVay said. He jumped down and took the bag from Egan. It was filled with something metal that clanked inside as the bag swung toward him. It was heavy. Egan took his rifle from the back.

"Thanks," he said.

"Going out trapping this morning?" McVay said.

"Just looking, really."

"Got a good lead?"

"No, just an old kill. Got to start somewhere." Egan pointed for McVay to put the bag down on the ground beside the other one. He laid the rifle down, then knelt and opened the bags.

McVay stood back thinking how lightly the old man moved. "Say, could I come along with you? I mean, something might happen out there that's newsworthy." It had come out of McVay's mouth, but it seemed someone else had said it. McVay was embarrassed at the lie.

Egan turned from the bags. His eyes swung up and locked onto McVay's. "I don't know when I'll be back. Maybe several hours, but you're welcome." His eyes ran over McVay. McVay could feel him noticing the combat boots and fatigues.

Egan prepared his gear carefully, taking only what he needed. He repacked what was left and replaced the bags in the truck. When he was ready, he faced McVay. The eyes asked if he was ready.

McVay nodded, and they started out across the prairie. They walked the mile slowly, both men scanning the horizon and neither speaking. The kill was at a watering tank, two old shrunken sheep carcasses. The sheep had obviously been partly eaten. McVay could see that from fifty feet away, where Egan had waved him to stop. They circled the carcasses several times. The old man was nearly crawling as they drew closer to the sheep. McVay walked behind him, crouching a little out of respect for the old man, but not knowing why. Around the tank the ground was bare and dusty. McVay had only gotten to the bare spot when he pointed to the ground. "Look."

Egan didn't look. He kept on walking toward the carcasses. He had already seen the track that McVay was pointing to. "Coyote," he said. McVay shrugged his shoulders, a little embarrassed.

"So coyotes killed them."

"Coyotes been eating them," Egan said. "Maybe something else killed them." He knelt down beside the first sheep. He took the front leg and bent it up under the sheep, making it look as if it were part of a grotesque nativity scene. He went to the second sheep and did the same. "Lightning," he announced. He answered McVay before he had a chance to ask. "Lightning-struck animals never get stiff," he said. "No rigor mortis."

"And the coyotes?"

"Just a free lunch."

Egan had walked away from the sheep, so McVay went to have a look at the chewed and stinking corpses. The smell reminded McVay of other bloated bodies, years before. He knelt ten feet away and looked at the way the coyotes had begun to eat them. They had started from the rear. It repulsed McVay, and he rocked back on his haunches. His thigh brushed a cactus, and he stood up cussing the thing. It clung to him through his pants. When he tried to remove it, it penetrated his fingers. Finally he pulled it off and flung it away. "Damn good-for-nothing things," McVay said.

Egan laughed. "Ain't good for much," he said. "Except maybe starting horse races." McVay shot a questioning glance at him. "We used to use them to start horse races," Egan said.

"How's that?" McVay said.

"They sort of explode when you shoot them. If two guys got to pestering each other, sometimes they used to race. We'd line them up with a cactus like that between them. That way one guy could start them by shooting the cactus and judge the winner, too."

"Pretty good shooting," McVay said. "Must have been short races."

"Quarter mile," Egan said.

McVay looked down at the cactus that he had thrown away. It was about the size of a baseball. "Shit," McVay said. He was forced to smile at Egan, but Egan wasn't smiling. He was serious. "Four hundred yards?" McVay laughed.

"They explode with a pop," Egan said. "GO! Before the sound got there. GO! Little pieces of cactus over everything." He smiled at McVay, and McVay, staring again at the steely eyes, was tempted to believe him.

"Four hundred yards?" McVay looked at the rifle. The tiny muzzle pointed upward; there were ivory inlays under Egan's gnarled old hands. "With this?" he said.

The humor sifted out of the talk and disappeared into the dusty soil. "Let's see it," McVay said. The old man had gone too far, made his claim too concrete. He had cornered himself.

Egan's eyes narrowed. He took the binoculars from his neck and handed them to McVay. "Find a cactus," he said.

McVay found a cactus with the binoculars, and in a moment Egan had located it in the scope of the rifle. It was over four hundred yards, but Egan said nothing.

"Starting horse races?" McVay said.

Egan looked cold across the prairie. He looked wild now, not like an old man. "Not just horse races," he said, "contests." He was wrapping the shoulder strap of his rifle around his left arm for better stability. "You watch that cactus, and when it explodes, you think of the word GO running through two cowboys' minds on each side of it and think of two half-wild horses leaping right at you through those binoculars. Think of those cowboys whipping those horses with a six-foot piece of rope. Think of them whipping each other."

The shot rang in McVay's ears, and an instant later, centered in the frame of the binoculars, the cactus exploded. McVay heard Egan whisper, "GO!" and McVay did see those cowboys lashing each other with stiff steer ropes, the hemp cutting necks and faces, and the horses running flat, their bellies only inches from the ground, stumbling, horse and rider running for their lives.

McVay jerked his eyes away from the binoculars where the pieces of cactus were still raining to the ground. He looked toward Egan, but the old man was walking away, the rifle swinging rhythmically with his easy gait.

The Indian camp was still mostly tents and pickup campers. A few people were living in their cars, but one family had started to build a house. The other structure was the school. James Lebeaux had insisted on a school. He said that it should be the first thing to be built; it would show the government that the community was permanent and that it was peaceful. But the newspapers had not made it look peaceful. They had somehow found out that there were several men living in the camp who were wanted on felony charges in other states—stories like that could hurt them badly. It was true, of course, that some of the men were felons, but most were not dangerous. Still, it would be better if the criminal element would leave.

Radicals were one thing. Given the situation, it was understandable that some Indians would take an extreme position. It was a sign of desperation that Lebeaux could easily understand. But the ones who used militancy as an excuse were simply those who did not fit into any society, who did not know what the camp was about, and were using it as a place to hide. Because they were Indians, they came to the camp. In their minds, Lebeaux supposed, they thought that violence was somehow following the old way, and perhaps it was. But the drinking and the laziness and the loud threats were not the old way. When Lebeaux looked at these people, he did not see anything that reminded him of the old ways. What he saw were more products of the white man's government. These misfits were mostly Indians, it was true, but they were corrupted, like polluted streams or shopping malls built on hillsides that were once holy places.

The worst of that bunch was Robert Lancaster. He called himself Robert Lance and was the leader of the most violent faction in the camp. Lebeaux had made an error when he had pointed out, in front of several others, that Lance was not from the Black Hills. He had implied that he was not even an Indian, and that had made Lance mad. There were people in the camp who listened to him, and it worried Lebeaux that Lance seemed to have a solid core of about six followers. When the newspaper published the article about convicted felons in the camp, Robert Lancaster's name appeared. It said that he had served two years for armed robbery.

Lance denied it, saying that he had served the time, but that he never committed the crime. In actuality he was surprised that the newspaper had not found out a few other things about him. Rumors that Lance was still wanted circulated through the camp, and Lebeaux was afraid that this would ruin everything that they were working for.

He knew that Lance and his followers were trouble, but there was very little that he could do about it. This was an Indian camp, not a white man's camp. This camp was run on trust, not on rules.

At ten minutes until six Jerry Stockton walked into Bailey's office. He sat down. Bailey was cleaning his pistol and thinking that he hadn't shot it for almost a year. It was dirty, and Bailey was ashamed that it had been so long since he'd used it. He put the pistol down on his desk and looked up at Stockton. "You here for the meeting, Jerry?"

Stockton nodded his head once, folded his arms, and began to wait. Bailey looked at him and thought of saying something more but didn't. He went back to cleaning the pistol and tried to forget that Stockton was even there.

Simmons was right on time. He walked through the office door just as the big wooden-framed clock clicked to six o'clock. Stockton jumped up and introduced himself to Simmons. They began to chatter about the articles that Stockton had written. Bailey tried not to listen but he could hear the tone of skepticism in Simmons's voice.

"Maybe we should get this thing going," Simmons said to Bailey. "I'm anxious to find out what new developments there have been."

"The reporter isn't here yet," Stockton said.

"Neither's Egan," Bailey said.

"Probably taking a nap," Stockton said. The comment was meant to be funny, but Bailey stared at him, making no pretense about his mood.

"He's out doing something, Jerry." Bailey was daring Stockton to make another crack. Stockton had the good sense to say nothing. He smiled, childlike, at Bailey.

They waited another fifteen minutes. Bailey stalled the best he could with small talk, but it was hard to be nice to men he disliked. He didn't want to say anything about the problem without Egan there, but he knew Egan could be very late, and he might have to talk to these men alone. He'd already realized that Egan was the only one who knew anything about what was going on, that Egan was the only one with any power to solve the problem, and that made him dislike these two even more. The men kept trying him, asking about what had been happening. Just as Bailey decided to go ahead and discuss it without Egan being there, the door opened and the old man slipped silently into the room. He stood at the door as if he had come to the wrong meeting. Behind him, almost like a shadow, stood McVay. The old man looked tired and embarrassed. It was clear that he did not enjoy meetings like this one. Bailey waved them to come in and sit down.

Simmons shook Egan's hand. "Good to see you, Bill," Simmons said. "I trust you got my note."

"Yes," Egan said clearly, without expression.

"All right," Bailey said. "Tom McVay, Mel Simmons." He let them shake hands. "Now let's get into this thing."

"I'll bring Mr. Simmons up to date," Stockton said.

Bailey rubbed his face and sat back in his chair. "I think Mr. Simmons knows what's happening here," Bailey said. "All we need is an understanding about where we go from here."

Simmons turned to Egan. "Bill, did you get a chance to look at any of the kills?"

"The calf and the heifer at Knutson's," Egan said. "Everything else was old."

"What did it look like?"

"It rained that night, couldn't tell much."

"Well," Simmons said, "we could save a lot of time if we could just establish that there is nothing out here except maybe a couple of dogs or some coyotes. Have you seen enough to say that?"

Everyone turned to Egan. The old man looked down, thinking. "No," he said. "I couldn't say for sure that there isn't a wolf out here."

"Of course not," Stockton put in quickly, "because there is a wolf."

"Shut up, Jerry," Bailey said.

"No, I can speak here." Stockton put his fist down on the desk. Bailey let his breath out slowly, closed his eyes, and nodded his head.

"There is a wolf here, Mr. Simmons. Has anyone told you about the skull? Have they shown you the skull, told you what Joe Standing Elk saw?"

Simmons shook his head. "No, I don't know what you're talking about."

"Show him."

"I was going to show him, Jerry. Settle down." Bailey took the skull and the envelope of hair from his desk. He handed them to Simmons. "Supposed to be a wolf tooth there," Bailey said, "and this is supposed to be his hair. Shepherd outside of town claims it killed his dog."

"Wolves do kill dogs," Simmons said as he looked at the skull. And he thought, They've always killed domestic dogs, almost like executing a traitor. He turned the skull over in his hands, then looked at Egan.

Egan shrugged. "Could be," he said. "Looks like wolf hair." Simmons rolled the skull over and over in his hands, thinking. McVay could see that Simmons, despite his skepticism, wanted to believe.

"So, it's possible?" Simmons said, more to himself.

"You're damned right," Stockton said, sensing support.

"Let's not jump to conclusions," Bailey said.

"I think we need to formulate a plan," Stockton said, "to kill this damn thing."

"No," Simmons said, and Bailey started to agree. But Simmons went on. "I think we would be making a huge mistake to kill this thing, if it is a wolf. We must catch it alive."

Bailey and McVay looked at Egan. The old man said nothing. McVay knew what Egan was thinking. He could see that he was against Simmons's plan. But he could also see that if anyone was going to speak against live trapping, it would have to be Bailey.

The telephone began to ring just as Bailey spoke. "No," he said, "if there really is something out there, I don't want to mess around." The phone rang again, and he picked it up. It was Ike Brewer, the daytime bartender at the Oasis.

"Sheriff," he said, "I got a problem." Bailey let him go on while he watched Egan. He knew Egan would quit if Simmons made him try to live-trap anything. Bailey didn't want him to leave. "Traverse Best didn't show up for work."

"So?"

"Well, I tried to call him, and there's no answer. I was wondering, if you got the time, would you go out and take a look?"

"Sure, Ike, when I get time." Bailey hung up the receiver. Stockton and Simmons were talking about what they were going to do if they caught the wolf alive.

"Wait a minute," Bailey said. "You guys are jumping the gun. We've got no idea what's out there, or even if there's anything out there."

"But we have to get a plan. We have to think ahead," Stockton said.

"You two can make all the plans you want to," Bailey said angrily, "but who's going to do the work, who's going to get out there and outthink your wolf, who's going to trap him?"

Everyone turned to look at Egan, but all they saw was the door closing gently. Bailey grabbed his hat, pulled it on. "I'll get him," he said.

Bailey found Egan just outside, standing quietly, looking up at the moving sky. "Come on," Bailey said. "Let's go for a ride."

Egan was still looking up at the sky. The clouds were flying past the moon. He began to nod his head. "Yes," he said, "nice night for a ride."

As they started for Bailey's car, the door to the office opened and McVay stepped out. "They're still trying to figure out what they said," he said to both Egan and Bailey.

"They'll never figure it out," Bailey said. "Come on, we're going for a ride."

They drove in silence. Bailey was mad. He squeezed the steering wheel hard, his hands like steel clamps. Egan was in the front seat with him, and Bailey looked at him. He didn't sneak a glance; he turned and looked full at him. Egan sat up straight, pale blue eyes forward. Nothing bothers him, Bailey thought, not really.

"We're going to find the bartender from the Oasis," Bailey said. Then, "I don't blame you. It's hard enough to trap a jackrabbit in a live trap," Bailey said.

"That's not it," Egan said. "He'll be alive when we get him, maybe a broken leg at the worst."

Bailey thought, sure, they could throw a net over it or something. It wouldn't be tough. "Well, what the hell?" Bailey said. "Why not play the game?"

Egan looked at him, and McVay sensed what the old man was going to say. "That's not the game we're playing," he said. "Nobody's going to make me do that sort of thing again."

"Make you do what?" Bailey asked, honestly confused.

"Make him do what they can't, for their kicks," McVay said from the backseat, and he had no idea why he'd said it. He had no idea why he was even with these men. He should have already found Katie, should be with her right now, he thought, getting ready for tomorrow at Billion's. But he wasn't, he was in the backseat of a sheriff's car traveling down a gravel road toward a man's house he barely knew.

Bailey shrugged. "Okay, but that's no reason to give up. You still thinking about leaving?" he said to Egan.

It was the first McVay had heard about Egan wanting to leave. That, he didn't understand.

"Depends," Egan said.

"You can't," Bailey said. "You can't leave me here alone with these morons. Christ, Egan, I'll go wacko."

"So would I," Egan said.

"Come on, Egan. Something will turn up, and you'll be able to catch whatever the hell it is we got, and it'll be over."

"Simmons can catch it."

"He couldn't catch a cottontail."

"Can't tell," Egan said.

"He's an ass," Bailey said.

"He sounds good," Egan said.

"He hasn't said anything you didn't already say. He said, 'Maybe there's a wolf.' Shit, I knew that."

"He was impressed with the tooth in the skull."

"Yea, but it could have been faked."

"I don't think it's a fake."

"You believed that old Indian, didn't you?"

"Can't see why he'd lie," Egan said.

"Then you're saying there's a wolf?"

"No," Egan said.

"That's double-talk," Bailey said, and they were both quiet for several minutes. Bailey wanted to ask something, but he was afraid to bring it up. It was like a secret between Egan and himself. It was as if they had agreed not to say anything about it, but Bailey had to know.

"What about Harmon Knutson?" Egan didn't answer, and McVay

slid closer to the front seat. "Egan?" Bailey slowed down and looked at the old man. "He was shooting at something out of the window of his pickup the night he got killed." McVay watched the two in the front seat. "What was he shooting at, Egan?"

McVay's eyes went to Egan. He knows, McVay thought. There is a wolf. No, he hopes there is a wolf. Egan looked ahead, at the road. "I don't know," he said.

"Was he shooting at something?" McVay asked Egan.

"Yes."

"Why didn't you tell Simmons that?" Egan didn't answer. They were at the lane that led to Best's house. The sheriff shook his head and turned into the driveway.

The cottonwoods around the house shone black against the lighted night sky as if they were one round, bushy tree. Bailey glanced at his watch. It was five minutes after eight. The lane wound into the yard of the ranch house, and they could see that there was no car in the driveway. Bailey considered going back into town. But they were there. He stopped the car. "Let's have a quick look," he said.

The three men got out of the car, each wrapped up in his own thoughts. Absently, Bailey said, "It's not like Best not to show for work." They went to the front door, and Bailey pounded with his fist. "Ike said he'd called. Sure doesn't look like anyone's home." He turned to the other men and put his hands on his hips. "Shit," he said, "now what am I supposed to do?"

They came away from the house, and Egan raised his head and looked around them. The clouds were still tumbling past the moon, and the night was bright. "How about a look around the yard?" Egan said, and without waiting for an answer, he walked slowly out toward the shed that stood to the west of the house. He kept watching the ground. Bailey and McVay came after him. Egan could feel them a few feet behind.

"Come on, Egan. There's nobody here," Bailey said. Egan stopped, squinted at the ground. "Come on, Egan," Bailey said again. But the old man knelt down. He could feel Bailey move to his shoulder. "What?" Bailey said.

"Blood," Egan said.

Bailey knelt beside him. He looked at the dark place in the grass in front of Egan. "Shit," he said. He touched it, not believing, as if to brush it away. His fingers came up with tiny rust-colored specks on them.

Bailey looked at Egan. "Is that blood? McVay, there's a flashlight in the glove compartment of my car. Get it, would you?"

"It's a day or so old," Egan said. They stood and looked around them. It was still and light. The moon was bright in the cottonwood branches. Egan began to amble off again.

"Egan," Bailey hissed. But the old man kept walking, his head down, scanning from left to right. Bailey looked around again. He could see the interior light go on in his car as McVay searched for the flashlight. Shit, Bailey thought, what if he sees the tape? But he shrugged and looked around, wanting to be busy. The shed was only twenty feet away. Bailey went to the door and looked inside. The moonlight fell on Best's shiny new pickup truck. He shut the door and hurried after Egan.

Bailey was excited. "His pickup is here," he said. "He must be here."

Egan pointed. "More blood," he said.

Now McVay had caught up with them. He shone the light on what Egan said was blood. McVay and Bailey looked closely. They didn't speak, but they both knew it was blood. Egan was ahead of them again, following the dark splotches. Both McVay and Bailey thought of going back to the car for guns, but the blood was old. There was no point.

Around the house was a woven wire fence. In the fence morning glories had begun to grow. Their tiny clinging fingers twisted themselves around the wire of the fence. The blooms were small, their leaves were a soft green, and the flowers themselves were shut to the night air. The men followed the trail of blood toward the fence. What had begun as blotches here and there was now one long stain nearly a foot wide. The trail wound across the yard toward the fence of morning glories. It branched, became two, then came back together. Whatever had been bleeding had had several wounds and had lost a lot of blood. No one spoke. McVay and Bailey stayed behind Egan and watched the trail as it divided again into two dark strips eight inches wide.

Nearer the house the shadows on the ground got deeper. The cottonwoods were thick above them, and the trail of blood blended with the shadows and became hard to follow. Bailey couldn't see it at all without the flashlight. Egan went on, very slowly now, with Bailey and McVay walking beside and slightly behind. The sheriff's eyes were strained. He squinted at the ground, saw nothing, rubbed his eyes with both hands and looked up to rest them. His mouth had been slightly open in a little yawn, and it stayed that way. He stopped, and an old reflex sent his hand toward where the pistol should be as his left hand pawed at Egan's back. Egan sensed it and looked back at him, then followed his stare to the corpse sprawled against the fence, tangled in the morning glories. The flashlight came up and shone on the back of Traverse Best's head.

Blood was caked hard on his pants. One leg dangled exposed, the flesh torn and peeled down to the ankle. The fingers of one hand were missing, and the arms spread against the fence were shredded and twisted. Best lay face down. The fence was bent down with his weight. There were long deep gashes in his buttocks. His head hung down on the other side of the fence and was covered with blood, the throat and one ear torn away.

Bailey found his voice. "Jesus Christ," he whispered.

Part Four

McVay had forgotten about his earlier plans. When they'd gotten back into town, it had been late, and all he wanted to do was to find Katie. Seeing Best hanging there in the fence, surrounded by morning glories with their tiny blossoms folded in on themselves, had given him a sickening feeling. It wasn't the corpse or the blood, or even the picture of the scene as it must have happened that bothered him. It was the fact that this was the middle of America, peacetime, as far from a foreign country as a person could get. It was the excitement in Bailey's voice, and the look on Egan's old face. Those were the things that bothered him about finding Traverse Best hanging in the fence. They made him realize that something very important was going on here. Finding Best got McVay's attention, focused life for him, and when he got back to town, he found he'd put his reason for coming to Medicine Springs in the back of his mind and that all he really wanted was to see Katie. He could not tell himself why.

So he'd asked the sheriff where she lived, and Bailey had looked at him and, without any question in his eyes, had told him how to get to the Hermany-horses place. Egan had heard him ask Bailey how to get there and had nodded and turned away. They were all tired by then—it was almost midnight.

Now McVay was making his way along the gravel road that headed out of Medicine Springs toward the northwest. The country started to roll just out of town, and by the time he had gone two miles there were pine trees, and the contour of the land changed dramatically into hills and canyons. He was in the Black Hills and felt their blackness. He could still see the calmness in Bill Egan's eyes as he scanned the area around Best's body, and it made him bull his neck against a chill along his spine.

For the first time he wondered if there really was a wolf in these hills. He had read the books that Johnny had given him, but he had never really thought about whether or not there was a wolf. It hadn't mattered to him until tonight. The Hills got darker, and the road began to twist as it climbed. He knew that he should be going about his business, should be camped out above Billion's house at that moment, ready to move at first light. He knew he should stick with his plan, but things were different now. He had to find out what had killed Best, and he knew that he had to know more about Katie Running.

When the lights of the house came into sight, McVay slowed the truck. He should have called, he thought. And what about her two roommates? If they remembered him, there could be trouble. Then he wondered if Katie was alone. What if she was with someone else? That sent a strange feeling into his stomach. He told himself that the whole idea had been an impulse and that he should forget it, but he knew that he could not. The truck moved into the driveway, and he watched a figure come to the window in the front of the house. McVay watched for a minute before he turned off the headlights. The figure was a man, he was sure, and again he thought of forgetting the whole thing.

But he did not. He turned the engine off and let his eyes adjust to the darkness. It reminded him of the darkness around Best's house, and instinctively he reached for the .45 in the glove compartment. He hefted it, enjoying the weight of the thing, and tried to think it through. Could the pistol be a liability? Might it save his life? He hefted it again and slipped it into his jacket pocket. By then the figure had moved from the window, and McVay could see that he was looking out the window in the front door. They both stared, though neither could actually see the other. If the brothers remembered him and could tell that it was him, there might be a shotgun waiting behind that door. McVay felt the flat side of the .45 in his pocket. It was probably a hundred feet from his truck to the house, very dark, except for the light coming from the windows in the house. Now there was a little game to it. He wondered why he really wanted to cross that open place between his truck and the house. Katie, he thought, that was the reason, and again he thought of just driving back to town, but he couldn't. There was Katie, and now this little game between him and the figure behind the door. The Lord hates a coward, he said to himself and opened the truck door.

The light from the dash silhouetted him, and he shut the door as quickly as possible. He put his hands in his jacket pockets and hunched his back, making believe that he was cold. As he started to move, he saw the figure at the door disappear, and before he had advanced twenty feet toward the house there were two figures. The Lord hates a coward, he kept telling himself, and that made him smile, but he watched the two figures, ready for any movement. He tried not to miss anything, tried to see at the periphery of his vision, and tried not to blink.

He was fifteen feet from the front door when he heard voices and saw the door knob move. There was an old picket fence around the yard, set on large wooden fence posts. McVay judged the distance to the nearest post, but then he recognized Katie's voice.

"It's Tom," she was saying, "go back to the TV." She stepped out onto the porch, with her white teeth reflecting all the light there was in the yard. He heard someone mumbling behind her, and he relaxed. "What the hell are you doing out here?" She laughed.

"Looking for you," McVay said. She came down the steps and moved very close to him. He could smell her.

"Good," she said. "I've been thinking about you." She smiled up at him, and he could feel the heat from her round face. They stood for a long time like that, and finally McVay began to feel uncomfortable.

"I wanted to talk to you," he said. "Something killed Traverse Best."

Katie was stunned but not surprised. She knew Best lived a more dangerous life than he let on. "Come on in," she said.

They had to walk past Jake and Pete to get to the kitchen. McVay noticed that Jake had a bandage over his left eye and that Pete's right arm was wrapped. He genuinely hoped that he hadn't hurt them badly. They didn't look at him. The television was on, and they watched it intently. When they got to the kitchen, Katie went about putting on a pot of coffee. McVay sat on one of the old wooden chairs and watched. She felt his eyes and knew that he would want sympathy. But Best's death affected her also. There was an impulse to turn and blurt out that she had known Best too, better than he had. There was a strange sense of guilt, but she forgot her own problems.

"You look tired," she said. "Rough deal?"

"Pretty rough," McVay answered.

"So what happened?"

"We found him out at his place. Hard to tell what killed him." Katie looked at him and wrinkled her brow. He shrugged as a sort of answer, but she didn't let him get by with it and shook her head. "He was cut and torn apart in places," McVay said.

"They're not saying it was that wolf."

"They're saying there isn't a wolf."

Now Katie shrugged. "It wasn't the wolf," she said. She said it like there was no doubt in her mind. McVay tried to see her eyes, but she got up to check the coffee. It was still perking, but she poured a little out to see if it was close enough. It wasn't and she turned back to McVay and leaned against the counter. That made her hips stick out, and McVay became aware of her body. She put her hands on the counter behind her, and the hips seemed to be thrust upward, her shirt buttons strained. "There's a lot of bad shit coming down around here," she said. McVay heard something different in her voice. He looked closely at the eyes but couldn't see anything. "Ought to give you a good story," she said, and then she looked at him. Neither gave in. She turned then, and poured two cups of coffee.

When she came to the table, she asked if he was hungry. He told her no, a lie, and they sat in silence. The television droned in the other room. McVay could see the blueness of the screen flicker against the kitchen window. Without warning, Katie spoke. "You going to stay here tonight?"

McVay shrugged. He hadn't thought about it. "Up to you, I guess," he said. "Don't have to."

"Shit's really coming down," she said.

McVay nodded. He didn't know exactly what she meant but knew that she was upset. To change the subject, he nodded toward the television room. "Those two pissed?" he asked.

"Only 'cause you're white," Katie said.

"They remembered me?"

"I had to fill them in a little."

"Thanks."

"I didn't tell them everything. There was a lot they missed." She smiled. "They wouldn't have understood it all."

McVay smiled back. "Should I be watching over my shoulder?"

"Hard to say. If you were Indian, no. Depends on what they think of you." She stood up. "You smoke?"

"Some."

She went to the cupboard and took out a plastic bag filled with pot. She rolled the joint in an instant and handed it to McVay. Then she slid a book of matches across the table at him and brought the coffeepot over to fill their cups.

The pot was rough, but McVay could feel it take hold almost with the first drag. She took the joint from him and drew in on it. They sat holding their breath and looking across the table at each other. Finally they shook their heads and exhaled.

"Christ," McVay said.

"Here we go." Katie smiled and handed the joint back to him.

McVay pulled on the joint again but not deeply. He had begun to think. Was this the marijuana Jimmy had been trying to buy? Had

Billion sold it locally after he'd killed Jimmy and stolen his mother's money? Then he thought about Best. Best and Jimmy, the damned marijuana. He tried to think of other things. Old Egan, he decided, he'd try to think of Egan. But he sensed that something was wrong and he opened his eyes. All he saw was Katie, then he realized that she was looking over his shoulder, and he spun in his chair. Jake Hermany-horses leaned in the doorway behind him. He jerked and started to stand, but Jake jumped back and put his hands in the air.

"Sit down, man. I ain't going to fight you," Jake said, and McVay sat back down. He could feel his heart beating in his chest. "You think I'm fuckin' nuts?" Jake said as he came into the kitchen.

"No shit," Pete said from the doorway. McVay jumped again, and when he saw the wrapped hand, he tightened in the chair. "We learned our lesson," Pete said. He smiled almost shyly. "I wouldn't come within twenty feet of you," he said, "'cept I could use some smoke." He laughed.

"Me too," Jake said and smiled the same shy smile.

Katie started the joint around again. McVay pulled on it but did not inhale. Now it reminded him of Jimmy and Billion. He hated it. Pete and Jake sat on the floor. No one spoke then, and Katie went to roll another joint. McVay told himself to calm down. It was the marijuana. He tried not to think of that night in the street beside the Oasis, but he could not understand how Pete and Jake could have forgotten it. In the light of the kitchen he could see that there were more signs of the fight on the men's faces than the bandages covered. He was surprised to see that the bruises showed even on Pete's dark skin.

The two Indians had been drinking and the marijuana affected them almost immediately. "Jeesh, I guess," Jake said.

Then there was more silence. Katie was smiling. The joint made another round. This time McVay passed it without putting it to his lips. "I thought I fell in a thrashing machine," Pete said.

"No," Jake said, "a cement mixer."

McVay smiled at them.

"Jeesh, like getting drug by a horse."

"Yeah, drug off a cliff by a horse."

"Jeesh."

Katie laughed, then Jake and Pete, and finally McVay.

"Boy, you were pissed, huh?" They laughed again.

"Or getting run over by a tank."

"My head still hurts."

"That's from the beer," Katie said.

"Beer?"

"What'd you hit us with?"

McVay held up his fists. "Felt like an iron pipe."

"Iron Fist."

"You an Indian?" Jake and Pete collapsed into laughter.

"Shit," Katie said.

"Good shit," McVay said.

"The best." Katie watched him from the corner of her eye. "Billion's," she said.

McVay nodded. He was looking down at the table. The joint was in his hand, and he knew that Katie's eyes were on him. He looked up and held the joint out to her. "Enjoy it," he said. "It might be hard to get in the future."

Katie took the joint and the stare from McVay. She did not smoke it but passed it on to Jake. She had to tap him on the shoulder to get his attention. "Jeesh," he said, took the joint and held it. Pete leaned over and took the joint from his hand. It was very short, and Pete dropped it on the floor. He took a toothpick out of his shirt pocket and stabbed the joint. But by the time he got it to his lips, it was out. He looked at it closely, then handed it back to Katie. She put it in the ashtray and they all sat quietly for a long time. The air seemed heavy to McVay, and warm. He felt like his body was about ready to go to sleep but his mind was alert. Katie's hand was on the table, and he reached out and touched it. She looked over at him, but he did not look back at her. He watched the hand, ran his fingers along the knuckles, and tried to touch it as softly as he could. His hand was much bigger than Katie's, and the color was different. His hands were tanned and older looking. Katie's were Indian. They were a strange color. McVay tried to think what color they were. They were not brown or red like he'd always thought an Indian's skin would be. But he could not think what color they were. He heard one of the men moving on the floor. Someone had mentioned going to bed. He wanted to say good night but he couldn't look up. He watched the hand and felt it until he heard Katie speak.

"Me too," she said, and her hand rolled over and took his. "You ready?"

McVay nodded and followed her. They stepped over Jake, who was still sitting on the floor, and moved down a dark hallway. It was so dark that it frightened McVay. All he could feel was the heaviness of the dark air and the pressure of Katie's hand as she led him down the hallway. Then they were in her room, and he felt her move close to him. He could smell her in the dark. Then the softness of her hair against his face and the taste of her.

The bed was very warm, and they lay perfectly still. Katie's head was on McVay's shoulder, and his arm wrapped around her back. McVay thought that she was asleep, but when he moved his arm, she moved, too, trying to make him more comfortable. They ended up lying on their sides facing each other with their heads on separate pillows but very close. Their bodies were touching. The marijuana was still in their heads, and absently McVay began to let his right hand run gently along Katie's side. He started just under her left arm and stroked her slowly along the ribs, to her waist and over her hipbone, then very softly along her thigh, letting his fingers trail off and return to where they had begun. Then again, along the curves, trying to barely touch her, petting her like an animal, trying to make her purr. Over and over again, each time trying to make it more gentle until she moved even closer to him and breathed wetly onto the soft part just under his chin.

"Go to sleep," he said.

"I can't. I want to talk to you."

"What do you want to say?"

She snuggled closer to him. "I wish I'd met you someplace else," she said. "Maybe on your home turf. Maybe Toledo."

It occurred to McVay that it would be nice to take her back with him, but he didn't mention it to Katie. "Toledo isn't much," he said.

"But you like it."

"Like you said, it is my home turf."

She did not speak right away. She moved her head onto his chest.

"You don't have to tell me," she said. "In fact, I'm not sure I want to know, but why'd you leave Toledo? What are you doing here?" She felt his muscles tighten a little, and she wished she'd never asked.

"Newspaper," he said. "The wolf story."

She shook her head against his chest. "You don't have to tell me, but I know it's not a newspaper story. You've got something to do with P.J. Billion."

McVay considered saying Billion had some information about the wolf, but he realized that he only had two options: he could say nothing or he could tell her the truth. He thought about the options. It would be easy to not say anything, but he wanted to tell her. He wanted someone else to know. He began to stroke her again. "Okay," he said. "I came out here to find Billion."

"A drug deal," she said evenly. McVay nodded in the dark. "Had to be," she said. "That's what Billion does."

McVay went on petting her. He was fascinated by the smoothness of her skin. "Did he cross you?" she asked.

"No. I didn't have anything to do with it, really. It's my little brother's deal," McVay said. He stopped stroking Katie's side and brought his hand up to rub his own face. "It *was* his deal," he said. "Now my little brother is dead."

They lay quietly for a long time, Katie thinking that she was very sorry for McVay, and McVay unable to stop thinking, for a reason that he could not understand, about Traverse Best hanging in the morning glories growing on the fence around his house. Finally Katie spoke. "And you're here to even the score?"

McVay nodded in the dark and went back to caressing Katie's side with his rough hand. He stared at the ceiling until the thoughts of Best and of his brother went away. When he looked toward Katie, he could see her white teeth, and her big eyes watching him. "So what's to smile about?" he said.

Katie brought her hands up and took hold of his face, letting her thumbs glide along his lips and into his mouth. "I can't tell you," she said, "how happy I am to find out you're just trying to take care of your little brother." She kissed him. "So what do you do in the real world?" she asked.

"Build tires," McVay said. "I like it."

Katie laughed. "Then what the hell are you doing out here?" McVay shrugged. "You like this, too?" she said.

"No," McVay said.

"Yes."

"No. I don't get off on this kind of thing." McVay stopped petting her. "People have always counted on me. That's all."

"And you never let them down?"

"I try not to."

"You ever think that maybe they're taking advantage of you? Ever think they're using you?"

"No," McVay said. "It's just that I'm there at the right time and place, and I can do the job, and they look to me. That's all." He was speaking louder than he needed to, and Katie put her hands back up to his face. She kissed him.

"Easy," she said, "just asking." She kissed him again. "You're messing with a creep," she said. "Billion will kill you if he gets a chance. I'd take even money that he had something to do with Best dying." He started to say something, but she held a finger over his mouth. "Don't press me," she said. "Just be careful. Bad shit coming down around here. You gotta be careful. I'd like to see you hop in that truck of yours and head back to Toledo and your job. I know you won't, but I'd like to see it." She took her hands away from his face and snuggled her head against his chest again. "Now I'm going to sleep," she said. "I'm glad you came out tonight, Tom." She rubbed her cheek gently against his chest, and he could feel her relax.

But McVay could not let her sleep. "How about you?" he asked. "What's your story?"

"Came here to get away from the city," she said. "The opposite of you, I guess."

"But you're from here."

"In a way." She whispered it very softly. Then, softer yet: "I don't know where I'm from. Don't know where I belong."

They lay quietly for a minute, and then McVay heard her breathing change. It became even and deep and he knew that she was asleep. McVay lay awake. He thought about what she'd said, about going home, about being taken advantage of. Then he thought about her. She was very different when she was alone with him from when they were in public together. In the Oasis bar she talked like Jake and Pete. She took on their accent and used their limited vocabulary. But she knew more than she was letting on. She knew a lot. McVay wondered if he'd told her too much. He felt her there sleeping against him, and he could feel how warm and relaxed she was. Her breathing lulled his mind and soon he was sleeping.

But there was a dream. He was at the pond out by the interstate highway, the pond where they had built the raft with the diving board—the pond where Steve Miller had made a high arching dive only a few weeks before and had gone too deep and hit his head. McVay had been there that day, too, stretched out on a blanket on the tiny beach, not twenty-five feet from the raft. He'd watched Steve make the dive and had thought at the time that it was very high and that there was a chance Steve would hit the bottom. So he was already on his feet when the other kids on the raft started to yell that Steve had not come up. It was as if he'd been waiting for something like that to happen. Not just that day but his whole life. That was the day McVay found out he could do it, he could act when the need arose, he could do things that others couldn't. The kids stood on the raft and on the shore while he dove into the water. He could remember the way the strokes felt. He felt he could move thousands of gallons of water with each pump of his arms. When he got to where Steve should be, he took in air, deep into his lungs, enough to last for as long as it might take to find Steve. And when he'd gone under, it had been really very easy. He had found the bottom and pulled himself along it until his head had hit Steve's leg. He had found his hair and with all his might had pushed off the bottom. In an instant he had him ashore, pumping the water out of him with the other kids around him. When Steve started to sputter and to throw up water, the kids began to beat McVay on the back. "Way to go, Tom. You did it, Tom. We knew you could."

But the dream was about a different day. It was after he'd saved Steve, and this time he was not wearing his bathing suit. He was sitting on a rock by the little beach when he heard the kids shouting again. This time it came from along the shoreline. There were three or four of the same kids who had seen him save Steve Miller. They were shouting for him to come, to help them. They ran up and down the shore, ran to get him, to make him hurry. And so he ran, feeling the same way he had felt when he swam out to save Steve; with the air pouring into his lungs, he was covering ten feet per stride. When he got there, they said it was Amy Johnson, she'd just gone under, right there, in front of them, not ten feet off shore. They looked at him, and the panic seemed to go out of their faces. "There," they said, and pointed to the water just off shore. He was in in an instant, surprised to find that the water was only as deep as his waist. He took strong, heavy strides to where they said she'd gone down. He went under, sure that she would be there, just like Steve. But she was not there. "Get her, Tom," he heard from the shore and down he went. Nothing again, up for more air, and down. Longer this time, stretching his arms out, searching the bottom for an arm, a leg, anything. More air. "Come on, Tom." The darkness of the bottom. Air. "Get her, Tom." His clothes were getting heavy and the air was not lasting as long as it should. And finally gasping and pitifully paddling the water, he found he was still only waist-deep in water, but worn out now. "God, Tom. Find her!" One more futile groping of the bottom. "Get her!" "God!" And now he was spitting water and coughing. "Find her, Tom." "God, Tom." "Tom?" Tom?"

"Tom." She held his face again. "It's okay, Tom. It's okay." He lay rigid in bed. "It's okay," she said and kissed his sweating forehead. "It's okay," she said again. She held him close and rocked him. When he tried to speak, she would not let him.

"Easy," she said and rocked him until the tightness left his muscles. She rocked him long after she was sure that he'd fallen back to sleep. She stroked his hair and thought how sorry she was. Sorry that he was a silly man. What a shame, she thought. He should go home where he would be safe. Home, no matter what, was the only safe place on earth.

Junior Bailey hadn't slept at all. He'd gone back out to Best's place to pick up the body. They'd sent an ambulance from Rapid City with a crew who would take Best back for the autopsy. Bailey wanted to be sure that they didn't mess anything up. He'd taken out some floodlights and lit the area. He pointed the lights at the body and the area immediately around it. The lights were white and made all the colors look unnatural. Behind the light was blackness; only the limbs of the old cottonwoods reflected any light at all. The scene had seemed weird to Bailey, like a movie set, and it became more weird as the night dragged on. After the ambulance crew left, Bailey had been alone. He'd left Egan in town with McVay. He wanted Egan to get some sleep. He'd have to go over the scene after the people from the state Division of Criminal Investigation had. But Bailey didn't want anyone in the area until after all the agencies had had their look. At six o'clock Bob Wilson, a part-time deputy, had taken over for him. But until then, he'd been alone. So he'd watched the yard from inside his car and listened to the Chopin tape. He had played it over and over and studied how the lights distorted Best's backyard. He'd found himself waiting for sunrise, wondering what color it might be this morning. He'd wondered what subtle pink would do for the backyard, or gold, or blood red. He'd wondered if the lights might not bring out the morning glories. He'd tried not to wonder what had killed Best.

Now he was back in town, and all he could remember about the night was the Chopin tape. It, and probably the adrenaline pumping through him, had taken the place of sleep. He was tired, but there was still a lot to do. The boys from the Division of Criminal Investigation would be out there by afternoon, and he wanted to be with them. He needed to get a little sleep, but first he had to let Simmons know what had happened. Stockton should be informed too, but he couldn't bring himself to face him. He went to the Oasis and was surprised to find Simmons standing in the lobby, surrounded by the remains of cardboard boxes. From the labels, Bailey knew that the boxes had contained live traps. One of the traps was already assembled, and Bailey could see that Simmons was proud of it. Simmons started to say something about the traps, but Bailey stopped him. "Need to talk with you," Bailey said.

Simmons could tell that this was a serious visit. "Certainly, " he said. "What can I do for you?"

Bailey motioned toward the chairs on the other side of the lobby. He looked at Johnny, who was all ears. "Let's sit down."

Simmons moved to one of the overstuffed chairs and Bailey lowered himself gently onto the leather couch. He ran his hand over the leather and pressed it to feel its softness. For an instant he forgot what he had to say to Simmons. When he remembered, he looked up and smiled weakly. "Had some trouble last night," he said. "We've got no idea what it was. This thing might not even concern you, but there's a man dead."

Simmons tilted his head. "Dead?"

Bailey nodded and looked back at the couch. "Could have been any one of a number of things that did it; machinery, maybe a fight with another man." Bailey sat trying to think what else might have mangled Best.

"A wolf?" Simmons asked earnestly.

Bailey sighed. "I suppose it's possible but not likely." He watched Simmons. "Certainly, not likely," he said. Simmons was not paying any attention, so Bailey changed his approach. "What I'm asking for is a little restraint. I don't want everybody to get all excited. The state crime boys are going to look it over this afternoon, then Egan is going to have a look."

"Yes, I'll have to talk to Bill."

Bailey breathed out. He could feel the staleness of his breath. "Don't think you and Egan are going to get along over this live-trapping deal. He's set against it."

Simmons bristled. "I hired him, and he will do as I tell him."

"I'm not sure he will."

"If not, I can fire him."

"If you fire him, I'll hire him," Bailey said quickly, then took an instant to calm himself. He was tired and didn't want to lose his temper.

"Well, Sheriff, I guess that is well within your rights, but let me remind you that I am the Chief Ranger of the Black Hills National Forest, and Bill Egan is not the only trapper in the world."

"But he's the best."

"He's an old man."

"He's still the best."

With effort Simmons dropped the subject of Bill Egan. "I'll want to have a look at the area."

Bailey was standing up slowly. "Yes, Mr. Simmons. As soon as the DCI boys are finished and my men have had a look."

"Your men?" Simmons smiled.

"Yea," Bailey said. "Me and Bill Egan."

He tried to walk unhurriedly toward the door, tried not to jerk the door open, but he could feel that he was squeezing the door handle too hard. The fresh morning air felt good and helped him forget his fatigue, but by the time he was halfway to his office, it was creeping up on him again. He had the paperwork to do, then back out to Best's place. There was no real sleep in sight. As he came closer to his office, he noticed a strange car parked at the curb. There were two men sitting in it. Bailey was sure he'd never seen them before, and there was something about them that bothered him. They were obviously waiting for him, but he didn't want to deal with anyone just then. He went to the door and started to unlock it. The car was behind him, and he heard the doors open. He pushed his own door open and turned around to meet the men. They were dressed in three-piece suits, young and very neat. Bailey felt grubby. He tipped his hat.

"Sheriff Bailey?"

Bailey nodded. One of the men reached into his coat pocket and came out with a wallet. He flashed his identification.

"FBI," he said. "We'd like to talk to you about the death of Agent Best."

McVay was in his hotel room now, thinking about the night he and Katie had spent in the pool room of the Oasis. He lay watching the ceiling, feeling the sun warm the room. He remembered how hot the lights had been, how bright, and he could feel the board bench of the bathroom pressing at his back. The sun lamps warmed him an inch deep the entire length of his body. And he remembered turning his head to see Katie coming, glistening with beads of sweat, from one of the booths along the side of the pool. McVay had felt the heat from the sauna rocks behind her as the door opened. She came to him warm, skin nearly red. McVay lay still, looking up at her. She had laughed then and touched the side of his neck. The touch came back to McVay as he lay exhausted on the bed, then the softness of the fingers, and finally the softness, the dampness of the body itself. He closed his eyes and could feel pine needles, tender, but armed with points. Then Katie, moving against the needles. Slowly, easily, then fast, rhythmic, like the kick of an automatic rifle. McVay's eyes opened, then closed again, and the image of Best, translucent, white flesh hanging away from his frame, pushed out the image of Katie pulsing beneath him. Then it was Katie again. Beautiful, McVay thought. She is. She is beautiful. His eyes closed and he slept.

And Bailey slept. He tossed and turned in the noon sun that spread into the curtainless living room and across the couch, and could feel that his mouth was open, sucking at the air in huge gulps, which were drying out the sides of his mouth and making him hoarse and sore-throated. But Bailey didn't care. There wasn't much time until he had to be back out at Best's place. He should be there now. Still half asleep, he put his hands to his face and rubbed hard. He sat up in the sun pouring from the window, saw that there was someone there, and waved at him to come in. It was Egan. Bailey stood up, and as he wiped his forehead with his sleeve, he saw that it was one o'clock. "Christ," he muttered as Egan stepped inside.

"It's okay," Egan said. "The fellows from the state crime lab showed up, so I figured I'd better come and get you."

"They're out there?"

"Yea," Egan said. "Probably about done by now."

Bailey tucked in his shirttail. "Did you take a look?"

"You said to let them have their look first."

"Right." Bailey stood up, disoriented from the too-short nap. He pushed his hair back with his fingers. "Well, the state boys will come up with something." He pulled on his hat.

"Let's get out there." They started for the door, and Bailey wondered whether to tell Egan about the FBI. He hesitated for an instant, then decided against it. The old man followed him out the door.

Larry Mullens watched the observation deck below Mount Rushmore through his reflector sunglasses. As usual for this time of year there were several hundred visitors looking up at the faces. There were people from every ethnic background. A lot of Japs, Mullens said to himself. It was because of the cars and the radios that they had the money to tour the U.S. There was no way Mullens would ever have the money to go to Japan. It wasn't that he'd ever want to—it just made him mad that the Japs had all that money. But Mullens wasn't looking for Japanese; he was looking for Indians. There had been some trouble down in Kansas somewhere. A carload of Indian activists had been stopped by the state police on a routine traffic check, and the police had found a case of automatic weapons and some explosives. The Indians had been thrown in jail, and during questioning one of them had said that they were headed for the new camp in the Black Hills. All of that made Mullens nervous. The Indian camp in the northern Hills was getting bigger every day, and Simmons wasn't doing a thing about it. Now explosives, Mullens thought. There were only a few things in all of the Black Hills that Indian activists would want to blow up, and one of them was his mountain.

He stood in the shadows of the visitors' center with his arms folded across his chest and watched the people. He'd never liked the way the monument was set up. There was no real provision for security. The government even supplied telescopes. For a dime anyone could look up there and check out exactly how to get to the faces. They could even see the cracks in the rock. They could plan just where to put the explosives, where they would do the most harm. Mullens didn't like it. The public was too close. There was no real way to tell what any of these people had in mind. He tried to watch them, tried to see if anyone was making sketches or looked suspicious, but there were thousands of visitors a day. There was no way he could size up everyone who came onto the observation deck, let alone the ones in the gift shop and restaurant.

But he could take a close look at any Indians who were hanging around. There was no real reason for them to be here anyway. What would an Indian care about the heads of four American presidents? All they ever wanted to do was to take the Black Hills back. Mullens shook his head. Too lenient, he thought. Government officials were too scared of losing their jobs to do what needed to be done. The politicians were trying to please everyone at the same time, trying to make up for what happened a hundred and fifty years ago. It was crazy, you have to start from where you are and forget the past. Bad things happened, sure. Big deal. There was no way to make up for all of that by letting a few people get away with things that others never could. Just thinking about it made Mullens mad. Guys like Simmons were living in a dream world, he thought, out chasing some wolf that hasn't existed for fifty years, while right here and now, radical Indians were living in an illegal camp, planning who knows what. Simmons was the one who should stop it. He was Chief Ranger. But that was the Forest Service. They always were a bunch of dreamers. All they thought about were trees, never anything important. They weren't like the Park Service. They're really just a bunch of tree farmers, Mullens thought. They didn't even think about things like security. Mullens shook his head again. And now explosives, Indians with explosives, and Simmons still wouldn't even answer his calls. He wished the Park Service controlled the area where that Indian camp was. He'd know how to clear them out. But Simmons didn't have the slightest idea—out chasing a wolf, Mullens thought. He pushed away from the wall that he'd been leaning on and began to circulate among the visitors as they looked up at the heads carved into the mountain above.

Monkey, monkey, how many monkeys? Were they planted or were they sowed? One or a hundred or a whole treeload?

Billion didn't move a muscle. He did not blink. He tried not to let his heart beat. Monkey, monkey, how many monkeys? He was determined not to move anything until he could remember what he had heard. Were they planted or were they sowed? One or a hundred or a whole treeload? He remembered talking to someone who knew someone in an FBI office. He should remember. Let's see, Billion thought.

A fly landed on his face, but he did not move. Wouldn't he be surprised, he thought, if he knew that I was alive. It's a trap, a trick. I'm going to fool that fly. Let's see, the word was that they were everywhere, and that I should lay low. Billion wanted to laugh, but he didn't move. The joke's on this fucking fly.

He thinks I'm dead. But I'm not. Don't laugh, you'll scare him. There was one monkey for sure, but probably more. More than one. A hundred? A whole treeload? The fly crawled across Billion's eyelashes. I'm going to kill it, he thought. When I remember how many monkeys were sent to catch me, I'm going to kill it. Still, Billion did not move, and the fly crawled onto his forehead.

He was on the track now. Monkey, monkey, how many monkeys? A tiny smile curled at the corner of his mouth. Don't move. Are they silver or are they blue? One or a hundred? No. Billion did not smile. Just two.

His hand snapped to his forehead. Two rat finks. The fly did not know what happened. "One more," Billion said out loud. "Best had a friend." He wiped the smashed fly from his forehead. One rat fink down, one to go.

Bill Egan took up a partial fistful of soil and squeezed it. He let his old broad fingers pulse. Between pulses he looked at the soil. The fingers made no impression. He opened his hand and let the soil blow away, then he sliced his hands together to get rid of the last of the dust and looked up at the eaves of Traverse Best's house. The paint was peeling; the sun reflected obliquely from the curls of yellowed paint. There were no tracks.

A week earlier the nagging rain had washed tracks away nightly. For a week the conditions had been perfect. Now things were drying out. But they should easily hold a track. Egan fingered another handful of soil. He moved across the yard and driveway, keeping the area that he was investigating between him and the sun. He searched every square foot, and by the time he was finished, he knew the yard as if he had lived there his whole life. He stood back and looked at it all at once. Five cottonwood trees, several small plum bushes around the yard growing up in the fence where Best had ended up. The yard was bluegrass with some western wheat grass, but there was no other vegetation until past the driveway, where the buffalo grass and sagebrush began. There was nothing else alive in the yard, no sign that there ever had been. He knelt again. The driveway should have held tracks, but there were none there except theirs, McVay's and Bailey's from the night before. He went to the blood spots that they had followed. He put his face down to within inches of them and blew lightly. Dust rose from the stains and revealed more hard-packed blood. Egan was on his knees now, bending low. He closed one eye and looked across the driveway with the other less than an inch from the ground. From that angle the driveway spread out in front of him in waves that had been invisible from above. Six feet out on this too symmetrical ocean Egan noticed a tiny ship. Rising up, he leaned out and plucked it from the waves. He held it in the sun. Turned it, then tasted it. A greasewood leaf.

Sheriff Bailey stood beside the cars at the edge of the yard, talking with the state people. When they'd finished their own survey, Bailey had sent Egan in to have a look.

Now Egan backed out, putting each boot exactly inside a print that he had made before. He stood at the edge of what he considered to be the area of importance, squinted his eyes, tried to reconstruct what had happened in his mind. Then he began to walk out from where they'd found Best's body.

He walked slowly, letting his eyes move from side to side. The sun was low in the west now and made the small ripples in the dust cast shadows and so reveal any ridges or imprints in the ground. The tracking conditions were good, but there were no tracks. It did not surprise Egan. The greasewood leaf had told the story. Greasewood is a tall, bushy, sagelike plant. There was no greasewood growing around Best's house. The area had been swept. Egan tried to figure out who would destroy the tracks. It didn't make sense to him. He could have sworn that the wounds on Best's body were from canines. Best had looked very much the way cows used to look after being attacked by wolves. Egan had been hoping in a way that there was a wolf. Now, he doubted it. But he didn't know who had swept the tracks away or why. A wolf was still a possibility.

He looked up when he heard the state car start. Bailey was still talking to the state crime investigators through the window, but they were about to leave. He stopped his search and waited for Bailey to say good-bye and to catch up. When he came, Egan waved him to approach from behind so he wouldn't spoil anything that might be in the dirt ahead.

"Well," Bailey said. "You know what they said?"

"Somebody swept the sign away."

Bailey shrugged. "Yea, that's what they said."

"Did they find anything?"

"Not here. They said the body will probably tell us more, but that's going to take a while."

Egan nodded, then looked at the sun. "Better hurry," he said.

"Christ, Bill, there's nothing here. Somebody covered it up."

But Egan was already moving. He walked slowly again, searching the ground in a large circle around the yard. Bailey followed him. "We're fifty yards from the scene," Bailey said.

"Nobody's been sweeping over here," Egan said. Bailey nodded and continued to follow him.

"Guess that blows the hell out of the wolf theory," Bailey said. He was already sure that there was something else behind this death. It was too coincidental that an undercover FBI agent would happen to get killed by a wolf supposed to be extinct for fifty years. Again, he thought about telling Egan that Best had been working for the FBI. It was not fair that Egan did not know, but he'd told the agents he'd keep it very quiet. The investigation that Best had been conducting was still going on, and they didn't want anything to get out. They wouldn't even tell Bailey much, and that made him mad. "Looks to me like we got a real nut on our hands," Bailey said. Egan did not look up. He still thinks there might be a wolf, Bailey thought. It's not fair to let him go on thinking that there might be a wolf. "Bill," Bailey said. "I had a couple of visitors this morning." Egan had bent down in front of him and was looking at the ground.

"Look at this," Egan said.

Bailey crouched and looked at the earth in front of Egan. The light was leaving the sky now, and Bailey had to squint to see what Egan was pointing at. When his eyes focused, he could see a large imprint in the dust. It was a track. "A wolf?" Bailey whispered.

"No," Egan said, "it's a dog."

Johnny heard Simmons say that he was formulating a plan. He was talking to Stockton, and Johnny pretended to be busy at the desk. "This makes everything different, if"—Simmons hestitated—"if it's a wolf." Stockton indicated that he understood, then noticed Johnny leaning over the desk. He took Simmons's arm and led him out of Johnny's hearing.

When McVay came down the stairs, Stockton and Simmons stopped talking. They nodded at McVay, and McVay nodded back. He did not like them and was walking toward the door quickly when Johnny stopped him.

"Where you going?" Johnny asked.

McVay bristled, then realized that the old man was just curious. "To the café," he said.

Johnny squinted as if this was very important information, then his face brightened, and he smiled. "Oh, there's a message for you." He turned and pulled an envelope from the pigeonhole for McVay's room. McVay took the envelope and, glancing quickly over his shoulder, caught Stockton and Simmons watching him.

He did not bother glaring at them. Suddenly a little walk seemed a good idea to him. He walked the entire length of Medicine Springs's main street. Originally, he had planned to come up the other side of the street to the café, but halfway back he changed his mind and crossed over to the Oasis bar. He felt off balance, out of step. There was a job to do. He had to get to Billion's and clear out, but now he couldn't just go. Then he remembered the envelope that Johnny had given him, and as the new bartender slid a glass toward him, he took it from his shirt pocket.

Bailey and Egan had just gotten back to Bailey's office. "All right, Junior," Stockton said. "What's the idea of withholding information from the press?"

"There was no intention of withholding anything."

"Why wasn't I told?"

"Jerry, we've been pretty busy. Besides, you obviously know as much as I do, anyway."

"All I know is that Best is dead."

"Me too."

"Junior, I want some facts and figures here."

McVay forced his little finger under the flap of the sealed envelope and ripped open the top. He shook out the note, a piece of lined paper. Expecting it to be brief, well written, an invitation to breakfast maybe, he smiled when he saw that it was typed. Katie was a surprising woman. He'd have bet that there wasn't even a typewriter in the house. McVay's glass came down slowly as he read the note. "Meet me at the old Gennings place at eight o'clock." Katie's name was typed at the bottom of the note.

"You must know something," Stockton said.

"Right," Bailey said. "The great state crime lab found a little less than what Egan found. They found nothing. According to the state, Best simply appeared on that fence, hacked to hell."

Stockton turned to Egan. "What did you find that they didn't?"

"Nothing that meant anything."

McVay asked for one more drink. It was only 7:15. When the bartender came with the drink, he asked where the Gennings place was. It was a good half hour's drive. Why the Gennings place? Why not the bathhouse behind the Oasis again? Why not her house? Or even the bar?

"How do you know it was a dog track?" Stockton said.

"It was a dog track, Jerry. Egan knows a goddamned dog track when he sees one."

"It could have been a wolf."

"No," Egan said.

"Are you saying that a dog killed Best?"

"No, we're not saying that. All we're saying is that Egan found a dog track near the scene of the death."

"How near?"

"Maybe fifty yards."

"That means nothing."

"That's what I said in the beginning, Jerry. We don't know anything about what happened. We don't know."

"But it could be a wolf," Stockton said.

Bailey closed his eyes and nodded. "It could be a wolf," he said. "Or a Tasmanian devil, a malfunctioning combine, an enraged tomcat, or a hatchet murderer. We don't know!"

McVay returned his glass to the bar. It was 7:25. He threw some loose change down and stood up. Best, he thought, would have been there to scoop up the change. He went out, searching for his keys in his pants pocket.

"I say that you get the highway patrol, or Christ, even the National Guard. At least get them ready, in case we should need them."

"That's silly, Jerry. Egan"—Bailey turned to the old man standing near the door—"tell this fool what you told me about the probability that Best was killed by a wolf."

Egan cleared his throat. "What I told the sheriff was that I'd never heard of any wolf ever killing a man. Never really heard of one attacking a man before."

"But," Stockton said, "it is certainly possible. Isn't it?"

Egan looked at him. "I don't know," he said.

The headlights of McVay's pickup filled the alley beside the Oasis. Shadows leaped from the darkness. McVay fumbled with the radio as he pulled out onto the main street and headed toward the edge of town. The radio reception around Medicine Springs was amazingly good: he had his choice between Chicago, Salt Lake, several southern stations, and two from Canada, but McVay wasn't in the mood for listening to music. It would be better just to try to think. He switched the radio off; by then he was in the country. The distorted forms of sagebrush and the uniform line of barbed wires and fence posts flipped past as if they were newsreels being shown on each side of him. The night was hot, the start of a dusty summer, and the sky was clear and bright with no clouds and a moon not quite full.

McVay had drawn himself a rough map on an Oasis napkin. He took it from his shirt pocket and switched on the overhead light as he drove. Six miles on the asphalt road, then a right for three miles on gravel, then left for several more. He refolded the map as best he could with one hand and forced it back into his pocket. But before he turned off the overhead light, he noticed his reflection in the window on the passenger's side. He looked transparent. The fence on that side of the road continued to pass through the staring face. The sagebrush appeared as explosions of darkness within the figure. He switched off the light, and immediately his vision became clear, his own image disappeared.

As he came to the first intersection, he slowed. Halfway across the road ahead stretched a huge snake. He stopped, letting the headlights pin the snake. It stopped also, raised its head, pecking at the light with its tongue. McVay let the pickup roll ahead a little farther. Sensing danger, the snake coiled itself. McVay looked closely. He was afraid of snakes and worked at controlling his fear. He wasn't sure what kind it was. He pulled up beside the snake and looked out the window. He could see nothing but knew that it must be in the darkness below. He guessed that it was eight or ten feet from the side of the pickup, so he opened the door to send light out to where he believed that it was coiled. He had misjudged. The snake was coiled less than a foot from him, and when the door opened above it, McVay had no chance to heed the rattle. The mouth opened white and struck up to where McVay sat. He accelerated, and the strike fell harmlessly against the door panel. The door swung shut, and McVay felt his breath coming in gasps. He threw the pickup into reverse and spun the tires. The snake appeared in the headlights again, and he raced forward, trying to line up the left tires on the coiled rattler, back and forth, until there was an audible pop. Then he backed up again until he could see the smashed snake on the road ahead of him. He shook his head and banged the heel of his hand against the steering wheel. He'd lost control. Damn. He banged the steering wheel again, then wiped away the beads of sweat from his forehead. It was just a snake, he said to himself. He drove slowly, trying to forget the scene. After a while he managed to put his own reaction far to the rear of his mind, but however he tried, he could not block out the image that his mind had created of the snake at the moment of its death, mouth wide in defiance, striking hard at the spinning tire of the pickup.

The road became worse, and after the second turn it deteriorated to two tracks with a center hump where grass and sagebrush grew. McVay could hear the bottom of his pickup scraping. Occasionally a jackrabbit would jump and run crookedly for its life. At the first movement McVay would hit his brakes. Then he would have to chuckle at the rabbit zigzagging from shadows. McVay supposed images of coyotes filled the rabbit's mind. He came to an auto gate, homemade from railroad rails welded six inches apart. The fence converged from both sides and joined the gate through two old metal wagon wheels that were welded to the rails. McVay's pickup bumped and rocked as it crossed. He had entered a new pasture. The road became even worse.

Finally the road began to ascend, and McVay could see buildings silhouetted against the bright night sky. An old homestead from the 1920s: a barn made of mud and some logs, a couple of sheds, broken corrals, and a house, the roof fallen in over the porch, the windows caved inward, black and vacant. The scene was desolate, the angles obtuse, and the contrast with the summer night sky striking. McVay stopped his pickup and sat for a moment with the engine running and the lights pointed at the tangled corrals. The headlights made the darkness to the sides of the truck unbearable, so he turned the lights to park and left the engine running. Slowly the outlines of more buildings grew out of the dark until McVay felt almost comfortable. He glanced at his watch. It was eight o'clock.

There was something about the pickup, just sitting in it, that was oppressive. McVay rolled down the window. He thought of trying the radio, but the idea of music from some warm, lively radio studio juxtaposed with the scene through the window of the car made him feel uneasy, as if the music might draw attention to the fact that he was there. He got out of the pickup and leaned against the door. It was better to be outside. He watched the sky. It was very light, as if there were a small town nearby with a football game that night and the lights reflecting off the clouds. McVay wondered how the pale moon could be making all that light. Then he realized that it was the moon reflecting off the silver-green of the sagebrush that made it seem so bright. The stars were tiny yellow pinholes in the sky. They seemed to be contributing nothing.

McVay looked at the forms of the buildings, tried to imagine the people who had built them. Monuments to shattered dreams, he thought. Homesteaders, hoodwinked into thinking they could raise crops on this land. He glanced at his watch. 8:15.

McVay was getting nervous. Katie's idea of a joke? It was 8:25. He'd checked the .45 in the glove compartment and laid it on the dashboard. Now he was outside of the pickup again; he was restless and pushed away from the truck. He took a look around the bleak homestead. A movement caught his eye. Something had moved between the house and the first small shed. He squinted. It could have been a lot of things, he thought—a deer, rabbit, anything. But he continued to stare and listen to the quiet that hummed in his straining ears.

Then there was a noise. Not a crisp sound, but something that blended with the stillness that comes with too much silence. A smooth rustling sound. A sheet of paper hitting the surface of water. McVay tried harder to hear, but the sound would not come again. He watched the gap between the buildings. Nothing moved. He became anxious; his thoughts went back to the rattlesnake, then to what he had done. He turned to open the pickup door, and the sound came again. Longer, the surface of the water raising up to devour the paper this time. The sound slurped, and McVay's head snapped to look. There was nothing to see, but the tightness of the muscles in McVay's neck proved that there had been something, if only a noise. McVay stood for a moment, wondering if he should take the .45 off the dash. He decided against it. He'd overreacted once tonight—that was enough. He knew that fear and all the little feelings that went with it were mind-made. He refused to give in to it, let out a little snort, and began to walk toward where he had heard the sound.

The area around the homestead was littered with pieces of broken corral rails and, along with the stubborn sage, they made the walking difficult. McVay's hand bounced off his hip as he walked, as if he was keeping time to a song in his head. The shapes of the buildings and the old fences changed as he moved toward them. His mind wanted to animate the silhouettes, but McVay would not let it.

Whatever he had seen had slipped from behind the house to behind a small shed, a smokehouse, McVay supposed. The sound had also come from that direction. McVay expected to surprise something on the order of a skunk when he peeked behind the shed. He touched the shed as soon as he was close enough, and that seemed to help control the feeling of disorientation he had experienced crossing the dim yellowness between his pickup and the shed. The planks were old and weathered, like the ones he had paid a dollar a foot for to remodel his apartment. Putting both hands against the old eroded wood, he could feel where the rain and blown sand had stolen the planed and painted surface. He wanted somehow to put his cheek against it. It felt alive with the heat it had stored from that day's sun. He looked back at his pickup and thought again about the .45. The truck was barely visible, crouched like a reptile in the weeds along the driveway. He moved along the wall, slowly and quietly, then, with hands against the wall, he carefully looked around the corner of the building.

There was nothing but another bowed wall of old barn planks and clumps of sage growing up and out of the foundation. McVay stepped out where he could see the entire wall. Still there was nothing. He took his hands from the wall and pushed them down into his pockets. The night was cooling off. He began to turn back and heard, much closer this time, the smooth flowing sound that had brought him this far from his pickup and his .45. His hands came out of his pockets, and the closest one touched the wall again. He peered into the dimness. This time the sound had come from where he had been. The sound was between him and his truck.

Moving back along the shed wall, he heard the noise again, this time to his right. Whatever it was, it had completely circled him now. His pickup showed up against the sky fifty yards away, black and massive. McVay looked hard after the sound but could see nothing. He stepped away from the shed, his fingertips clinging to the warm wood as long as they could, then he was in the open. The cool swishing noise came from the wall where he had just been standing. He turned and backed toward the pickup, staying low and on the balls of his feet. He heard no more sound but continued to back across the sagebrush-strewn opening between the buildings. As he got closer to his truck, his breath began to come easier. Twenty feet from the vehicle he began to relax. After backing almost the entire distance, he straightened up and turned toward the pickup.

The snarl was very short, but crisp, and very close. It grew from the silence, and though it was short, McVay had time to respond. Instinctively, he raised his arms in time to catch the smashing jaws and protect his face and throat. The snarl had exploded into a whining, ghoulish rattle at the very center of the massive body whose weight now held McVay to the ground. The teeth were inches from his face, the head forcing downward in twisted jerks. McVay had gotten hold of the thick fur beneath the pointed ears, and for an instant there was stalemate. He wanted to reach for his boot knife but he could not afford to let the animal go. The big head jerked savagely from left to right and jerked itself loose. McVay rolled in the dirt, reaching for the knife, then felt the teeth sink into the back of his skull. The pain brought him up to his knees, but the teeth remained embedded in the back of his head. He felt the wild breath mixed with blood running down into his shirt. Then he fell forward, over a sagebrush, and the teeth began to shake his head like a puppy would shake a shoe. His hand had found the boot knife, but as he brought it out, he was shaken again and the knife flew into the darkness. Over his own head McVay grabbed the ears but could do no good. Finally his arm stretched out in front of him in pain. His right hand fell upon a piece of the old corral post, a four-by-four. He took it in both hands, and with a huge effort got back to his knees. He raised the four-by-four and brought it down hard over his shoulders. A solid thud. The teeth loosened slightly. Down came the club again, and again, and again, and the teeth let go. McVay struggled to his feet and ran headlong to the pickup.

He jumped in and pulled the door shut, and with his right hand turned the ignition, while his left hand worked frantically at closing the window. He wanted to grab the .45, but it was on the other side of the dash and there was no time. The sound of the starting engine was drowned by his own roar of pain. The teeth were buried in McVay's left shoulder. The window, halfway closed, had been smashed by the animal's chest. McVay held his head back, staring into the emerald green eye not three inches from his own. He felt himself being pulled from his seat. This animal is going to kill me, he thought. His right arm and fist beat mercilessly at the head that seemed to fill the window. Finally his right arm gave up and held to the steering wheel. Then, McVay felt the engine running. He thought of the .45 again, but his right hand fell from the steering wheel onto the gearshift lever, and he slammed the accelerator to the floor. He did not steer. The right fist began to beat more savagely on the head. Beat out the eye, McVay told himself. The pickup spun in the dust and sagebrush, and finally the teeth began to loosen their hold. Then the head was gone. McVay flipped on the headlights and jerked the steering wheel to the left. The truck bounced from the ditch and found the wheel ruts. McVay was going seventy miles per hour when he gained control.

Egan and Bailey talked for nearly two hours. Bailey was upset by Stockton and by the whole set of circumstances. The hardest part of it all was keeping to himself the fact that Best had been an FBI agent. Egan went over everything that he'd noticed around the site of Best's death. He thought out loud, hoping that Bailey could help him put something together. Bailey could see that Egan was unable to add things up, and that it bothered him. And Bailey felt he was somehow lying to Egan by not telling him all he knew. It was unfair to let the old man go on trying to figure things out without all the facts.

"Doesn't add up," Egan said, and shook his head. "Something killed Best, and I'm guessing it was an animal, but somebody covered up what happened."

"That part sounds a little like murder, doesn't it?"

Egan nodded. "Best have many enemies?"

Bailey could stand it no longer—after all, Egan was kind of like his deputy. "He probably had a bunch. He was an FBI agent."

Egan looked across the desk at Bailey. His old head began to bob up and down. "Well, that might change things."

Bailey was embarrassed. "An agent by the name of Kring stopped in this morning and told me that little piece of information. Made me promise not to tell anyone."

"Thanks." There was a silence and then, "Well, what was he investigating?"

"Kring wouldn't tell me. Said it was an ongoing investigation. Should be wrapped up soon, and they didn't want any foul-ups."

"That's a big help."

"But I got a couple ideas. Whatever it is that they're investigating must be in the Hills. My jurisdiction stops at the county line—that's the edge of the Hills. If it were in my county, they'd have to tell me what they're doing. But at the same time it's got to be close to Medicine Springs. There's only two things worth the FBI's time around here. First, there's P.J. Billion, who deals dope out of his ranch up in the Hills. Then, there's the Indian camp. They're illegal up there in the Hills, and that's federal land. Christ, they probably got agents all over this place."

"So one of those two outfits could be responsible for sweeping away all the signs at Best's place?"

"Could be they got wind of Best and decided to do him in."

"Could be." Egan rubbed the stubble on his chin. "But what actually killed him?"

Bailey shrugged and they lapsed into silence.

Now Egan was in his room, thinking that he had no real business in Medicine Springs. He was a trapper, not a law enforcement man. He should leave, he thought. The chances of there being a wolf were even slimmer now than they had been when he arrived. It had all been kind of a dream anyway, just a dream of the past. A dream of rolling grass and the cottonwooded creeks winding endlessly. It was a dream from his past, a past that he'd helped to change. Old Egan's face twitched peacefully as he sat in the chair by the window. The light was eerie from the warm summer night, and though it was calm outside, in his dream there was a wind, and a sense of everything moving. It was a floating sensation, moving over the prairie. It was a dream about dying. Egan was sure. His heart? He didn't know, but it was peaceful. He enjoyed it.

Egan was jarred to consciousness by the sound of his own name. "Egan." It came slowly to him. Then the knock on the door. "Open up, Egan." The old man sat upright and shook off the sleep. "Egan." And onto his feet. The voice was not loud. It did not seem excited, but just before Egan opened the door, he sensed fear. He smelled blood.

McVay leaned against the doorjamb. The blood was dried over his ears and down his neck. It had run into the corners of his mouth, and Egan could see where he'd tried to rub it away. His shoulder lay open to the air, the flesh torn and black with dried blood, but McVay had control. "May I come in?" he asked.

The old man reached for him and could feel that the strength was nearly gone. He discouraged McVay's resistance with a strong grip, brought him into the room, and sat him in a chair. There were footsteps in the hall. McVay looked up through swollen eyes. "Johnny saw me come in. I don't want to deal with him."

Egan nodded and went to the door. "It's all right," he told Johnny, shifting to block his view.

"That reporter looked funny when he came in."

"No problem," Egan said. He patted Johnny's shoulder. "Everything's all right." He shut the door.

McVay tried to sit upright in the chair. Egan went to the sink and wetted a towel. He handed the towel to McVay. "Shock?" he asked.

"Not bad, I'll be okay." He wiped the blood off his face.

"You're going to need a doctor."

"Yeah, but I need to talk to you first. I'm no expert, Egan, but I think your wolf's out there." Egan sat on the bed. "Christ, Egan, that's a powerful animal." McVay winced, and Egan could see that he was losing strength. "Goddamn," he said, "I am going to need a doctor."

Egan went to him and took hold of his good shoulder. "Hang in there, boy."

"Goddamned bastard. Bad way to go, Egan. Best went out in a bad way." His eyes were closed now.

"I'm going to get you a doctor," Egan said. "But first, tell me something."

"Goddamned green eyes," McVay said.

"Do you work for the FBI?"

"No."

Egan pushed him gently back in the chair. "Take it easy. You messing around that Indian camp?"

"No." McVay's eyes were still closed, but he had fought off the nausea.

"You know a guy named P.J. Billion?"

The eyes came open, and McVay watched Egan, trying to understand the question. Then he shook his head. "Christ, Egan, get me a doctor, would you?"

Egan looked down at him and nodded. "Sure," he said, and touched McVay softly on the shoulder.

Simmons knew that he was going to have to do something about the Indian camp. He'd talked with his assistant on the telephone twice in the last two days. The camp was getting larger everyday. There were rumors that there were weapons and explosives in the camp, and Larry Mullens was pulling his usual paranoia trick. But Mullens had a point. The camp was definitely illegal. There was no doubt about that now. The Indians had been there for a month already, and his assistant had said something about their wanting to build permanent structures. It was all very much against Forest Service policy, and Simmons knew that he was going to have to get into it soon. But the possibility of a wolf roaming around the edge of his forest was more important to Simmons than a bunch of Indians camped up in some draw. And now that that reporter had been attacked too, there was even more reason to put the wolf issue at the top of his list. He'd worry about the Indian camp the next day. Today he wanted to get out to the Gennings place and look around. He'd have help soon, and then he could take care of the Indians.

After he got to the Gennings place, Egan circled the buildings ten or fifteen times, starting where the attack had taken place and slowly spiraling out until now, watching the loaded station wagon pull into the yard, he was half a mile away. The sun had been up for over an hour. It was warming, and Egan knew it was destined to be blazing hot by noon. He stood on a small rise, south of the buildings, and watched Simmons step from his car cautiously and begin his investigation. Egan wondered if he should go talk with him or continue his circling. The circling was futile. Egan was convinced that there would be nothing out here to find, but he did not want to talk with Simmons. He sat down to think and to watch the land.

Simmons began his own circling, more like wandering, around and around the place where he had been told that McVay was attacked. The ground was hard, which was immaterial to Simmons, because it had already been too long; and the fact was, even in the old days, he could only recognize a gray-wolf print for certain if someone like Egan pointed it out to him. He crossed Egan's prints, but missed them because he was thinking of what Bailey had said when he called. Even over the telephone Simmons had known that Bailey was disturbed. The voice was low, overly calm, and had a certain rasping quality. "The wolf attacked McVay," he had said simply. Simmons was still stunned. Bailey hadn't said, "McVay has been attacked" or "Something has attacked McVay." He had said, "The wolf . . ." A certainty, as if there was nothing truly incredible about what he was saying. A gray buffalo wolf, Simmons thought, as he passed over Egan's tracks, unnoticed for the second time, and he looked up, imagining what it was like. The largest wolf to exist since dinosaurs had stood here, within yards of where he was standing. And he thought of it in the enclosure at the state capital, with his name under it.

Egan watched Simmons zigzagging through the area as if looking for a lost quarter. Had Simmons gotten there before him, Egan would have been infuriated at the man ruining the picture written in the dirt. But it was all right. There had been no picture anyway—not even pencil lines that would point to anything. All Egan had found were the marks where the area had been swept and a handmade boot knife with the initials *TM* engraved on the handle. The initials had to stand for Tom McVay. Strange equipment for a reporter.

Egan watched Simmons, wondering what the man was doing, what he was thinking of. He was now engaged in tracking what he took to be McVay's footprints and which were, in fact, Egan's. He fumbled along in the same general direction that Egan had methodically taken, moving away from the scene of the attack. Egan recognized what Simmons was doing, and noticed that Simmons was on the wrong side of the tracks. He was fighting the sun, kneeling to touch the tracks as if he could judge their age by the warmth left in them. He left them disturbed, useless for rereading. And he was walking too close, looking almost straight down at the tracks, distorting further anything they might have to say. Egan looked away from Simmons. It was coming clear to him. He scanned the surrounding slopes and sagebrush, and further, to the Black Hills. It was all very much the same, he thought, only now there were no wolves. He looked from the dark green hills back to the man slowly meandering his way across the prairie toward him. Simmons had not seen him yet. Egan had an almost uncontrollable impulse to circle the man, slip back to his pickup, and leave him to wonder. But he could not do that, nor could he slip up behind him and let out the wolf howl he had been famous for. No, this was serious, Egan thought, though somehow, just now, it was funny.

But there was no time to laugh. Simons wound his way up the slight grade toward where Egan was standing. He walked with his head down, no idea that Egan was standing in plain sight at the top of the rise. He walked steadily, except for his detours around sagebrush and cactus, one boot plodding in front of the other as if he were counting the steps. Egan didn't move until Simmons's gaze came to his feet and turned up. Egan smiled then and nodded his head to a frightened and embarrassed Simmons.

"Good Lord," Simmons said. Then, regaining his composure and not stopping to explain, he said, "Well, what do you think?"

"Didn't find a thing," Egan said.

"No," said Simmons, "me neither." He turned and looked back toward where they had come from, where McVay had been attacked. "But there has to be something," he said. "Bailey says the reporter was really chewed up."

Egan nodded. "Something chewed on him."

"It's a wolf, Bill. A goddamned wolf, and probably a buffalo wolf." They stood without talking for a while, then Simmons went on. "This could be really big, Bill. Biggest thing that's happened to either of us. It could put this forest on the map, make us big names." Egan watched as Simmons talked. The words came out in rushes. Simmons was still winded from the climb up the hill. His face was red, and he was sweating. "Something like this only comes along once in a lifetime." He paused and smiled a little. "If you're lucky," he added, and wiped his forehead with his shirt-sleeve. "This could be a real crowning achievement. Something to go out on that would make them remember that you were there." He stopped again, and they listened to the slight wind in the prairie grass. "We've got to catch him, Bill." And Simmons turned to look Egan in the face. "Alive."

Egan returned the look calmly. His head wagged from side to side slowly. "He isn't out there," Egan said. "But if he was, I'd kill him. And I'd bury him in a draw somewhere where he could rest and not have to bear the sight of you and people like you staring at him."

"No, Bill. You can use the steel traps, damage a leg, but once you get him, I want you to bring him in alive."

He hadn't heard what Egan said. "It wasn't a wolf," Egan said again.

"Bill, you don't know that."

"No," Egan said, "but I'm pretty sure." He began to walk away. "I'm not that lucky," he said.

"But you are," Simmons said, coming after him. "We're both lucky. We're here on the scene. We're right where the action is."

Simmons touched Egan's arm. The old man wheeled around. The old eyes were on fire. "The action? The spearhead of progress, right?" Egan's face was red. "We're two of the dumbest bastards that ever lived. Only you're even dumber than I am."

"Bill."

"At least I know what I'm doing. I know what I've done. You're going to keep right on doing what you're doing and calling it right." Egan pointed to the Black Hills. "That's yours, right? Yours. Well, look at it. It's sick. You're torturing it." He hesitated. He was looking at the Hills now. "I helped," he said. Then his eyes snapped back to Simmons. "But it's tougher than we are. It can come back, we can't. We die with what we've done."

"But there is a wolf," Simmons said. "It's still here. You're the one that wants to kill it."

Egan's face began to shake, and Simmons drew back. "It's all very simple to you, isn't it?" Egan said. "Let it live." He pointed back to the Hills. "You call that living? Stop the fires. Let the trees grow. They're pretty. Let the people see the trees. Never mind what is supposed to live in those hills. Never mind what those trees are choking out. Never mind the things that need those fires." Egan turned back to Simmons. He looked a little embarrassed now. "And never mind any dignity that we might be able to preserve." He said it softly, the oldness back in his voice.

"There isn't any wolf out here," Egan said. "But if there were, I'd do my best to see that it at least died with some dignity." Egan shook his head. "He's probably a little like me," he said. "He's probably very tired." Egan turned and walked down the hill. Simmons watched him go.

Joe Standing Elk had seen them die before. He'd seen them hung in fences, wedged between rocks, frozen to the ground, crushed at the bottom of cliffs. But never this many. He counted on losing a few in the spring to weather, and maybe one or two during the summer. If there was odd weather, or coyotes, perhaps a few more. It was early summer now, and the lamb that he had just thrown into the back of his pickup was the sixteenth to die this year.

Old Joe looked down at the woolly carcass. Its eyes were dried up and sunken, the mouth had started to shrivel, and the teeth showed through the pale green of the lips. He had no idea what had killed this one. It was just dead, lying out on the grass, with its mother standing beside it. There was not a mark on it. It was fat with the grass that it was lying on. There had been plenty of water near it. There had been no storm for weeks, no lightning at all. The lamb had simply died.

The ewe stood close beside Joe, bleating softly, confused. And Joe turned to look at her. His left hand remained on the pickup box. He scratched at his chest under his too-warm woolen clothes and shook his head at the ewe. "There's nothing I can do," he said. "It is the Evil."

In the clinic, Tom McVay had a dream. Egan stood over the wolf and shot it. There was no struggle. He simply shot the wolf in the head, though McVay had tried to stop him. As Egan raised the gun, he tried to scream, but nothing came out, just McVay's open mouth, no sound. But when it was done, the sound came: "Egan!" It drifted like an echo, and McVay felt two hands grab his legs and pull him from the pile of rocks where he was standing. "Egan!" It rolled and tumbled with him. But finally the name reached Egan's ears far away.

McVay hit and rolled. The cactus and yucca stuck in his back and side. Rocks rumbled down with him. He lay dazed, his head spinning, his side on fire. As his vision came and went, he heard the laugh and finally focused on P.J. Billion's smiling face.

"You took a bad spill, boy," Billion said. Already he was backing away, hefting his rifle as though guessing its weight. "You should be more careful about where you stand"—he smiled even more broadly—"and who you mess with."

McVay was on his knees then. His head had cleared, then fogged again with fear. His voice was gone. He could only shake his head. Billion responded by nodding his head in rhythm with McVay.

"Oh, yes. I am the piper. It's time to pay up. You ever seen a .30-06 hole in a deer or something?" Billion backed up a little farther. "You're going to hate it. Just hate it." He laughed again, hollow, fading slowly.

Billion was fifty feet away, standing in the center of a small basin formed by the pile of rocks that McVay had been dragged from, with another pile behind him. "Now see if you can't stand up, you gutless fucker." Billion's voice had changed from a singsong to a snarl. "Get up. I'm going to take your head right off."

McVay was shaking, almost in convulsions. He knew he should stand. He knew he should try something. But he couldn't get to his feet. It was like he had no muscles.

"Stand!" Billion screamed.

And so slowly McVay rose until he was upright, as if hung from wires, his shoulders slumped and his arms limp in front of him. He was terribly tired. His eyelids were nearly shut, and for an instant the world went out of focus and threatened to go black. Billion stood in the center of McVay's pulsing vision, and McVay tried to think of something to do. Billion was shouting again, but the sound came slowly to McVay. He could not understand and looked past Billion, to the pile of loose rock that loomed above them.

At the very top of the rocks stood Egan. The old man stood motionless, his cheek tight against the stock of his rifle, his right elbow out at a right angle, his eye steady in the scope, and his finger poised on the trigger.

McVay saw the muzzle blast before he heard the rifle fire. It was as if he could see the bullet traveling. There was time to look down at Billion, who hadn't heard the shot yet. He was shouting to McVay again. His mouth came open and shut slowly, until the noise from Egan's rifle reached him. Then he began to turn. Fall, McVay thought. Die. The bullet seemed to have passed through Billion, harmlessly.

Billion did not fall as the sound of Egan's rifle smacked against McVay's ears, and he watched Billion turning, raising his rifle at Egan. Now something was exploding at McVay's feet. Egan was watching. He had lowered his rifle and was watching Billion turning. Particles were spinning in the air, tiny green particles, and suddenly the lingering crack of Egan's rifle changed to "Go." It was cactus. Spinning, shattered cactus. "Go." And Billion's gun was up and firing. "Go." Billion was recoiling. The old man's mouth came open, his chest ripped open from Billion's shot. Egan's lungs pulled at the heavy air, and he tumbled forward. "Go." Then falling, the eyes still open. "Go. Go." And cactus falling. "Go." And McVay began to move. Ripping at the damp sheet, his legs churned in his bed.

McVay woke up in a small clinic in a town twenty miles from Medicine Springs. It was almost nine o'clock in the morning, and McVay still did not feel rested. It must have been the dream, he thought. But he could not remember the dream, only that he had dreamed and that it had frightened him. He was all alone. There was another bed in the room with him, but it was empty, the khaki blanket tucked neatly at the corners. He sat up on the edge of the bed and began to look around for his clothes.

His arm and shoulder were bandaged, and as he ran his hands over them, he could feel the stitches. There seemed to be only a few in his right arm, but in his left arm and shoulder he could feel several rows. He stood up and felt pretty well. He was not doped up and could feel the pain in the wounds, and that made him confident that he was all right. Standing in the middle of the floor in the long nightshirt, he felt a draft coming up from underneath. He took inventory of himself. The fingers were chewed but all still there; the legs seemed sound, and he tried a couple of steps toward the mirror. There were a few scratches on his face, but nothing bad. The back of his head was full of stitches and felt swollen to the touch. Patches of hair had been shaved, but he was all right. An odd feeling came over him, and he smiled into the mirror. He looked silly, he thought. He felt silly. And he knew why. It had happened before. It was the feeling he got when he found out that everything was all right, that he was still alive. If there was pain, it proved you were alive. He laughed at his image in the mirror, and that made his shoulder hurt, and that made him laugh again. He went into the bathroom and urinated. Even that made him laugh.

When the male nurse came in, McVay was searching through the closet for his clothes. "So where'd you hide them?" he asked. He was still feeling silly.

"Looks like you're going to make it," the young man said.

"Fuckin-A," McVay said. Then he laughed.

The young man looked at him oddly. "The old guy that brought you in here last night told the doctor you might try to sneak off, so the doc told me not to give you your clothes until he could see you."

"So when's the doctor get here?"

The young man looked at his watch. "Real soon."

McVay took two quick steps and jumped back in bed. "I'll be right here," he said.

"God," the young man said, "doesn't that hurt?"

"Yea," McVay said. "Feels great."

When the doctor came in, Katie was right behind him. McVay nodded to the doctor and smiled at Katie. His mood was still light, but he was beginning to wonder about what had happened. Katie reached out and took his hand. He could tell that she was upset. The doctor began to check the bandages, and McVay smiled again at Katie.

"Just to be sure," he said, still smiling. "You didn't send me a note last night, did you?"

She shook her head. The words came hard. "No," she said. Then,

"I don't know." She sat down and would not look at him anymore.

They waited until the doctor had checked him out thoroughly. He asked McVay a few questions, then turning to the nurse who had been standing beside the door, shrugged his shoulders. "Give him his clothes, Karl," he said. And as he stood up, "The sheriff's on his way over here. He wanted me to be sure not to let you out of here until he had a chance to talk to you."

McVay nodded. "Thanks, Doc." He patted the bandage on his shoulder. "Pretty handy," he said.

When they were alone Katie began to shake her head again. "God, Tom. I'm sorry."

McVay looked at her. "You didn't bite me." He was having a problem being serious. "It wasn't your fault."

"I'm not so certain."

They heard voices outside.

"What are you getting at?"

"I talked with the sheriff and Egan this morning. It looks like you were set up."

Then it hit him. How could the person who wrote the note have known that the wolf would be at the Gennings place? He heard Bailey and Egan just outside the door.

"They've got a theory," Katie said. "They don't know it, but it could have been my fault." She turned away again. "It was a big mistake," she said.

The two men came into the room and nodded. Egan looked older to McVay. He leaned against the far wall and watched the floor. Bailey pulled a chair up beside the bed and began to ask how he felt. McVay answered, but he watched Egan. It was as if the life had gone out of him. His skin looked different, and his shoulders seemed to sag. The sheriff went on asking routine questions, and he went on answering them. Now his eyes moved from face to face. They know something, he thought. They all know something that I don't know. Do they know why I'm in Medicine Springs? It's all right, he told himself. You've done nothing wrong. You haven't had a chance. He looked at Katie. No, he thought. It's something else.

"Bill said you got a good look at what attacked you."

McVay nodded. "Yea," he said.

"He said you could see the color of its eyes."

Now the questions began to interest McVay. He nodded again, trying to understand what the sheriff was getting at.

"Green, you said?"

"A little brown," McVay said, "but mostly green, yea."

Bailey turned to Egan. "Tell him your idea," Bailey said.

Egan pushed himself away from the wall and looked up. "Might be wrong," he said, "but I don't think it was a wolf that attacked you." He rubbed at his stubbled chin. "Wolves usually have yellow eyes. I figure somebody sicked his dog on you."

What Egan said hit McVay like a rifle butt. He remembered sitting on the hillside over Billion's house, and he knew what they were going to say. "There's a fella outside of town," Bailey said, "that had a kind of reason to hate Traverse Best." Everyone was looking at McVay now. "Don't suppose you know him," Bailey said. McVay was cornered. He couldn't tell Bailey that he was in town to even a score. He couldn't admit that he'd lied about being a reporter. "His name is Billion, and I checked around. He's got a German shepherd out there." Bailey's eyes came up. "Somebody thought they heard you ask about him." McVay was thinking, trying to stay calm. He couldn't tell if Bailey was questioning honestly, or if he had something in mind.

"Well?" Bailey said. "There wouldn't be any reason for Billion to want to kill you, would there?"

Egan was watching McVay now. He looked ready to say something, but Katie spoke first. "Maybe it's me," she said.

The three men looked at her, and McVay used the time to steady his nerves and to get his brain working. But there was no need—Katie had taken him off the hook.

"We're talking murder now, and attempted murder. That's a pretty strong reaction to—" Bailey stopped and looked first at McVay, then back at Katie. "How do you figure into this?"

Katie had gone sullen.

"How well do you know Billion?" Bailey asked.

"I don't know him like that," Katie said. "I knew Traverse." She hesitated. "I had business with Traverse. Maybe Billion was after me, got mixed up, went after Tom by mistake." McVay glanced at her, but she had turned away.

Now the room was silent. Bailey pushed his hat back and shook his head. "Well, I don't get it," he said. "But I'm betting there's no wolf. I'm betting on Billion and his dog." He looked at Egan, who was looking down toward the floor again. "Guess we'll be going out there," he said.

"I want to go, too." It was McVay.

Bailey shook his head. "You're still pretty hurt," he said. "Besides, under the circumstances, it's probably not too good an idea."

"I need to be there," McVay said.

Bailey was shaking his head, but it was Egan who spoke. "Might need him," the old man said. "He's the only one that's ever seen the dog." Egan was trying. McVay knew that Egan wanted him to go.

"Christ, Bill. I know a dog when I see one."

"What if there's more than one dog?" McVay said.

Bailey's head began to nod. "Okay, you clowns. McVay, you can come, but stay clear. Understand?"

McVay nodded, and Egan smiled. McVay reached for his clothes. "Not yet," Bailey said. He looked at his watch. "Say, six-thirty. At my office." He stood up to go. "You sure you're all right?" McVay nodded. Then Bailey looked at Katie, tipped his hat, and they went out.

When they were gone, the room went silent again. McVay and Katie didn't look at each other. Then he spoke. "Thanks," he said. "But what was all that about Traverse Best?"

Katie shook her head and refused to look at him. "I was mixed up with him. I never thought anyone would get hurt."

McVay's eyes went to the ceiling. He was thinking. "Mixed up how?" he asked, as if he was talking to the ceiling.

"You ask too many questions."

"I don't even know why he did in Best."

"Look, dummy." Katie came and sat on the bed. "Traverse Best was a Fed. P.J. Billion is a nervous guy. He doesn't like Feds. He killed Best because he was a Fed, and he probably tried to kill you because he thought you were a Fed."

"I'm no Fed," McVay said. "Where would he get that idea?"

"Best had informers," Katie said. "Maybe he thought you were one of them."

She looked away again, and McVay knew she was finished talking. He reached out and touched her black hair. Then he took it in his hand, brought it to his mouth, and kissed it gently. She was so different, he thought—but in a way that he liked. He knew that she had lived in a city for much of her life, and he couldn't help wondering how she would do in a place like Toledo.

Egan stood waiting in the sheriff's office. He watched out the window at the street and on toward the sky, which was pitching in the west. It looked like it might blow up a storm, but not that night. And if it did, it would be a rough one. The sky was a strange color, pink with the setting sun, but a greenish cast ran through it, or maybe above it all, or behind it. Perhaps behind that setting sun, days behind it, was the greenness that Egan saw. He wasn't sure. He looked back to the street and even that seemed odd: he sensed there was a tornado somewhere. The dust lay still, but somehow there was the sensation of moving air, and the people of Medicine Springs moving through it, unaware, going about their late afternoon affairs. Egan let his eyes close. It was over for him. It was a dog, not a wolf. There was no chance now. Egan felt silly; he'd wanted it to be a wolf. He'd even convinced himself that it might be, and now it turned out to be a dog, a pet, a trained killer. But what about the animals that had been killed? That wasn't something a man would let a trained dog do. Egan shook his head. You never give up, he told himself.

The door to the office was open, and Bailey came in. He took off his hat and sent it flying toward the filing cabinet. It hit and slid off onto the floor. He was obviously feeling better. He looked at Egan after he'd sat down.

"Ralph," he said. "Rancher up the canyon says the dog's name's Ralph. A real sweetheart, he says." Bailey looked up, one eye closed and his mouth pushed into an idiot's grin. "Do we arrest Billion or Ralph?" he said.

Egan shook his head. Bailey answered his own question. "Both of them. Christ Almighty, Egan, we don't have anything on anybody."

He stretched his arms above his head. "But I ain't letting either Billion or Ralph spend another night on the loose."

"So we're going out there?"

"Yea, we'll worry about how to stick him with it later." Bailey looked at his watch. "Six-thirty," he said. "McVay should be here." He rubbed his hands together. "Now we got something to do," he said. "It's nice that this thing is working out to be fairly conventional. Not nice that it looks like murder, but at least everything is starting to make sense. Everything that's extinct is turning out to be still that way." Bailey frowned. "What I mean is, at least we don't have a wolf."

Egan watched the sheriff. He looked better now than he had for a week. He sat up straight in the chair, and the tiredness seemed to be gone from his eyes. His heavy head and jowls were smiling as if it were all clear-cut from this point on. Egan didn't have the heart to tell him what he was thinking. Egan was wondering about those first sheep that had been killed. Had Billion ordered them killed, or was it coyotes? Had Billion been out on that rainy spring night and sent the dog to kill that calf and maim that heifer? And Egan wondered about Joe Standing Elk's old dog. They heard the sound of footsteps outside. Bailey stood up as McVay opened the door. All his bandages were covered; he looked as though nothing had happened.

"Ready?" Bailey asked.

"Ready."

Neither Stockton nor Simmons knew about the existence of Billion's dog. They were convinced that there was a wolf now more than ever. They sat in Stockton's office, and Simmons told how Egan had acted that morning. Stockton had already begun to make plans for when the wolf was captured. He had an entire publicity plan mapped out that made Simmons glad he had taken him into his confidence about capturing the wolf.

"But what if Egan kills it?" Stockton said.

"Then we won't have anything but a wolf skin to show," Simmons said.

"Well, we've got to get him out of here then," Stockton said. "Fire him."

"I think he quit. If he's trapping, he's trapping on his own."

"How about a law or a regulation? Is it legal to kill wolves?"

"I think technically there is still a bounty on them."

"How about an injunction of some kind then?" Stockton banged his hand on his desk.

Simmons sat thinking. "Might be possible," he said. "But we have to be careful. This thing could get pretty emotionally charged. Especially if the wolf can be definitely connected to the attacks on humans."

"The people just want the wolf caught. They don't care if it's dead or alive, but most of them could see the biological value of a live capture." Stockton shook his head. "I still think we should try to get an injunction against killing this thing."

"Then what happens if we do get it made illegal to kill the wolf, and Egan says, 'Fine, catch it yourself'? That's pretty much what he told me this morning."

Stockton and Simmons looked at each other. They knew that, if there was a wolf, Egan would have to catch it. They began to think. Simmons tapped his index finger on the desk top. Stockton made a clicking sound with his tongue.

McVay, Egan, and Bailey walked down the street from the sheriff's office. McVay felt slightly dizzy but didn't let it show. The sun would be setting soon. The shadow from the buildings on the west side of the street was halfway up the facades of the buildings on their side of the street. McVay looked up at the line of shadow five feet above his head and wondered if he were to jump as high as he could, whether he could touch it. It seemed like a silly thing to be thinking about, but McVay knew what his mind was doing. It was trying to keep him from thinking about what was happening. It was avoidance, a way McVay had found of preparing for confrontation.

Bailey was in a good humor. He joked about Billion and about the dog, Ralph. He checked his pistol for ammunition and asked Egan if he had a gun on him. Egan nodded, though he didn't show it. Then Bailey asked McVay how he felt and asked if he wanted to carry a gun. He said he'd deputize him, so it would be all right. But McVay refused; his .45 was already tucked inside his jacket pocket.

"Suit yourself," Bailey said. "But watch out for Ralph, even if he is a sweetheart." He laughed. Egan smiled and nodded, and McVay flashed a grin at them both, then looked away, catching the sun still holding on, spilling its rippled pink like the side of a salmon. The last direct rays shot like distant searchlight beams over the town.

Egan tried to get into the backseat, but McVay had beat him to it. McVay didn't feel like sitting in the front with Bailey, especially with Bailey in the mood he was in. He wanted to sit alone, and as they started out, he began to wish that the two in the front did not know that he was there. He watched them. Bailey was smiling, joking, his meaty left hand wrapped around the steering wheel and his right arm draped over the back of the seat. Egan was the same as always, acknowledging the jokes and the lightness in Bailey's voice, but not adding to it. He did not show what he was thinking.

As they drove, McVay became more interested in the things that Bailey was saying. They began to seem funny to McVay. He laughed a couple of times when Bailey talked of catching petty criminals in the act. He didn't know what was funny about what Bailey was saying, but he laughed. He had begun to catch Bailey's mood when Bailey said, "And this goddamned Billion, I've been waiting for this character." Then the reality of what was happening flared in McVay's imagination. He was anxious to see Billion's face. "You'll get your sweet revenge," Bailey said, leaning back and looking at McVay over the seat. McVay sat quietly in the dark and heard the air rush from between his teeth.

Bailey had been right about McVay wanting revenge, but he had no way of knowing the real reason or how obsessed McVay was with getting it. Sitting in the backseat of the car, McVay thought of Jimmy, dying in an alley. He imagined again how the murder must have taken place. Billion had pulled the trigger. Pulled it three times. And he would pay for it.

Even in the dark McVay recognized the area. Bailey dimmed his headlights and slowed the car a quarter of a mile from the house. "We'll drive up like it's just a visit," Bailey was saying. "I'll go to the door, and you two stay in the car. Egan, if anything happens, you get around to where you can watch the back door. You stay low, McVay. Until I've got him in custody." Then he looked at Egan. "I'd like to get the dog alive, but if he gets growly, kill him."

It was dark now, but still gray in the west. The clouds Egan had been watching that afternoon were closing in just as the last of the sun disappeared. In five minutes the night would be solid black. Only the hollow eyes of Billion's house would give light. It was cooling off. McVay didn't like the setup. He didn't like not being in charge. They came closer to the house, and Bailey said, "Duck down when I open the door. I don't want him to see you."

The overhead light flashed on for an instant, then the door slammed, and Egan and McVay were in the dark again. Now McVay wanted to be in the front seat but it was too late. He watched Bailey walking toward the house and wondered what Egan was thinking. The old man squirmed in his seat, then put his right arm and shoulder out the window. He leaned to his right and watched Bailey through the open window as if the windshield was too dirty for him to see well. McVay felt better. He wondered if the old man was nervous, too.

They were parked beside the house. Egan had already decided how he would get to the back door if he needed to. He was leaning out the side window, ready. As Bailey reached the front door and sounds of his knocking drifted back to them, Egan felt McVay lean forward and put his arms on the back of the front seat. He wanted to look at McVay, to see what was happening with him, but there was no time. He studied the doorway where Bailey stood silhouetted, but found it hard to concentrate. The old sensation came to him. The sensation was unmistakable, but he was old and didn't trust it anymore. He forced himself to concentrate on Bailey.

When the door opened, Egan felt McVay move. Billion stood clearly in the porch light which he had switched on. He smiled a cocksure smile. They began to talk. Billion motioned Bailey to come in, but Bailey declined with a shake of his head. Bailey continued to talk. Finally, Billion shrugged his shoulders and smiled broadly. He stepped out onto the porch, turned, put his hands up against the building, and Bailey began to search him. He's got him, McVay thought. Easy. But at that instant he saw something move at the corner of the house. Before he could speak, the arm that he thought Egan had absently dangled out the window came up with a cocked .357 in it. The old man was trained on the movement before it was recognizable as a dog. McVay's .45 was up too, and he saw that Egan had noticed it but concentrated on the dog. They both held on the dog, steady, eyes open, unblinking. They watched the dog come up behind Bailey and sit down, watching him as he read Billion his rights. Egan eased out of the car with McVay right behind him. The muzzles of the pistols were still trained on the dog.

When Bailey turned to wave the two to come, he was face to face with the big German shepherd. He jumped visibly and fumbled for his gun. Egan and McVay came into the light in time to hear Billion tell Bailey to take it easy. Egan let the hammer of his pistol down to half cock. The pistol swung in his hand, but his thumb remained ready to reset the hammer. McVay put his away but kept his hand in his pocket.

Billion looked right at McVay. McVay returned his stare. "Don't let Ralph worry you, fellas. He's a pet."

"Right, Billion," Bailey said as he jerked his handcuffs from their leather pouch. "Turn around." He took hold of Billion's shoulder, and the dog came to his feet.

"Easy, Sheriff," Billion said. And McVay heard the two clicks from Egan's Magnum as he tightened his grip on his own .45. "Here, let me." He took the cuffs from Bailey and clamped them on himself. The dog sat back down. His head came up to Bailey's waist and was the size of a volleyball.

"All right, Billion, tell that dog to get in the trunk of my car." He pulled the keys from his pocket and tossed them to McVay. "Open it." The gashes under the bandages began to throb. The three men and the dog followed McVay around to the back of the car. It was dark there, away from the house, and McVay turned sideways to keep everyone in sight. He opened the trunk and stood back.

"Tell him to get in," Bailey said.

"What do you want him for?" Billion grinned.

"He could be carrying some valuable facts, Billion. Tell him to get in."

Billion laughed. "What kind of facts?"

Bailey smiled back. "Like particles of blood, maybe." Billion glared at Bailey, who kept smiling. "Tell him to get in."

Egan was having trouble concentrating again. There was a strange sensation in the air. He held the .357 Magnum ready while Billion took the dog's collar. The smile was gone from his face. He looked around at the three men: Bailey with his hand on his gun now, Egan standing a few feet away, and McVay standing with one hand in his pocket. Billion smiled as if he didn't care and said in a firm voice, "Go!"

The dog leaped, but not at the car. Into the night. Egan's gun was up in time, but Billion put a shoulder into him before he could squeeze off a shot. McVay's gun started to come out, then stopped. Bailey stepped up and fired twice into the dark. Egan, Billion, and Bailey stood in a line. Billion was grinning again. Bailey's gun was still up, being held with two hands. He stepped backward with his left foot and brought his hands, gun and all, around and into Billion's smiling face. Billion sprawled, and Bailey cussed him on the way down, but neither Egan nor McVay saw what Bailey had done. McVay stood calmly with his hand still in his pocket. He stared after the dog. Egan took two steps into the woods, gave in to the sensation that had been bothering him, and listened to the night.

Egan and McVay were the first to hear it. In the background Bailey and Billion bickered, but as the sound grew louder, they became quiet. The three faces drew closer to Egan, who was standing facing the screams that were building somewhere out of their sight.

"What the hell?" Bailey whispered. The screams continued, became shriller. They pushed out of the night at the men. McVay moved in closer. "Egan," he said softly, being drowned by the shrieking. "Egan, what is it?"

When Egan turned from the sound that had begun to fade into pitiful moans, all three of the others watched him. "What is it?" Bailey said. There was a moment's silence.

There was a smile on Egan's face. "It's the dog," he said, "being killed by a wolf."

Part Five

Bailey wanted to talk. He'd locked Billion away in the cell in the back of his office, sat down at his desk, and started. Egan and McVay both knew that he was relieved and worried at the same time. The talk was only that, just talk. He wasn't trying to find out anything or to tell them anything. McVay wondered if he was trying to keep from being alone.

Both Egan and McVay wanted to leave. They both had other things on their minds. As Bailey talked, Egan was making his plans. There was a wolf. Now he wondered if he could kill it before Simmons made a curiosity out of it. Simmons would turn it into a sideshow if he caught it, Egan thought, like the whole Black Hills, but Egan wasn't going to let that happen. He would be moving before light in the morning. Moving toward a special place in some insignificant draw where he would meet the wolf and kill it and leave it and not tell anyone where it was. He wondered how long it would take him to find that draw, and while Bailey talked on, he pictured it in his mind. He hoped that it would be treeless like the prairie was supposed to be. He hoped that there would be a trace of a fire, maybe a charred stump of a pine tree that had encroached on the native grass. He hoped that there would be a spring and a cool place for the wolf to sit while he thought about whether to investigate the bottled scent that Egan would use to bait the trap. If there was a cool place in the draw beside a spring, it might be a good place to bury him, Egan thought.

McVay was thinking that he should be moving now, that now was the perfect time. With Billion in jail, the house would be unguarded. He could search it at his leisure, get his mother's money back, or if worse came to worst, there was the marijuana. It would take an afternoon to convert it to cash in Toledo, a crummy business but better than nothing. He could settle with Billion later. There was no real reason to think that he would stay in jail long. In fact, he wondered what charges Bailey was holding him on. But that was not his concern—he was there to even a score. Then there was Katie. If he found what he was looking for, he'd have to get out of the area fast, and he would want to see her before he left. And then he noticed Egan pretending to listen to Bailey, and his desire to search Billion's house flagged. There had been a change in the old man. Now he looked younger, a little impatient, and keen. McVay could see the wheels turning and, as before, he was drawn to the old man, curious about his thoughts.

Egan looked at his watch. "Going to be an early morning for me," he said.

Bailey glanced at the wall clock. "Christ, yes," he said.

Egan and McVay stepped out onto the street but did not stand and talk. The old man made his way to the Oasis for the rest that he knew he needed, and McVay went to his pickup. He was eager to get out to Billion's place and have a look around. At first, things seemed to have fallen into place for McVay. But by the time he pulled up in front of Billion's house, it seemed certain that nothing much would come from searching for money. Sitting in the pickup with the engine turned off, McVay realized that what he was really after was Billion. In a way, Bailey had cheated him by throwing the bastard in jail. Now the money or marijuana did not seem important to McVay. He wanted Billion, he wanted Katie, and in a strange way he wanted Egan to get the wolf.

It took him only five minutes to search the house and the outbuildings. As he had expected, he found nothing that would replace his mother's money. He did find Billion's medals and a shed filled with contraband from his service days. From the stash of military weapons that Billion had hidden in his shed, it was clear to McVay that he would have to be careful if he ever got the chance to deal with him. The souvenirs were interesting, but they were not what McVay was looking for. He drove back toward town feeling empty. It was not until he saw that Egan's light was still on that he knew what it was that he wanted to do.

As McVay stood on the sidewalk looking up at the light, he pictured the old man going over his equipment. Equipment that had not been used in thirty years. And McVay pictured the tender way Egan would handle the traps, the light film of oil that he would be spreading on the barrel of his rifle. As he watched, the light went out. Egan would be asleep soon. McVay moved to the door of the Oasis. He would need his sleep too.

The sky was turning from black in the west to a purple, only slightly lighter in the east. Egan stood looking over the contents of his pickup with a flashlight. He had not really expected that he would ever need any of it again. The tools that had hung for so long in the shed behind his daughter's house were laid out in a certain order in the box of the truck. The wicker basket-pack was filled with the essentials. He tucked the brown paper bag that held his lunch into the top of it, surveyed it all again, and as he flipped off the light, he heard someone walking down the sidewalk.

The .357 was strapped to his belt under the light jacket that he wore. Instinctively his hand slid under the jacket and touched the handle of the pistol. Subconsciously he checked to see that the rifle was in the rack in the rear window. Standing still, he waited for whoever it was to come close enough to be recognized. The footsteps were confident. He thought that it might be Bailey, but it was not. It was McVay.

The young man stepped up to him, and they stood without a word for an instant. Egan looked closely at him and could see what McVay wanted. Egan wondered if he hadn't really been waiting for McVay to show up.

"Can I come along?" McVay said.

Egan stood expressionless. "You want to?"

"Yes."

They looked at each other an instant longer, the old blue eyes staring evenly into the young green ones. Then, quickly, as if Egan had just remembered the business at hand: "Okay, get in, we're running behind."

Bailey knew that he'd made a mistake as soon as he'd done it. What he should have done was to take the cuffs off Billion as soon as Egan had said that it was a wolf that they were listening to. But he hadn't. He had brought him into town, busted lip and all, and set him in a cell for the night. Bailey hadn't gotten much sleep. He'd sat up thinking until after midnight, then laid on the couch in the office, staring at the ceiling, until dawn. He could justify the arrest by saying it was for McVay's protection; the wolf had nothing to do with the murder of Best and the attack on McVay. But no attorney with a brain would fail to see that the existence of a real wolf shot Bailey's theory to hell. He'd be lucky to get off with a false arrest charge.

Standing in front of the bathroom mirror, he tried to make himself look presentable. He wasn't looking forward to the day. There would be a lot of questions that he didn't have answers for. That goddamned wolf, he thought. Then he thought of Egan, and he knew that Egan had to catch the thing. He had no faith in Simmons—the local trappers were no good—it would have to be Egan. Bailey splashed cold water on his face for the third time and glanced at the clock through one eye. Six o'clock. The buzzards would be gathering soon. Then the telephone rang. "They just couldn't wait," he said.

It was Stockton. "What's up?"

"Well," Bailey said. "I guess we've got a wolf again."

"We've always had a wolf."

"This time for sure, I think."

"What about Billion and this arrest thing?"

"Word travels fast. But scrap it."

"You didn't arrest Billion?"

"Afraid so." Bailey frowned into the telephone. "Look, Jerry, it's early. Come on down in a couple hours and we'll talk."

"But the paper deadline is noon today."

"I'd hold it up if I were you. See you about eight." Bailey hung up quickly. He could hear Stockton starting to say something more but hung up anyway.

Billion's lawyer showed up before Stockton. "Sheriff," he said, "I think you made a mistake, honest perhaps, but nonetheless a mistake."

"Yea?"

"You shouldn't have arrested my client."

"The judge sets bond."

"But there won't be a hearing for three days." The lawyer shook his head. "I've been on the road since six this morning. My client's willing just to let this slide." Bailey acted as if he weren't interested. "But if he has to wait for the hearing and has to put up bond, well, that would be a lot of trouble for him. Not to mention the wounds that were inflicted on him during the arrest."

"You want me just to let him go?"

"An honest mistake." The lawyer smiled.

Just then Stockton came in the door.

"I'll think about it," Bailey said. "Get back to me in an hour or so."

"I'll be at the café."

Bailey turned to Stockton as the lawyer closed the door. "How long am I supposed to hold the paper?" Stockton said. Bailey shrugged. "It's pretty important that the citizens of Medicine Springs know what's going on here."

"There's a wolf, Jerry."

Stockton let out a long breath. "Well," he said, "that's what I've been saying all along. Me and Joe Standing Elk and Simmons, but you wouldn't believe us. What convinced you?"

"Egan identified the sound."

"You tell Simmons? He'll be happy to hear that."

"I haven't had time."

"Well, he's out of town for today. Up at that damn Indian camp. Got to get them moved out. What are you doing about the wolf?"

Bailey winced. "I'm"—he hesitated—"I'm thinking about calling for the National Guard." He expected Stockton's face to light up, but it didn't.

"Well, Junior, do you think that's wise?" Stockton said.

"Shit, Jerry, you've been yelling that for weeks."

Stockton rolled a pencil across Bailey's desk, back and forth. "There are other considerations. I have to admit that Mr. Simmons and I believe it would be better to use live traps. Mr. Simmons has another trapper on the way. The National Guard might shoot."

"Jesus Christ," Bailey moaned. "Look, I haven't made up my mind. Maybe the Guard's a bad idea. Give me some time to think."

Stockton nodded violently. "Sure, I know that a decision like that can't be taken lightly." He stood up to leave. "Weigh everything," he said.

"I will, Jerry. Just give me a couple of hours."

Stockton was nodding gravely now. He stopped at the door. "Better hold the paper, huh?"

"Yea, Jerry, better do that."

Katie Running had been doing a lot of thinking. Everything seemed to be coming too fast, and there were feelings inside of her that she didn't understand. Ever since she had come back to the Black Hills, she had felt good and bad at the same time. Her quiet times, when she was alone on the porch of the Hermany-horses place or just walking in the Hills, gave her a feeling of calm. It was a feeling she was not used to. She was more used to the choking feeling she got at the Oasis. She was confused but couldn't figure out why. There was Tom McVay of course. He was strange and attracted her in ways that were familiar. But he was a man—she knew men and could deal with them. That part of her life seemed nearly normal, but there was more bothering her than that.

It had something to do with the Indian camp and James Lebeaux. Since the day she had seen him drive into the camp, she had felt guilty. Maybe it was the fact that he had known her parents and was older that made her feel that she must respect him. It had something to do with authority—not the kind that a government or school principal has, but authority that really meant something. Katie Running had thought all of that through and decided she had to talk with Lebeaux. It reminded her a little of the Catholic boarding school on the reservation. Her guilt was smothering her, and she needed to confess.

The camp had grown to seventy people. There were tents, truck campers, and even a few crude buildings. She found Lebeaux sitting on the steps of the shack they had built to use as a school. There were a dozen school-age children at the camp now, and Lebeaux had insisted on a school. He smiled when he saw her coming. "Little Katie Running," he said. "What brings a lady like you to our humble camp?"

Katie stood before him with downcast eyes. It was the posture she had learned at the boarding school. It was not the way she stood on the streets of Minneapolis or the way she stood when she was alone in the Hills. But she could not help it. She wanted to look him in the eyes and speak, but she couldn't. Finally, Lebeaux stood up and touched her shoulder.

"What is it, Katie?"

She shook her head. She was like a little girl. "I'm all mixed up," she blurted out.

Lebeaux let his arm slip around her shoulder and hugged her. "Let's walk," he said.

They went along the side of the school and into the forest. A stream started at the spring where the camp got its water. Silently they followed it until it came to some boulders and tumbled a few feet to a pool. Lebeaux led Katie to one of the boulders and sat her down. He sat across from her.

"Now," he said, "what's the trouble?"

Katie felt herself begin to go silent, but being surrounded by trees had eased the tension, and she resolved to talk. "I don't really know," she said as she looked into the pool below the boulders. "I've been all tight inside."

"Do you have any idea what's causing it?"

She thought for a moment. "Maybe it's coming home," she said. "Maybe I should have stayed away."

Lebeaux swiveled on his rock, trying to catch her eyes. "Were things better in Minneapolis?"

"Not really," Katie said, "but it made more sense."

Suddenly Lebeaux reached out and grasped her arm. "What's bothering you?" he said.

The quickness of the move startled Katie, and she looked up into Lebeaux's face. Before she could think, she said it. "I was an informer. I took money from an FBI man."

Lebeaux looked at her sternly. "Is that all?" he asked.

"I got all mixed up. The FBI man was killed. But I didn't have anything to do with it. Then a friend of mine was almost killed, and I think it was because of me." Tears started to come to her eyes, but she held them back.

Lebeaux's grip eased, but he continued to look at her. When she dared to return his stare, she saw that he was not mad. "That's not so bad," he said.

Then he let go of her arm and let his gaze wander to the trees and grass around them. "We are in a difficult time and place," he said. "We are like a lost tribe. All of us are wanderers without a home. But in a way it's worse." He looked up to the blue sky. "Because our home is here. We know where our home is, but still we are lost. Our problem is that right now, for a short time, our home is hostile. But this is where we belong. This is where you belong." He reached out and turned Katie's face toward him. "Your home loves you. If you let the spirit of these hills come inside, the confusion will be gone."

Katie had been watching him, but now she looked away. The sun was coming golden through the pine trees, and the forest was absolutely still. She closed her eyes and let the sunlight warm her face. She wanted to stay right there, forever.

The dog was torn into two pieces. A front leg and shoulder had been pulled, along with most of the skin from that side, away from the rest of the body. Part of the insides and the back had been eaten. Egan and McVay stopped thirty feet from the carcass. Egan studied it from that distance, then, waving McVay to stay where he was, moved in for a closer look. It took him several minutes to cover the thirty feet to the carcass. He studied the dog up close for several minutes, not touching anything, then steadily backtracked, placing each step on top of one he had already made. When he got to where McVay stood, he turned sharply to his left and walked to a small knoll fifty yards away. He stopped at the top and looked back toward the dog. "This is where he was sitting," he said, pointing to an area of grass a couple of feet in diameter. "He's a big one," Egan said and indicated a patch of soft sand as he passed it.

McVay looked to where Egan had pointed. He looked hard into a smooth dishlike impression in the sand. It meant nothing to him. Then he noticed four more dents in the sand smaller but still large enough to hold twenty-five-cent pieces. He let his vision expand, and when he saw the holes poked deep in the sand just in front of the four impressions, the picture came clear to him. It was a footprint. He held his hand over it. His palm covered the imprint of the largest pad. His fingers barely reached past the places where the claws had punctured the earth. When he looked up, Egan was moving through the trees toward the open prairie. Ahead of him the sun had just come into full view and was ready to pass over the first of the shattered, cream-colored clouds that became heavier toward the west.

McVay ran to catch up. The old man was taking six-foot strides. As they started up the slope, the strides became shorter, and when the slope became a steep grade, the steps became short and choppy.

When they reached the prairie, the land flattened out, the strides lengthened, and the two men headed directly for a place where they could see for miles. Egan carried the basket-pack, and from his left hand swung the rifle that McVay had seen him shoot. When they stopped neither man was breathing heavily. They looked out over the prairie and back to the Black Hills. With the exception of a single barbed-wire fence, there was no sign of man.

"Why don't you follow the tracks?" McVay said.

"We will," Egan said. "I wanted to see the land first." He scanned the country, back and forth, his eyes squinted as if focused on the distant hills.

"Do you think we'll see him?"

"Not today. Two, three days, maybe."

"Then he's still in the area?"

Egan's eyes ran across the horizon again. His head nodded slightly. "He's here," he said, "somewhere." And he raised his arm to point. "Maybe there."

McVay looked out across the prairie that opened below them and saw, hazy in the strange light, a line of buttes. As he stared, they became purple and pulsed in his strained vision. When he looked up, Egan was gone again, striding back in the direction they had come.

Simmons had no idea that the meeting would be so large. There was a representative of every government agency and bureau in the Black Hills. Apparently it was no longer simply a Forest Service problem. Everyone had a concern. It was not just a matter of camping without a permit. They talked about the problem of waste disposal, vegetation destruction, erosion. Larry Mullens showed a map of just where the camp was in relation to Mount Rushmore. It was surprisingly close, and on the map he had drawn a big arrow representing the direction of the prevailing winds. His concern was the open fires and what a forest fire would do to the aesthetics of the monument. One of the state people made the mistake of saying that forest fires were part of the ecology, and Mullens flew into a rage. "This is a national monument. Without trees growing around it, it would look ridiculous. Nobody would come to see it." He was nervous and fidgeted with his sunglasses, which protruded from his shirt pocket. "Those open fires are a hazard to the monument. Those people must be moved out."

Then a federal attorney talked about the Indians' right to be there. "There was a treaty, like Lebeaux said, but we feel that it will be held to be null and void when the court gets hold of it."

"When will that be?" Simmons asked.

"Hard to say," the attorney said. "The federal court dockets are packed. It could be years."

"They're too great a threat to let them go years," Mullens said. "And what about the explosives, and the felons that are living there?"

A federal marshal took the floor. "We don't know what's going on inside the camp. There are all kinds of reports. Some of our sources are saying that there could be a connection between the camp and a robbery of explosives from the mine in Deadwood. We don't know that for sure. We do think that there are several convicted felons in the camp and perhaps a fugitive. But, of course, none of that is an indictment against the camp itself. After this meeting we plan to go out to the camp and talk with Lebeaux. At this point that is about all we can do."

"What about the pneumatic tools that were stolen from the quarry in Rapid City?" Mullens asked. His smile was smug. He'd found out about the report from a friend of his in the Rapid City Police Department. The smile grew broader. He'd caught the Feds trying to keep the report under wraps.

"The quarry operator said they might have been misplaced. They could have been missing for a long time."

"But they're capable of drilling rock, right?"

"Not by themselves." The marshal was trying to get off the subject. He looked around the room for other questions, but Mullens wouldn't let it drop.

"A simple two-hundred-dollar air compressor would run those tools. You can buy one anywhere."

"Mr. Mullens, we don't consider that report to have any bearing on the Indian camp."

"Isn't it a little strange that you have reports of explosives disappearing and also the equipment to drill and set charges? For crying out loud, it adds up to an assault on the monument."

"None of those reports are confirmed."

Mullens was standing up now. He had his sunglasses out and shifted them between his hands. "Well, the monument is under guard, and it will stay that way until that Indian camp is shut down."

The marshal nodded, wanting to give the floor to someone else. He had already said too much, could see Agent Kring smiling from the back of the room. He wondered if the FBI's reports were jibing with theirs. "I think we all agree that something has to be done here. But it is a very sensitive situation. The public, for the most part, doesn't understand what we're dealing with out here, and they are very influential." The two men representing the press scribbled on their pads and the marshal resolved to shut up. He sat down.

Simmons was overwhelmed. He had thought that it was only a few Indians camped in the forest trying to make a point about their homeland and some treaty or other that had been broken. It had all seemed very insignificant a couple of weeks ago, and to Simmons, in light of the fact there was a real gray buffalo wolf roaming the edge of the forest, it still seemed trivial. But he could see that he would have to go out with the marshal and whoever else was going out to the camp and make sure that one of the other agencies didn't try to make policy for the Forest Service. He wondered what Egan had found, and he knew that he had to get back to Medicine Springs soon if he planned to beat the old man to the wolf. But his own man should be arriving soon, and he'd be back in town himself by late afternoon. He directed his attention back to the meeting and could see that it was about to break up. The men from the press were asking questions. He hoped that they wouldn't ask him anything hard.

Four cars left Forest Service headquarters and began to wind their way toward the Indian camp. Simmons was in the first car with his assistant and a state man. The second car carried the federal marshal and Larry Mullens. Then there was the car with the FBI, and last, the car with the newspapermen. Simmons's assistant was filling him in as fast as he could.

"There are several blatant violations," he was saying. "The most obvious is camping without a permit. Then the open-fire violation, littering, waste disposal, and of course the building of permanent structures." He paused and thought. "There are some others, but those are the big ones."

"Permanent structures?" Simmons said quietly. He hoped that the state man in the backseat would not realize that he had not heard about the building.

"The big one is a school," the assistant said. "There are a couple more, but the main one is the school."

"Then they plan to stay?" Simmons said.

Both men looked at Simmons incredulously. "Yes," the assistant said. He was embarrassed and lowered his voice in the vain hope that the state man was not listening. "It's a settlement. They plan to stay."

"But this is federal land." Simmons laughed. "They can't just move in."

But when the cars pulled up at the clearing in front of the camp, it was apparent to Simmons that they had indeed moved in. Now there were forty cars parked beside tents and trailers, and he could see the roof of the school above it all. He stared through the windshield at the camp. He'd had no idea. "But," he said, "they've cut down trees." Neither the assistant nor the state man answered him.

They stepped out of the cars, and Simmons could feel the others standing behind him. As they looked over the camp, most of the people ignored them, going on with their work. Some were sawing firewood, others carried water from the spring near the school or worked on their tents. There were cooking fires everywhere and children running in all directions. A few people were watching them, and the children, as they noticed the strangers, stopped their play and moved closer. Simmons saw one small boy with long black hair poke another and point at Simmons. "He's the honcho," he said. Simmons looked quickly around and saw that all the other white men were standing behind him. "The honchos always wear the uniforms," the small boy said.

Simmons became self-conscious and looked back at the other whites. He was the only one with a uniform on. Even Mullens wore civilian clothes, and Simmons could not remember ever seeing Larry Mullens without his Park Service uniform. They've set me up, he thought. Then—no, it is my forest. I'm the one who should do the talking.

A man stepped forward. "I'm James Lebeaux," he said, but did not offer Simmons his hand.

Simmons tried to smile. "Are you in charge here, Mr. Lebeaux?"

Lebeaux shook his head. "No," he said. "But I speak for many of the people." Lebeaux spoke softly but he did seem to be the leader. His height shocked Simmons. He stood for a moment looking up at the man, then came to his senses.

Simmons looked around the crowd. "We'd like to talk to you in private," Simmons said.

Lebeaux shook his head. "No," he said. "We can talk in front of everyone." He knew they would try to get him alone, and he knew that anything he said should be heard by all. If the people thought that he was saying one thing in front of them and another in private, there could be problems. It was hard enough to present a united front the way it was; he didn't need for anyone to get the wrong idea.

"I'm afraid that you cannot set up a camp here," Simmons was saying. "The Forest Service regulations are quite clear on camping restrictions." He had intended to go on, but Lebeaux was shaking his head. "You will not be able to get away with this," Simmons said. "This is federal land and we will have to evict you."

"This is Indian land, and we have been evicted for the last time," Lebeaux said. Simmons heard Larry Mullens snort behind him.

"Now see here," Simmons said. "You have open fires, and if they would set the forest on fire, there would be a tragedy."

"It is only a tragedy in your mind. There were open fires and forest fires here for thousands of years before white men ever saw this place. It is only since you initiated your silly policy of putting out fires that the forest has begun to die. Only white men could presume to improve on the plan of the Great Spirit."

Simmons shook his head. He was suddenly very tired of it all. He was caught in the middle. His mind wandered back to Medicine Springs, and he wondered what Egan was doing. He heard the federal marshal talking.

"If there are any fugitives from the law here, we will have to come in and take them out," he said.

"If there are fugitives, they are fugitives that you have made," Lebeaux said. They had struck a tender spot. There were fugitives in the camp, Robert Lance for one, and Lebeaux was afraid that they were not there for the right reasons. It would be hard to keep them in line, but they were Indian, and that was enough. "You do not understand," he said to the federal marshal. "Your laws do not apply to natural things. They are made up. You have made everyone a fugitive. Even the land is a fugitive from you." Lebeaux swung his arm around. "You have not learned to live in harmony with these hills. You have no right to them."

"You know you're setting yourself up for every weirdo in the country to show up here," Larry Mullens said.

Lebeaux shrugged, then he smiled. "Anything would be an improvement over the weirdos that come here every summer."

Simmons had had enough. "We're getting nowhere," he said. He could see that this was a waste of time. All he wanted now was to get out of there and get back to Medicine Springs. "We'll be in touch with you," Simmons said simply.

James Lebeaux stood in the center of a group of people. He watched the men climb back into their cars. The people talked encouragingly to him. Some even slapped him on the back, but Lebeaux did not let his success go to his head. He had noticed a few who stayed at the front of the group, who watched him jealously and sneered among themselves. He knew that this division was a chronic problem with his people. It had destroyed their efforts many times before. As usual, if they failed in their mission, it would not be the whites alone who caused the failure. The seeds were within.

By ten o'clock Bailey had talked to a dozen people. He was back where he had started from, only worse. Now there was a wolf for sure, and he had no idea how to find it. People were mad and scared, and he'd arrested a man whom he didn't have a prayer of sticking with the charge. One of the dozen people he'd called was the state's attorney. He'd asked him what he should do, explained the whole situation to him, and ended with the statement that he still thought Billion was guilty, it just didn't look like it. He could almost feel the state's attorney shaking his head through the phone.

"Let him go, Junior," the attorney said. "We wouldn't stand a chance. I'd be afraid to go anywhere near the court on that one."

Bailey wasn't surprised—that was about what he had expected—but letting Billion go would be tough. It would be almost impossible to endure that smirk and the fancy words of the lawyer, and Bailey was sure that letting him go would be dangerous. Billion was not the kind of person who would be scared by what had happened. It wouldn't bother him in the least to know that Bailey was watching him closely. He was sure that Billion had done exactly what Egan had said: he had trained that dog to attack and had sent it first after Best, then McVay. Bailey hated the thought of letting him go, but it looked like he'd have to.

The sky seemed bright at first, but when he put on his sunglasses, it was too dark. He took them off again and crossed the street to the café. Billion's lawyer was sitting at the counter, leaning over a newspaper, sipping coffee. His legs were crossed—like a woman's, Bailey thought. Bailey took the stool beside the man and ordered a cup of coffee.

"Sheriff," the lawyer said, as if he was surprised to see him. Bailey nodded. "You've put me off for two hours. Have you given my proposal some thought yet?" Bailey leaned back, stretched, and rubbed his neck at the same time. He straightened up and rubbed his face as if he was only now making up his mind.

"Yea," he said, "I'm pretty sure that your boy did what we said he did, but as usual, it would be hard to stick him with it."

The lawyer smiled. "You going to release him?"

"Well . . ." Bailey acted undecided.

"I'm sure we can get him out one way or the other," the lawyer said. Then, "And there's that busted lip, and I think maybe even a couple of broken teeth."

"I tell you," Bailey said, "I think we might just forget it."

"We'd probably forget it, too, if there was an immediate release." The lawyer's voice became a little demanding.

Bailey's jaw tightened, but he said, "Okay, let's go."

They walked across the street in silence. The cell was in the back of the office. An old man, Earl Peterson, was watching it for Bailey. "Let him out, Earl," Bailey said.

"Out?"

"Yea, he's going home." They waited while Peterson fumbled for the right key. Bailey refused to meet the lawyer's eyes.

When Billion came out, the smile was already on his face. Bailey was happy to see that it was distorted by the puffiness of the lip. He hoped he'd break it open again with the smile. "We're turning you loose, Billion."

"Wonderful, knew you weren't serious, Sheriff." Bailey had an impulse to fatten the other lip.

"Go on. But watch it," Bailey said.

"Watch what? Why, whatever do you mean?" Billion grinned. The lawyer took his arm and led him toward the door.

Bailey waited in the back of the office until he was sure that they had gone. He didn't say anything to Peterson. He stood with his hat pulled down and his arms crossed. His foot tapped slowly and lightly on the concrete floor. The whole thing stank. Letting a creep like Billion free in his county was almost unbearable for Bailey. He'd have to find McVay and warn him. He'd already been over to the hotel and knew that McVay was gone. He could be with Egan, he thought. That was where he'd start—if he could find Egan, which he probably couldn't.

He waited until he was sure that he wouldn't run into Billion or his attorney and then left the office. As he got closer to his car, his tension began to ease. It felt good to be in his car again. He stretched out, relaxing as he listened to taped piano music, and was doing eighty miles per hour before he caught himself. He shook his head as if he was tired, straightened up, and slowed down. Opus Fifty-three. It reminded him of a movie. An old one. He wondered how anyone could tell when it was played wrong.

Simmons knew that the best he could do was to catch the wolf before Egan, and he knew that was unlikely. Still, he had to try. The romance of the situation had built in Simmons's mind and created an urgency. The Indian camp had just intensified Simmons's interest in the wolf and made him even more angry at Egan. Why Egan refused to leave the wolf alive was a puzzle to Simmons. It was a simple matter of roping the wolf while its leg was held in a steel trap. It had been done thousands of times. The leg was usually broken, and that would be too bad, but the wolf, the specimen, would be alive to be seen as a representative of days that were gone forever. The procedure was simple. Keeping the wolf alive was more a matter of not killing it. But Egan didn't see it that way. He didn't seem to have any idea what that animal would be worth in terms of science and history, let alone the personal prestige involved in having trapped it.

Simmons was no trapper, even though he'd supervised trappers years before. He knew, if he was going to beat Egan to the wolf, he needed help. So now he sat across the table in the café from one of the best coyote men on the Great Plains. The man's name was Jenkins, and he was skeptical about the whole idea.

"I don't know the first thing about wolves," he said.

"Neither do I," Simmons said. "But we have to try. Egan is an old man. We have that much of an advantage."

"That's a disadvantage," Jenkins said.

Simmons paid no attention. "Jerry Stockton, the newspaper editor, is supporting us and will help in any way he can. But basically it's up to you and me."

Jenkins sipped coffee and shrugged. "Okay, what's the plan?"

"First, I think the best place to start is east of town. There's an old sheepherder out there who's seen the thing hanging around his sheep. We'll make our sets out in that country. Now, I've had a couple of live traps sent in, and we'll use them."

Jenkins put his coffee cup down, looked Simmons in the eye, and said, "No." He shook his head. "I don't know anything about that kind of trap, and even though I don't know anything about wolves, I know they wouldn't come within a mile of something like that. It'll be hard enough to hide a steel trap from him, let alone a big mess of wires and levers."

"Look, we want this wolf alive and healthy."

"The best I can do is a broken leg."

Simmons looked at him and rubbed his ear, thinking. "I don't want it hurt," he said. Jenkins made a face. "We'll just wrap some cloth and tape around the jaws of the traps."

"I don't know. Might pull loose."

"We'll just check it more often. I think that would work."

Jenkins shrugged. "You're the boss," he said.

Early that morning the truck lights had reflected from the jackrabbits' eyes, and twice Egan had eased to a stop and reached for the .22 express that hung in the rear window. McVay watched him bring the rifle over his head, never taking his eyes off the rabbit. In the same movement he opened the truck door just a crack, enough so that the rifle muzzle would slip between the door and the frame of the windshield, but not enough to switch the inside light on. He shot left-handed. McVay was sure that the last time he'd watched him shoot he had done it right-handed, but it didn't seem to make much difference. Egan let out a low whistle that increased in volume and in pitch, and when the rabbit lifted its head, it exploded.

Egan picked the rabbits up with a pair of wooden tongs and wrapped them in plastic. Before they started off again, he checked to see that the empty cartridge had been ejected and a new one had taken its place in the firing chamber. He took out the clip and added a shell, pulled back on the safety, to be sure, and replaced the finely inlaid rifle in the rack behind the seat.

They were walking before it had even begun to show light in the east. McVay stayed with Egan, but behind, knowing that the old man should lead. Egan had it timed so that they reached the high spot he had noticed days before just as the sun appeared. McVay was behind him, and as he looked up, he saw Egan silhouetted, higher than himself, against the gray morning. The old man had never looked taller or straighter to McVay. He stood facing the sun as it rose, the woven basket backpack making him look as massive as McVay imagined that he had looked twenty years before. The rifle cradled in his right hand hung loose, as if for balance. McVay came up beside him and stood quietly while the old man swung his head from the river to the Hills, studying the twenty miles between them. He let his eyes come back to the flat land and back again to the Hills.

Without looking at him, Egan said, "Follow right in my tracks, no sense making two trails," and he was off, down the grade of loose gravel as if it was a paved road. McVay came behind doing his best not to slip and stepping exactly where Egan stepped.

The grade led down into a gully with sporadic cedar trees and a spongy hint that, in the wet months, water flowed there. The bed of the gully looked washed and was void of vegetation. Egan did not walk there, but walked just on the edge and watched the wash carefully. They had walked the gully for over a mile when McVay first began to realize that Egan was following something. He strained his eyes at the fine soil of the wash but saw nothing.

The cedar trees gave way to sagebrush and buffalo grass, and the wash widened. It became a broad cut in the crust of the earth with crumbling red banks. A single last cedar grew straight and ten feet tall from the edge of the cut. The soil around its roots had been eroded away, and the two main roots, one growing straight down, the other at a ninety-degree angle into the bank, had developed a thick yellowish skin that served as bark. The tree was managing to survive. Egan stopped, still fifty yards from the tree. He looked hard and long at the floor of the cut. Then he looked up the cut and turned and looked down it. He swung his pack off and set it lightly on the ground. From a side compartment he took a pair of gloves and put them on. He said nothing to McVay as he took out a rolled piece of canvas, two very heavy plastic sacks, a small hammer and shovel, a sieve, a two-foot-long stake, a smoked and waxed steel trap, and the two rabbits wrapped in plastic. He took one rabbit from the plastic and replaced the other one in the pack. With a pocketknife he made a slit in the skin of the rabbit's leg, between the two bones. From the side of the pack he cut a piece of bailing wire and wired the rabbit's legs tight, leaving eight inches of wire. He put plastic sacks over each boot and tied them tight around his ankles. He slung the rifle around his shoulder from the strap, put the tools under one arm, held the roll of canvas and rabbit in the other, and with the trap dangling out away from his body, made his way to the single cedar tree.

McVay stood beside the pack for an hour. He watched Egan lay out the canvas and kneel down. The trap was set between the exposed root of the cedar and the red clay bank. First Egan dug a shallow hole, being careful to put every bit of clay onto the canvas where he knelt. He put the trap into the hole and sifted soil back over it. For the chain he dug a channel to the stake that he had pounded in to secure the trap. He covered it all with sifted soil. Then, from the root that was growing into the bank above the set, he wired the rabbit carcass. He stood and rolled up the canvas, then with his plastic-covered boots Egan retraced his steps to where McVay stood. The tools were put back into the pack, and they walked on. A quarter mile from the set Egan stopped and shook the extra soil from the canvas.

It was nearly noon when they came to where the land rose into the Hills. Egan turned sharply to the east as if the Hills were dangerous to walk in. From then on he concentrated his vision to the north, back in the direction that they had come, and east. They walked along a boundary defined by an abrupt change in vegetation. To their left the plants were rugged—sage, yucca, greasewood, and the tiny flat cactus that grew in clumps. To their right the trees began, the ferns and leafy bushes.

After Egan had made his second set and they had walked a distance away and had cast the leftover dirt to the winds, they sat down. It was nearly three o'clock, and they had made only two sets. Egan sat looking, for the first time, toward the Hills. "We'll make another set if we find the place," he said in answer to McVay's questions. Now he was looking at something on the grasslands. "No sense in wasting time if we don't find the right place." Then he looked at the sun, which was beginning to be covered by the strange clouds that had been hanging in the sky now for two days. "We'll have to start back soon, anyway," Egan said and got to his feet. "I'll be right back," he said.

McVay watched him walk out in his long strides across the grass that they had been walking beside for two hours now. Egan stopped beside one of the ferns that speckled the grassland. He bent over and touched it, scratched at the soil around it with his finger, stood looking at it again and returned. "Let's go," he said as he passed McVay.

They made a huge loop and started back toward the pickup. This time they walked a narrow ridge, and again Egan seemed to be seeing something in the hard-packed earth. McVay looked but could see nothing. The clouds were building again like they had done the day before, and McVay began to feel fatigue. Suddenly Egan stopped. McVay watched as he again took out tools, canvas, and a trap. A hundred yards ahead the ridge came to an end and dispersed into a lower land. Water from the ridge had cut a gash three feet deep, but only eighteen inches wide. Halfway down that natural alleyway there was fern like the one Egan had investigated before. Here Egan made his third set. He lay on his stomach for nearly two hours, the canvas keeping the smell of him from the earth. This time he used no bait. This time he hoped the earth would bring his prey to the exact spot.

The sky was darkening fast when they got to the pickup. McVay stood beside the truck, thinking of how tired he was and watching the sky while Egan stowed his gear in the back. McVay listened to him arranging things as he watched the doves twisting among themselves above, heading for water. Slowly the sounds Egan was making faded from his hearing and were replaced by the vague unsettling sound of the wind. But he felt no wind against his face, and when he looked around he saw that Egan had moved to a point overlooking the country they had walked that day. Though Egan's back was to him, he could sense the old blue eyes. They were not open wide, not fixed in a stare, but unblinking, looking at the final rays of sunlight over the flat grassy tops between rough eroded breaks in the earth's crust. The river winding along the north marked what Egan knew was the boundary. To the south, the boundary was the Hills, black and mystical, seventy-five, maybe a hundred square miles, so familiar, yet new to him now. They knew the rules by heart: Egan through years of learning, and the wolf through centuries of selection.

The blue eyes narrowed, taking it all in for the last time in its totality, committing the overview to memory. From there on it would be the small things that were important, tiny things that Egan understood—understood so well that there was a hint of remorse in the eyes. Egan knew that he would win, and that it would not take long. Then it would all be over. He raised his head slightly and focused on the distant Hills, the blue eyes not straining but letting it all come to him. And from those Hills, old yellow eyes stared back into the sun fighting its way down through unsettled clouds, and somewhere in the middle there was a collision and shreds of color hurled themselves across the land.

Old Joe Standing Elk watched the sun setting. It seemed to be taking too long. The sunset had been building all day. He didn't know exactly what to think of it, but he knew there were things that were not supposed to make sense to men. It was summer now, they seldom got rain at this time of year, but something was happening somewhere. He stood outside of his tent and watched it boiling in the west between the sun and the earth. It was new to him, dull gray clouds that seemed to be layered, hanging still in the west all day, not moving with the constant west wind. Now, with the sun going down, the purple and reds shot through the layers, coming out of the clouds above his head where the sky became abruptly blue.

The way it should be, he thought, blue, like it was almost every day at that time of year. Or maybe billowing, tall thunderheads, black with wind and electricity. But not like this. He kept thinking tornado. They came at this time of year sometimes, and the clouds always looked odd before they came, but the air was always calm. When a tornado was coming, you could feel the eerie heavy air on your face and shoulders. This was different. The wind was moving as it should. When he tried to put a name on what was wrong, he could not. Just strange clouds in the west at sunset. A pretty evening. It would make a nice postcard for the tourists to buy in the cafés and the gas stations and the roadside attractions. They would like it and send it to people, and they would think there was nothing odd in it, that this was the way *Paha Sapa* always looked. But Joe Standing Elk would never buy such a postcard. He knew that the sun was taking too long to set.

Simmons and Jenkins didn't tell Joe Standing Elk that they were setting traps in the area of his sheep camp. They figured he'd be glad to have someone trying to catch the wolf. Jenkins was a good trapper. He just didn't know anything about wolves. What he and Simmons lacked in knowledge they made up for in enthusiasm. They started early and worked late. Jenkins, using what facts about the habits of wolves that Simmons could recall from the old days and from books, and his own knowledge about trapping, placed his sets well. He did not take the time with each set that Egan did, but he put out many more.

Simmons knew that wolves travel a certain territory, passing the same place every few days. The path that a wolf took, though not exactly the same each time, usually ran by ridges, gullies, fence lines, natural highways. By marking down on a map the sight of all the known kills, Simmons had come up with an approximate course of travel. It was along that course that he and Jenkins began setting their traps.

The night before, Simmons had sat up until after midnight, wrapping the jaws of the steel straps in burlap that he had washed four times in the washing machine in the rear of the Oasis office. The burlap was soft and pliable, but even more important, it was scentless. Simmons struggled to tie the pieces of washed twine with plastic gloves that would keep his smell from either the metal or the cloth. Finally he was finished. Twenty-two traps hung on a wire in his bathroom, wrapped with burlap and smelling, he hoped, of nothing.

When Jenkins saw them the next morning he shook his head but didn't say anything. He took them from Simmons and stored them in a special plastic-lined wooden box in the rear of the pickup. When Simmons showed him the map in the dome light as they drove, Jenkins raised his eyebrows, impressed. Simmons had been doing his homework; they might have a chance after all.

Jenkins set the traps as he would for a coyote, more carefully than he would have for a bobcat, but not with the care he would have used for a fox. They set sixteen in various places along a huge ridge that ran for five miles along the border of what the map indicated should be the edge of the wolf's territory. The plan seemed good. If the wolf was indeed traveling that route, he must certainly be using that ridge as a highway. Jenkins baited several of the sets with grouse that he had shot. Grouse were not in season, but under the circumstances, Simmons had "opened the season" on them. The other sets were placed in such a way as to catch the wolf as he walked between two rocks or stepped over a fallen cedar tree. If any of them were to work, Jenkins knew that the wolf would have to make a mistake. He simply didn't know enough to force a wolf into making a mistake.

They moved on into the afternoon, bouncing their pickup across the prairie, turning off the ridge to intersect a low broad washout that led to where a sheep kill had been made several weeks before. Jenkins set the twentieth trap of the day. The routine was beginning to have a depressing effect on him. He was tired, but Simmons kept at him, asking after each set what he thought the chances of success were. Jenkins answered with, "You never can tell, could catch him in an hour." But he knew that the chances were slim. If they were to catch him before Egan, they were going to need some luck. As they came over a small rise, with two traps left and the sun going down, lady luck revealed herself to Jenkins and Simmons in the form of an old ewe.

Simmons heard her first, and he waved Jenkins to stop the truck.

The bleating came to them in worried, frightened moans. "What is it?" Simmons said. Jenkins listened.

"It's a sheep," he said, and opened the pickup door. He listened again to get the direction right and headed toward the bawling. Jenkins and Simmons were together when they came to the top of a narrow wash and saw the old ewe tangled in plum bushes below them. "She's got her wool twisted into the thorns to where she can't move," Jenkins said. He reached into his pocket for a knife. "We'll do her a favor and cut her loose," he said. But Simmons caught his arm as he started toward her.

"Wait," Simmons said. "How long do you think she'll live?"

"Not long like that," Jenkins said. "Maybe a day." He was looking at Simmons, questioning, but already knowing what he was thinking.

"It's a perfect setup, isn't it? I mean, she's right in the middle of that draw, we have two traps left, one for each side of her."

Jenkins's face was tense. The ewe had seen them and was bawling for help now, but he had to admit, it was perfect. Simmons was looking at him. "Okay," Jenkins said, "get the traps."

Only his lack of confidence in the other sets allowed him to suffer the sounds of the old ewe as he worked, carefully, the best he knew how, concealing the two traps—constructing a set that he knew was nearly irresistible.

P.J. Billion sat in his kitchen and thought about making another pot of coffee. The table that he sat at was covered with dishes. Yesterday's eggs, separating juices, small portions of sour milk and soggy cereal lay deteriorating in the dishes. Billion took the last drag from a cigarette and tossed it perfectly into a glass. It sizzled briefly in the stale soda. It was almost noon, and Billion had not been outside yet. He'd had the feeling before. There didn't seem to be any reason to do anything. All he really wanted to do was sleep. Ten hours last night in the jail and he was thinking about a nap. It was just like it had been after he got out of the service—nothing seemed worth the effort.

Billion was angry. A strange pulsing anger that would grip him until tears would rise in his eyes, then leave him calm and sluggish, staring for long periods without thinking of anything. Over some little thing, like the toaster burning his toast, he would strike out physically, beating his fist into the kitchen cupboards, screaming at what he was pretending was the source of his anger. But Billion knew, sitting there at the table, what was making him angry.

He got up from the table, slid his chair back gently, and went to the window. It was bright. The morning clouds had burned off, and it was getting hot. He rubbed his hand across his face and felt the stubble. A shave would make him feel better. He took a deep breath and blew it against the glass of the window. Had to pull himself out of this, he thought. He'd have to start at the bottom and make it right. He ran his hand over his face again. He'd start with a shave.

The room seemed twice as narrow, the ceiling twice as tall. McVay lay in bed, exhausted but unable to close his eyes. It was not yet ten o'clock. He hadn't even eaten dinner. He was tired and knew that the next day would be worse than today. Dawn was not nearly far enough away. Light radiated up and spread out from the window. The ceiling was lighted by what McVay knew was neon from the Budweiser sign. Before McVay went to bed, he had stood at the window and watched the café, like he had done the night he had first seen Katie. As he watched, he had wondered where she was. There was something in him that wanted to see her, wanted her there with him that night. But there was something else that tried to make him laugh, that wanted him to say, "Easy come, easy go," something that wanted him to go on as if nothing had happened.

There was also something in him, and growing, that wanted to be done with the whole thing. He wanted to go back to Ohio, to his job at the tire plant, but he wanted to take Katie with him. He had gotten caught up in too many things. He tried to focus his mind on what he was there for, but Katie kept drifting in and out. Katie, and the steady, bright eyes of Egan. He lay in bed thinking, and now more than ever his thoughts went to Jimmy, to the fact that the time was now. Billion was out of jail. He would have to confront Billion and get it over with. Bailey had found him after they got back to town and told him that he'd had to let Billion out. He'd been concerned. He didn't realize that McVay had been hoping that Billion would get out. If there was money or marijuana at Billion's, McVay couldn't find it. He had to have Billion to get what he wanted, and he'd have to do it soon. Tomorrow, he decided. He'd go out with Egan, but no matter what happened, he would slip away in the afternoon and go to Billion's. By tomorrow night he would be finished in Medicine Springs. But sleep would still not come. It was Katie. He knew that he would have to see her again. Tomorrow night, after he'd dealt with Billion. They could go to the bathhouse again. The thought of the hot spring water flowing over their bodies relaxed him, then the warmth of the sauna, and finally McVay rested.

What no one had figured out yet was that Robert Lance was wanted for murdering a gas station attendant in Utah. It was known that he had done time and that he hated white men, but nobody knew about the warrant for his arrest. Even if Lebeaux had known, there was little he could do. Lance was influential. His radicalism was appealing to some of the younger Indians, who could not see it for what it was, just violence. People like Robert Lance were a fringe element that Lebeaux had often pointed to as the residue of what was once a great people. They were a force that was negative, and he had to keep them under control. Now, with the energy building in the Indian camp, he was having problems doing that.

Robert Lance had been talking around the camp about the need to "shake things up." He was calling himself a soldier and trying to get others to see themselves as soldiers. But Lebeaux knew Robert Lance was no soldier. He knew that Lance had no discipline, that he was opportunistic, and that if things got tough he would crumble. Lance's motives for embroiling the others were clear to Lebeaux. Robert Lance wanted to draw attention to himself. Violence was his way, and he would push for violence every time, even if it made a mess of things.

So Lebeaux had gone to talk to him. They walked away from the camp and stood in the trees, out of earshot of the others.

"So what you want to talk to me about?"

"Nothing much, really. Just I heard you were talking to some guys saying we ought to raise some hell."

Robert Lance nodded. "Yea," he said. He put his hands on his hips.

"Things are a little slow around here." He was a small man and, Lebeaux thought, not too tough.

"So what do you have in mind?" Lebeaux said, watching the man. He tried to see if what he'd heard had any truth to it.

"You know, James, you think you're a pretty big deal. You figure you should make all the decisions." Lebeaux had not expected this. "Well, there are other guys here who know what's going on. There're other guys in the world who can think. And we got ideas of our own."

"Like what?"

"You were sickening the other day. Those assholes made a fool out of you. We should have fucked them over."

"That wouldn't have gotten us anywhere."

"It wouldn't have gotten your picture in the paper. That's for sure." Robert Lance sneered at him. "But don't worry. We've got a plan. We're taking care of you chicken shits."

"So what's the plan, Robert?" The little man worried him. He was talking very confidently.

"You know there's a few of us here that know our way around."

"You mean know your way around prisons?"

"That too, big man. But we know what needs to be done, and we know how to get it done."

"Why don't you just tell me what you're planning?"

"Oh, I'm going to tell you. 'Cause I know that you can't really say anything that any of us will listen to. And even you wouldn't turn us in. That wouldn't get your picture in the paper."

Suddenly Lebeaux had a sickening feeling that what he had heard was true. He hadn't believed it, thought it was just a rumor, but something in the way Robert Lance laughed told him that it was all true. "Rushmore?"

Robert Lance laughed again. "Smart boy," he said. "We've been planning it since before the camp. Ever since they chased you down from there."

"Last time there was a chance of changing things."

"Last time it was a joke, a few cans of paint. That's what we had. This time we're serious."

"Then you're the one who stole the explosives?"

Robert Lance raised his eyebrows. "You are a smart boy. But it wasn't me that actually stole them. I just helped."

"Where are they?"

Now Lance's laugh changed in tone. "I can't tell you that. I've got enough volunteers. There are six of us. We've got guns and ammunition, and we can handle it. Nobody is going to tell you where the explosives are."

Lebeaux shook his head. "Don't do it, Robert. First, you'll never get away with it, and second, if there still is a movement, it will put it back a hundred years."

Robert scratched his head in mock thought. "Let's see, a hundred years." He squinted, pretending to be thinking hard. "What's the difference?" Then he smiled. "Oh, I see what you mean. A hundred years ago that mountain didn't have a name. It was just a mountain, without those fucking heads on it. You mean that when we get done, it will be just a mountain again." He laughed. "I hope after we're through that not one single white man ever comes to see it again. I hope it is a wasteland for them."

Joe Standing Elk was missing a ewe. They had all been there that morning, he was sure. She must have gotten lost in the afternoon, before he had gathered them for the night, somewhere along the breaks where he'd scattered them to graze. Joe looked back from the high ground where he was standing, to the breaks where the sheep had been grazing. Then he looked at the sky. It was dark, but there was a moon. It would be possible to find the ewe with a moon like that. He took one last look around the flock to see that they were calm and took up his rifle, which had been leaning against a tree. He started down toward the rough country to where he knew the ewe would be.

The trail was shorter on the way down. It took him only half an hour to reach the area where the sheep had been. Finding the straggler might take much longer, but Joe Standing Elk was no beginner at searching for lost sheep. He had found thousands, maybe tens of thousands of them in his life. He knew sheep and knew their shortcomings. It was their shortcomings that always seemed to get them into trouble. They were careless animals. Not stupid like many people thought, just careless. They lived a life that was only partially conscious of their surroundings. Their instincts seemed to fail them much too often. A rain and subsequent freeze would leave them shackled to the ground by their own frozen wool, and their strength was not enough to free them. Many starved to death, frozen there to the ground. Or a ditch that narrowed gradually would funnel them in a long line to a place where the first sheep could no longer move ahead, and the ones behind would press on in until they were smothered. But most often, Joe knew, it was a question of a single sheep falling into a hole, or in some way being detained and so separated from the others, and when that happened they were lost. Panic preys easily on sheep, and when a sheep panics, there is nothing it can do for itself. That is when the shepherd must do his job. How well a shepherd can anticipate the actions of a panicked animal is the measure of his skill. Joe Standing Elk was a good shepherd.

He did not bother to look on the top parts of the breaks where the buffalo grass grew richest. That was where a sheep would go when it was thinking straight, calm, knowing where the herd was in relation to itself. Joe went into the breaks themselves, into the gashes that water had cut into the earth, where the deer like to lie in the daytime and where the grouse stay crouched under bushes, safe from the heat of summer. And there, after an hour of searching, he heard a faint bleating. He stopped still, in the bottom of the break beside a chokecherry bush, and listened. The sound came from up ahead of him, and he could tell that he was just in time. The voice of the sheep was beyond desperation. She was giving up. So Joe hurried, the old rifle swinging at his side, past another clump of bushes and into a clearing where some grass was trying to grow. Ahead of him, in the next group of bushes, he could see his lost ewe. Her wool was tangled terribly in the thorny, wild plum bush and he could see her eyes rolling in an effort to bleat once more. He could see the ewe and the bush and evidence of the struggle she had made with the clinging thorns, but what he could not see was the trap that was set between him and her, or the trap behind her, now sprung, holding the wolf tentatively in its padded jaws.

Joe smiled at having found the ewe in time, and began to walk toward her, pulling his knife out to cut the wool. He moved toward the trap, but his foot missed it. Two more steps and he put his hand on the ewe and spoke to reassure her. The man's voice made the wolf flatten even more into the short grass near the bush. It had felt the trap snap shut only seconds before it had heard the man. The trap had frightened it, and it had leapt sideways hard enough to hear the chain snap tight. But the trap had not hurt him, the padded jaws only felt snug on the leg. The wolf knew that the trap could not hold him, but there was a man, and so the wolf had crouched to let him pass in the dark.

But the man had not passed, and though the wolf was calm, even curious, there was a pinpoint of fear somewhere in his brain. He watched the man lay the rifle down and begin to cut the wool and rub the old ewe's head. The man was not threatening now. He was not advancing, just holding his ground, and so the wolf waited.

The ewe was acting strangely, obviously glad to see the sheepherder, but wary, still terribly firghtened. Joe was in the middle of the bush and had cut most of the wool that held the ewe. The moon was bright and shone through the branches of the bush, leaving its light in the gossamer of the spiderwebs that were suspended between the branches. When Joe cut the last of the wood that held the ewe, he stood up suddenly.

Too suddenly.

The pinpoint of fear exploded in the wolf's brain, and it stood, shook the leg that was in the trap, and then growled. The sound was low and menacing. It rumbled in the throat, and before Joe turned to meet the wolf's yellow-eyed stare, he knew what the sound was.

The wolf was too close, and Joe began to back out of the bush, slowly, watching the wolf but trying not to stare at it. The ewe had run blindly into the night, bleating out its fear, but now the night was still. The wolf had growled only once, but now it stood watching Joe. It was much larger than any wolf that Joe had ever seen. Its head was huge, and the hair flared out under the ears, making it seem ever larger. Joe backed steadily away from the bush. He felt as though he might get away, but then his foot found the second trap and he felt the dull snap as it closed on his leg. At first there was panic, but almost instantly Joe relaxed. Now the man and the wolf watched each other, and Joe thought of the rifle. It was lying on the ground at his feet, and slowly he knelt to pick it up.

Then the wolf was in his sights, not twenty feet away. He held just between the yellow eyes. The wolf stared steadily at Joe. He did not move. He did not blink. But he watched the man. They stood like that for several seconds. The tension eased out of them both, and finally the wolf moved. But not toward the man, to the side and away, until the trap chain stopped him. Then he looked back to the man, and without glancing at the trap, shook his leg violently. The padded jaws slipped easily from his leg, and the trap fell to the ground harmlessly. Then the wolf turned and faded into the moonlit night.

Part Six

A delicate night breeze blew toward the dawn, and McVay and Egan moved with it. It was the predawn of the day that Egan had said they would catch the wolf and the day that McVay had resolved to meet Billion. They drove into the brightening east in separate trucks. McVay said that he would be needing his truck, but had not told Egan why. Egan had not asked. The old man seemed distant that morning in the alley beside the Oasis as he went over his equipment, and though McVay did not want to interfere with what he was thinking, he watched the old man and saw that Egan did not look the way he had looked the day before. The color that filled his face had drained. He looked thinner now, his face a pallid white, but he moved the same, going over the tools, picking them up tenderly and laying them back into the canvas bags. McVay sensed the specialness of this morning, felt it himself, and thought that this day was his, too.

McVay saw the other truck, parked not too far from them, heard the rough voices, and heard the tools being tossed carelessly into the rear. Egan paid no attention. He was confident and calm, though slightly sad, and when they had gotten to where they would leave the trucks, McVay felt it all as one feeling and considered letting Egan have this day alone. But when he mentioned it, Egan touched his shoulder and caught him with the still bright eyes and said that, no, it was important that McVay be with him. They said nothing more but set out exactly as they should, Egan in the lead, and both men walking easily, gliding over the ground, toward the rising sun.

The other pickup stopped just before the crest of the hill behind Egan and McVay. It coasted to a stop with the lights turned out. Now Simmons and Stockton sat in the cab while Jenkins walked ahead to a place where he could watch Egan and McVay with binoculars. They had talked the night before. Neither Simmons nor Jenkins had much faith in their sets. The only one with any chance at all was the set where they had found the ewe tangled in the plum bush. The others would not work. They were almost sure of that. So they decided to check the set where the ewe was first, then come to where Egan and McVay were starting out and try to follow them. Simmons and Stockton were determined not to let the old man simply bury the wolf in some unknown spot on the prairie. When Jenkins came back, he nodded decisively. "They parked a quarter mile ahead and started walking straight east."

"Do you think we'll be able to catch up with them?" Simmons said.

"Depends," Jenkins said. "If we fan out and head east, we ought to be able to find them." He shrugged. "Lot of country out there."

"I don't want it to look like we're following them."

"We can start from right here. We don't have to go anywhere near their outfits. The land is higher here anyway, better chance of seeing them."

Stockton hadn't said anything, but now he spoke. "Well, let's get going," he said. He was excited. "Let's see if you got him." Jenkins put the clutch in and let the pickup roll silently down the hill. When he thought that they were far enough away so that Egan and McVay could not hear them, he started the engine.

But Egan's old ears heard the sound. He did not stop walking or turn toward where the sound had come from. He walked on, the .22 express swinging gently with the rhythm of his walk. He walked slowly through the dark, letting the old rifle move as if it were part of his body. And, in a way, it was. It was like his claws. His teeth. His way of being part of the prairie. The rifle moved with Egan's easy, almost limber strides—Egan moving quietly through the dark. Slow as a cat and for the same reasons. Not because there were obstacles in the dark, but so nothing would know he was there. The predawn walk was what he had dreamed of the night before. That, and arriving at the sandy hill and the cedar tree at just the right moment. He was right on time. He did not want to arrive before he was expected.

An owl flew over Egan and McVay as they walked. It would be heading for the pine trees of the Hills to roost for the day. Egan looked in front of him. The land fell away in the rosiness of first light. He was sure that the wolf would be in the last set that they had made. The wolf would hear them long before they got to him, and it would crouch as low as it could get. It would feel vulnerable on that sandy hilltop. Egan closed his eyes and could see the scene. It would be caught by a rear leg. The trap would have sprung from its hiding place and caught the wolf above the main leg joint. Around the chain stake the sand would be dug out as if by a shovel. The cedar tree would be torn beyond recognition. But first they would check the other sets, just in case. Wherever the wolf was, it was waiting. Now it was dawn.

The owl glided within ten feet of Stockton and Simmons as they slid out of the pickup cab. Neither man noticed the bird. It sailed on toward the blackness of the Hills. They had driven to within a few hundred yards of where they had found the old ewe. The sky was brightening fast, and the men stood for a minute wondering at the speed at which the morning had come. Jenkins took his rifle from the rear window of the pickup.

"Remember," Simmons said, "don't use that unless it's absolutely necessary."

"I'm not taking any chances," Jenkins said.

"No, of course not," Simmons said. "But remember the value of the thing."

"The skin would be valuable enough," Jenkins said.

"Yes, probably the most valuable skin in any collection anywhere." He smiled. "But better alive."

Stockton had brought all his camera gear. He waddled along behind, nearly bogged down by the cases and bags. He tried to take a light reading as he went, but the country was rough and he almost stumbled several times. When Jenkins got to the top of the ridge and could look down to where the ewe had been, Stockton was far behind. But by the time Jenkins had surveyed the area with his binoculars, he had caught up.

They saw nothing. The ewe was gone. They came down the hill cautiously. Simmons caught Stockton's arm and held him up while Jenkins went closer. They watched him searching the area. The morning sounds of the prairie were beginning to taper off. The animals were getting ready for the heat of the day, and so there was quiet in the draw. Then a dull clunk came from down the draw. Jenkins did not hear it, but Simmons and Stockton did. They looked at each other. Simmons shrugged, and their eyes went back to Jenkins. It was obvious that he was finding nothing. "Is this the right place?" Stockton asked. They heard the noise again.

"Of course it is," Simmons said. He tried to ignore the noise, but it came again. "What is that?" he asked. Stockton shrugged.

Then Jenkins was back. "I didn't find a thing. I mean the traps are even gone. There isn't a trace of anything. Just a few strands of wool still stuck in the bush." He shook his head, then he heard the noise for the first time. He looked down the draw.

Together they walked toward the sound. The draw flattened out on its way toward the lower land. As they came to the place the sound became louder. It came dully and at irregular intervals. When they came out onto the flatter area, they saw Joe Standing Elk, his left boot off and his foot bandaged, carrying a heavy stone from the eroding bank of the draw. As they watched, he came to the center of the flat area in the bottom of the draw and lifted the stone up high. He placed it carefully at the top of the tower of stone that he was building. The sound of stones meeting each other came to them, and Joe looked back. But he did not look at them. He looked beyond, to where the white puffy clouds careened past the sun, to where the blackness still lay heavy beneath the pine trees of the Hills.

There was nothing in the first sets, as Egan had been sure there wouldn't be. The wolf would be in the set beneath the cedar on the sandy hill. Now there was no doubt. But he did not tell McVay. Together they moved on. Egan slowed even more, and he could feel McVay watching him. He was feeling very old now, and he wondered if McVay could see that. He wondered if McVay could imagine what had been going through his mind as the sun had come up that morning. He wondered if McVay had guessed at the pain in his chest. But there was no sense in asking. He either did or he did not, and all Egan could do was to go ahead with what he had to do. Everything was moving now, set in motion years ago, moving on a collision course. Egan knew that now it was out of his control.

They could see the sandy hill from a long way off, and McVay had the urge to glass the hill with his binoculars. But Egan did not seem to want to look at it; he seemed sure that the wolf would be there. As McVay walked, he, too, began to know that the wolf was caught, and then it was not important anymore. He began to watch Egan. He studied the stride and saw the grimace on his face. The boots plodded forward, toward the sandy hill, like the pistons of a machine, and McVay found himself hoping that Egan would get away with it. He found himself hoping that no one would ever know this place, this sandy hill with the cedar tree at its top. And he vowed to himself that he would never tell, that the secret of the wolf's burial place would be safe with him.

Then they were in clear view of the set. Egan had not yet looked up at the hill. He was sure that everything was as he had imagined it, and so he turned to McVay, who stood behind him looking up at the hill through binoculars. He did not speak but let McVay's sparkling eyes tell him that, yes, he was there, lying flat, almost invisible in the grass tufts to the right of the cedar tree. He's big. Magnificent. And he is yours, the eyes said as they shifted back to Egan. The old man nodded.

He looked terribly tired. The old blue eyes had lost their brightness. "Would you mind?" he asked.

McVay nodded his head as Egan swung his pack to the ground. "I'll be leaving," he said. "I've got business."

"Yes," Egan said, "and so do I." He reached into his pack and pulled out the knife that McVay had lost at the Gennings place. "You might need this," he said.

McVay took the knife from the old man and looked into the clear blue eyes for the last time. They watched each other for an instant, then McVay turned on his heels and walked away without looking back. He forgot the place where the wolf would die and be buried, pushed the contour of the land from his mind, tried not to notice the position of the sun or the way the vegetation changed as he walked. He moved slowly, the way Egan moved on the prairie, and tried to visualize what was happening on the sandy hill. But he could not. Egan had a trenching tool with him for digging the hole to bury the wolf. McVay wondered if he would dig the hole or shoot the wolf first. He would shoot first, McVay thought. He would not make the wolf wait.

McVay had been walking for ten minutes when he heard the shot. He stopped and looked up at the sun, letting the brightness of it make his eyes water. It had been a faint sound, more of a snap, but it made him think of gunfire and of firefights and of what a rifle shot could mean. Before they had always frightened him. They had excited him and made his blood flow in great pulses. The sound of rifle fire had always caused his heart to raise up in his chest and to beat hard and fast. Rifle fire had always meant that the chances were great that the man who had pulled the trigger would regret what he had done. Now he began to walk again. The sound of Egan's rifle had been different. It had been the simple sound of penance, and McVay's heart did not leap. It beat steadily as he walked, and he put all of it behind him. Now he began to think of what he must do. He let himself breathe deeply and began to relax.

Simmons, Jenkins, and Stockton heard the rifle shot, too. They had been walking for twenty minutes in the direction that Jenkins had seen Egan and McVay walking earlier that morning. They had missed McVay, who was now in his pickup truck, and they moved as fast as they could toward the sound of the rifle. Simmons had cringed when the report had reached his ears. At first he'd hoped that it was not Egan, but he knew that it was. Then the possibility of a miss flashed in his mind, but that too was impossible. The wolf was dead. They had lost the great prize. They would never be able to exhibit the last gray buffalo wolf. Now the best that they could hope for was the skin. Just the skin, the carcass—but priceless. Experts from all over the world would come to see it. It would attract scientists as well as ordinary people. It could be a source of revenue for the Hills. But first they would have to find Egan. The three men fanned out and hurried in the direction of the shot, but the land was rough and the going was slow. Stockton was having a hard time keeping up, and so, while they waited, Jenkins and Simmons surveyed the land ahead with binoculars.

Lebeaux's face went white. "No," he said.

Robert Lance laughed, and Lebeaux could smell the whiskey. "We're as good as gone," he said.

"It won't work. That Mullens will be ready for you. They got guards and Feds, and I don't know what all."

"Then we'll kill the fuckers," Robert Lance said, and brought out a pistol from under his coat. "We've got dynamite and we've got guns," he said defiantly.

Lebeaux shook his head. "You'll ruin it all." He pointed to the school. "Look, we're getting what we want."

Six others stood behind Robert Lance. They were laughing at Lebeaux and passing a bottle among them.

Lebeaux stared hard at Robert Lance. He spoke calmly. "Occasionally," he said, "white men learn from us. Once in a while a white man learns that we are all part of the whole, and not to respect any part of the world is not to respect yourself. If a white man can learn this, how can you forget it?"

There was a flash of recognition in Lance's eyes. But it did not last. "You are just a coward. We," Lance said and pointed to his chest, "are all that's left of the Indians."

"If that is so, then the Indians are all dead," Lebeaux said. "The whites and their government of rules have beaten us."

Robert Lance laughed. "Beaten you, maybe."

"There are things more powerful than governments or violence," Lebeaux said, but his voice was drowned out by Robert Lance's.

"We're leaving," Lance said. He waved to the others, who stepped up and followed him into the trees.

Too hot to dig in sand, Egan thought, and he gasped for the air that had been coming hard for him. Sweat rolled down his face, and the pain in his chest came again, but he dug on. The hole caved in nearly as fast as he could dig, but this was the place, the proper place for the wolf, and he would see that he was left here. He was pushing himself too hard—he knew that—and so he stopped to rest. He looked over to the wolf, who lay thirty feet away as if it were sleeping. It was stretched out with its rear legs underneath and its front paws out straight. It was exactly as Egan had found it, the massive head resting on the front paws, except now there was a single hole and spot of blood between the eyes. Egan's head was swimming, and the vision of all the other wolves he had killed and helped to kill came to him. The memory of the killings did not affect him, but when his mind brought up the old picture of him standing beside the hanging wolf, his hands came to his face, and he rubbed at his eyes. His vision broiled in red. He was sweating too much, and he was dizzy. Then he heard the voices, or thought that he heard them. Was it Stockton calling for someone to wait for him? Were there people coming? He opened his eyes, but the churning redness did not leave. He went to the wolf and wrapped his arms around the chest. The grave was deep enough. It had to be. He pulled hard at the bulk of the dead wolf.

In Egan's head the redness took over, and he gasped for air. The last thing he remembered was the incredible weight of the wolf, the excited voice, "Here, over here," and the pain and redness. "My God." And then a suffocating feeling and finally the warmth of the wolf's coat as his face sunk into it. "My God," the voice said again. "My God."

As Simmons climbed to the top of a hill to use his binoculars again, McVay took his own binoculars from his shirt pocket and scanned Billion's house and yard from the same hill he had watched from before. He had driven his pickup halfway down Billion's road this time. Now it was noon, and the sun was hot. Nothing moved in the Hills. Nothing seemed alive. There were only the black trees, shading the ground, taking away the life-giving sun. It was cool where McVay stood. Billion's pickup was parked beside the house, and so McVay knew that he was home. He breathed deeply as he shifted the binoculars from one window to the next. The weight of the .45 in his jacket pocket anchored him to the spot. The binoculars were steady, and finally he saw a movement. Billion walked across in front of the kitchen window. He was in the back of the house. McVay came quickly down the hill.

When he reached the house, he pressed himself against the wall. The .45 was out and held high, level with McVay's head and pointing straight up. McVay metered his breathing, thinking hard about its calming effect. He pressed his ear against the wall and listened, but he heard nothing. He planned on Billion being armed. He did not want to give him a chance to use his weapon, and so he moved to the back door and, crouching down below the glass, tested the knob. It was not locked. On his way back to the wall where he had listened, he picked up three small stones. He crept to a place midway along the side wall, where he could see the corner of the front porch but was out of sight of any of the windows and doors. He pressed his ear tightly against the wall. If there was movement in the house, he would hear it. Then he tossed the first stone onto the front porch. The sound of the stone hitting the porch vibrated in his ear, but he heard no other noise. He tossed the second stone and thought that he heard something move inside.

When the third stone hit the porch, Billion pulled a .32 automatic from his pants pocket and went to stand behind the wall in the hall where he could see the porch through the window without being seen. He stood quietly for several seconds, then moved on into the living room and cautiously peered out the front window. He saw nothing in the yard and slipped the pistol back into his pocket. When he turned around, the first thing he saw was the muzzle of McVay's .45 pointed squarely at his forehead.

"I guess you fooled me," Billion hissed.

"Never mind," McVay said. "First, I want twenty-five thousand dollars."

Billion looked puzzled. Then he laughed. "You're on the take." He laughed again. "What makes you think I've got twenty-five thousand dollars?" He moved slightly to McVay's left.

McVay shook his head, telling Billion to stay where he was. "Because you stole it from my little brother."

Billion's smile faded and his eyes narrowed. "Brother," he said. "I don't know nothing about no brother."

"You should," McVay said. "You killed him." McVay's foot snapped up and took Billion at the left knee. The pistol never wavered, but Billion went back to the wall. He started to scream but didn't. His face contorted as he rested against the wall.

"It must have been a little like this when you killed Jimmy," McVay said. "Did you make him crawl or just blow him away?"

Billion did not look up until the pain eased in his leg. "You monkeys are all alike. Nothing but talk," he snarled. "Why didn't you take me out?"

"Didn't want to, yet. First we talk money, then we get serious. We pay up on the real debt. Turn around, spread out, hands on the wall." McVay kicked his legs apart and patted him down. He found the .32 automatic and the knife. Billion tried to turn back before McVay told him to, and McVay kicked his legs out from under him.

"I can go on like this all day," McVay said to him, "or you can tell me where the money is."

"There ain't no money," Billion said from the floor.

"Grass then. I'll take your dirty marijuana if I have to."

"Okay, there's no money, I'll give you the grass," he said.

It was too fast, too easy, and McVay was set on his guard. Billion started to move, and McVay rocked up onto the balls of his feet to kick him again. Billion threw up his hands. "Easy," he said. "We got to go outside if you want the grass."

McVay nodded and stepped back. "You first," he said, and followed Billion toward the back door. When they stepped outside, the heat of the afternoon hit them. It was too hot, McVay thought as he concentrated on the back of Billion's head and on what he would do if Billion tried something.

"It's there," Billion said. He pointed to the stack of hay bales beside the shed that McVay knew was filled with weapons.

McVay waved the pistol again. "Let's see it," he said.

They walked to the stack, and McVay told Billion to pull off the first layer of bales. They were hay, but the second layer was marijuana. Billion threw out four bales. "They're over fifty pounds apiece," he said. "Pretty slick, huh?"

McVay was being cautious. He didn't like the lightness in Billion's voice, but he went to the bales and took a handful of the marijuana. It was good stuff, green with a lot of leaves. Then he saw Billion glance at the shed. He must have seen that the lock was broken, because McVay could see that there was surprise on his face, but he hid the surprise when he looked back at McVay.

"Makes it easy to haul the stuff," Billion said. "Where's your pickup?"

"Just down your road," McVay said. "We'll take a little walk."

Billion shrugged as if it sounded like a good idea, but McVay saw him move toward the shed and shift his weight. McVay couldn't believe that he would try it. Even if one of the weapons was loaded and ready, there was little chance he'd make it to the shed. "Try it," McVay said.

This time Billion's laugh was more genuine. "Let's go get your pickup," he said.

McVay nodded and let up for an instant.

That was enough. Billion was on him with both feet. He had covered the distance between them before McVay had registered movement. He spun into McVay, the fists and feet darting out with bone-crushing force. The .45 flew from McVay's hand and landed near the hay bales. It had been cocked and ready, and when it hit the ground, it went off. The report crashed back and forth across the wooded valley, but neither man noticed it. McVay had stopped Billion's charge by leaping sideways, and now the two stood coiled with six feet between them.

McVay tried a snap kick to test Billion's lateral movement. It missed, and McVay noticed that Billion had moved left to avoid it. Billion continued to move, trying to put the sun at his back, but McVay would not let him have the sun, and so they moved parallel for several steps. Both men were judging the distance to the .45, knowing that it would have cocked itself when it went off and that it would be ready to fire if either got their hands on it. Billion also measured the distance to the shed door and wondered if it had been McVay who had broken the lock and if he knew there were weapons inside. McVay watched Billion's solar plexus and tried to concentrate his energy into his own. They stood gathering energy for several moments, then they both began to move. Billion threw a sweeping roundhouse kick that did not come close. McVay knew that it had been intended to set him up, but he had not taken the bait. He moved backward, out of range, then faked the attack that Billion had expected, to see what Billion had had in mind. Billion's body continued to spin after the first roundhouse. It gathered speed, and the other foot followed with twice the force of the first. But McVay was standing back now, waiting, and when that foot passed his head, he attacked, landing three body punches and nearly taking Billion's feet out from under him with a leg sweep. They were standing apart again, thinking, trying for a balance, and concentrating on each other when a whiskey bottle landed between them.

"What the fuck are you white assholes doing?" It was Robert Lance with his six followers.

It took a moment for the two to bring themselves back, and even then there was a dreamlike quality to the voices that taunted them.

Robert Lance held the .45. "You boys should be more careful with guns." The others laughed. They were drinking from another bottle now. "A bunch of Indians can't even take a hike in the Black Hills anymore without being disturbed." There was more laughter, and McVay began to ease off of the plateau that he had been building to deal with Billion. He began to try to understand what was happening now.

One of the other Indians stepped forward. "What you guys fightin' about?" he asked.

"White men always fight."

"If they don't have no Indians to fight, they fight themselves."

"But this is the famous P.J. Billion. He's the pusher man, right?" Lance was moving toward them. The .45 was still in his hand. "You guys shouldn't have been shooting up here. Us Indians get a little nervous when we hear shots."

"'Specially today," another man laughed.

Lance smiled. "We're a little bit edgy today, for sure." And they all laughed. "Back up," he said. "What you got baled up there?"

Billion and McVay backed away from the Indian with the .45. But McVay did not back up straight. He angled for the shed door. "Hey," Robert Lance said, "this ain't your basic alfalfa."

The others came up closer to him. They pulled at the bale. "Wow," someone said. "It's grass." They crowded in to look.

"Now that's a generous lid," another said, and there was laughter. But no one laughed when they looked up and saw that McVay was holding the AK-47 on them.

"Put the .45 on the bale and clear out," he said.

Robert Lance tried to stare him down, but he was sure that McVay would kill him if he didn't do what he said. "Okay, fucker," Robert Lance said. "We got business anyway." He knew that his own pistol was within easy reach. "We're leaving," he said and laid the .45 on the bale.

They backed away grumbling and calling McVay names. McVay held the rifle at his shoulder and tried to watch Billion at the same time. The Indians were in the trees now, moving toward the area where McVay had found the marijuana growing and the stone building on that first day. He began to give Billion more attention as the Indians got farther away. He had changed his stance so that he could face Billion and still watch the Indians when he saw a movement that was too fast. Gunfire came from the trees, and he returned it as he rolled into the shed.

Then the forest came alive, first one more gun, then two and three, until the firing became almost continual. The bullets shattered the wood of the upper portion of the shed, but McVay lay flat behind the rocks of the foundation. With the barrel of the AK-47 he knocked all the ammunition to the floor. Then he thought of Billion, but when he looked, he was gone. The shed was shaking, splinters of wood flew in all directions, and McVay was certain that he would die. But he could see the Indians now and shot in their direction. It didn't seem to faze them, and he knew that he had to do something. Then his eyes fell on an LAAW 66-millimeter rocket launcher. He scrambled for it, the bullets still hammering the upper part of the shed. It was all automatic. He armed the weapon as he crawled back to the door and, without thinking, held it up to his shoulder and picked out a target.

The Indian that he picked had just taken an automatic weapon from the stone building where the dynamite had been hidden, and when the rocket came, he did not know what hit him. The building went up with a billowing roar, and the shooting stopped. McVay watched the orange cloud rise, igniting the trees around it, and from where he lay on the floor of the shed, he whispered, "Goddamn." The explosion flattened out and the trees popped with red boiling flame. McVay saw the remaining men, led by Robert Lance, running away from the fire. He sat still for several minutes before he dropped the weapon and stood up.

The fire spread as McVay loaded the bales of marijuana into the back of his pickup. By the time he turned onto the main road, he could see the faint redness of the flames reflected off the evening clouds. He tried not to drive fast. He did not want to attract attention. But on the lonely road winding down from the Hills toward the town, there was no one to notice and so, as he drove, his speed increased. He knew that he should just keep going, but there was Katie, and as he came to the turnoff to her house, he slowed and in the last seconds decided to give it a try.

But Katie was not there. The house was dark and silent. He paused for an instant in the driveway and thought of the night that he had spent there. The desire to see her again grew stronger. He pulled out onto the main road, driving faster than before, gaining speed as he descended into the town. Now he could see the light from the fire in his rearview mirror, and he imagined the sound that it was making as it leapt from tree to tree.

The town was quiet. Only an Indian man stood on the street and looked toward the Hills. McVay slowed the pickup and ran his fingers through his hair. There was the Oasis bar. That would be his last chance of catching her before he left. He took several deep breaths as he pulled the truck alongside the building. When he got out, he glanced into the back to be sure that the tarp was still stretched tight across the top of his load. It was, and McVay knew that no one would guess what was under it. He tucked in his shirttail and walked to the door of the Oasis.

The bar seemed familiar to him, but dreamlike. He stood in the doorway and let his eyes pass over the people sitting at the tables and playing pool. They did not seem to notice him, and this surprised McVay. He was sure that the last few hours would show on his face. You must be doing a good job, he told himself, no one knows. But when Katie turned and saw him standing there, her smile faded, and she left the man she was talking to and came to him. They looked at each other, and without a word Katie took his arm and turned him toward the door. They let the door close on the people in the bar. It was as if McVay had not come in. Only one man noticed that he was there at all, and as the door closed, the man moved to the window to watch where the two were going.

Katie did not see the faint glow of the forest fire, and McVay did not let his gaze linger. He turned to her, took her shoulders in his hands, and held her firmly. He began to speak, but she shook her head and held a hand to his lips. His grip eased, and she said, "Come on. Come with me." She took his hand and led him around the corner of the building to the pool room door. She opened the door, and they went inside. But the door did not close all the way. McVay took her in his arms again and forced her face against his shoulder.

He was surprised by the tension that was in him, and he savored the feel of it slipping away as they held each other. They could smell the warmth of the water through the darkness. The sound of the water moving and the heaviness of the humid air took away the last of the tension, and they relaxed. Then McVay let his hands fall to Katie's waist, and they stood feeling each other's presence. Their faces were only inches apart. "I'm leaving," McVay whispered. "Come with me."

There was silence and the darkness became eerie. Katie did not speak. It would be the easy thing to do, she thought, and let her hand come up to McVay's face. She felt the tightness in his jaw and found that the green eyes were closed under her touch. McVay felt her fingertips moving in slow circles on his face, and he breathed in, ready to speak.

But he did not get the chance to speak. Suddenly there was light everywhere, and he heard the door close behind him. When he turned, Billion was standing with his back against the door and his pistol pointed at McVay's chest. "How does it feel, Monkey?" Billion smiled. "You're dead."

McVay tried to move away from Katie, but she would not let him. She had already looked at Billion and seen the tightness in his jaw, the crooked smile. Now she watched McVay, wondering what was going through his head.

He was thinking about Jimmy and the marijuana in the truck. He was thinking that if Billion killed him now, it would have all been for nothing. The brightness of the room was dazzling, and for an instant Billion went out of focus. McVay could feel the water moving behind him, and he knew that this would be a poor place to die. Katie was still in front of him, her eyes set on Billion now. McVay put his hands on her shoulders and was amazed at the strength in them.

"Move," Billion said to Katie. "You're too good-looking to blow holes in." But she did not move. McVay felt her hatred for Billion and knew that he must do something, that he would have only one chance to do it.

Billion began to move the pistol in the direction that he wanted Katie to go. It swung to Billion's left, fluidly, back and forth, and McVay let his eyes fix themselves on the motion. "Move it," Billion said. Back and forth, back and forth. "Move it!" The sound of Billion's voice had changed, and McVay could feel that Billion might shoot her, too. Back and forth. He watched the pistol. Back and forth. He let the rhythm of the movement relax him. He put all his energy into what he was doing. Back and forth. He knew that the instant Katie moved there would be a chance, a single chance, and he must be ready. Back and forth. He felt the energy sliding into his right leg. He let it go and felt it begin to pulse there in the lower part of the leg, so when he pushed Katie gently out of the way, he was ready.

Concentrating then on the pinpoint that was Billion's wrist, he waited until the pistol was at the end of its last arch, when it was pointing to the right of his heart. When the pistol was at the best place, he released the energy and his foot snapped up so fast that Billion did not see it. But the pistol was not dislodged, only pushed farther to Billion's left. McVay followed the kick, and suddenly he was inside the pistol's arc and clawing at Billion's face. They crashed to the floor and struggled for control of the pistol, which skidded across the concrete and out of their reach.

Out on the street, where the people had gathered to look at the wolf in the back of Simmons's pickup, they did not hear McVay and Billion roar at each other. There was too much noise. The people filed from the bar and the café and shouted to one another. They noticed the redness of the sky to the south and commented that it looked almost like the Hills were on fire. They laughed nervously to themselves and gazed at the dead wolf as they listened to Stockton telling them about the old man who died trying to hide it. They shook their heads and told each other how big the wolf was and how they would have liked to have had just one clear shot at it when it was alive. But all the time they watched the sky and wondered if the fire made it so light. Then old Johnny told them to hang the wolf up on the light pole outside the café, and they all agreed that that was where it should be hung. But once it was hung, it called attention to the sky, and they knew that the Hills really were on fire. The sky was too red, and it seemed to them that they could almost see the flames.

Old Johnny picked up a dried cottonwood stick from the gutter and poked the wolf's body with it. He made a noise like he imagined the wolf would make if it were alive. All the people laughed, except the sheriff, who came out of his office where they had just laid Bill Egan's body to wait for the ambulance from Rapid City.

Larry Mullens could see the flames from behind the barricade that he and his men had constructed on the trail leading to the top of the mountain. He looked at the flames and could not believe what he was seeing. Swearing to himself, he began to talk frantically into the radio.

While he called for a helicopter to evacuate them, he waved his free hand in the air and looked down toward where he had thought that the Indians would be. But he saw only the flames, leapfrogging from tree to tree, popping, rolling along the mountain crest. The barricade would have stopped an assault on the monument, but it was nothing against a forest fire. The mountain would be burned, ruined as a tourist attraction. But even knowing that, Mullens had to lower the radio for an instant and stand in awe of the phenomenon that boiled below them. For the first time in his life, Mullens recognized the power of nature.

"Protect the school!" James Lebeaux shouted to the children. "Get buckets! Use the spring!"

Behind the children carrying buckets, the Indian camp was coming apart. Cars were lined up to go; belongings were being thrown into the backseats. People ran in all directions, but the children stayed. And with order and calm they began to bring their buckets filled with spring water to the school. They splattered the cool water against the wooden walls of the school. Lebeaux directed them. He tried not to let his bitter disappointment show. He tried to give the children something positive to remember. Their hopes were crumbling again, as they had so many times in the past. But Lebeaux was determined to hold things together, to give the children something to carry with them into the future beside chaos and failure.

McVay and Billion rolled from the concrete into the warm, moving water of the pool while Katie regained her feet. In the water Billion shook loose. Billion had gained the advantage. He beat McVay with both hands, standing over him, screaming, and from somewhere there was blood. The water was pink in front of McVay's eyes. Billion held him under by the hair, his free hand still beating at the side of McVay's head. It was like a dream now for McVay: everything slowed, and he tried to fight the feeling of wanting to give up. The water was warm. He did not fear it anymore, and the fist pounding his head did not hurt. Then when he tried to breathe, the razor edge of panic struck him, and he began to struggle. But the struggling was pitiful, and Billion's hands held him easily.

Suddenly the hands went weak, and McVay burst from the water, gasping and screaming for air. His lungs burned with the humidity, and when he could focus, he saw that the water was dark boiling red. He coughed and spit up water, gagged, and struggled for the edge of the pool.

And then he was standing on the concrete, looking down at Billion's body floating in the pool. Blood still rolled from a huge hole in the back of his head. When McVay turned, Katie was standing beside him with the pistol still in her hand. McVay looked at her, tried to keep the panic off his face and his breathing slow.

"Come with me," he said.

Katie looked down at the body. She was calm. "Go on," she said, and began to shake her head slowly.

"You can't stay now," McVay said.

"No, Tom. I have to stay," she said. "I belong here." Then her expression softened. "Please?"

Slowly, he nodded. Her calmness had infected him. He pushed his wet hair back and nodded again. Then he reached out and touched her shoulders. He leaned toward her and pressed his cheek against hers. Their eyes met for only an instant before he turned and moved toward the door.

Now the whole sky was ablaze. The people in the street talked loudly and laughed their nervous laughs. McVay moved quietly to his pickup and slid behind the wheel. He could see that he would have to drive past the crowd to get out of town, but he was sure that no one would try to stop him. He turned his truck around in the alley, wanting to be heading in the right direction when he came out onto the street. He did not want to have to stop once he started toward the edge of town. When he pulled out onto the main street, he was surprised at the size of the crowd. He had assumed that they were watching the fire that lit up the entire southern sky. But when his headlights swung over them, they showed him the real reason for the excitement. The wolf hung heavily from the light pole in the center of the crowd. He saw Stockton and Simmons standing beside it, looking up and smiling. He saw that the rope had been put around the wolf's back legs, its tongue was sticking out, and there was dried blood at its mouth. Some of the people in the crowd turned and waved for him to turn off his headlights, which shone brightly in their eyes. But McVay did not turn off his headlights. He pulled closer. He drove steadily toward where the wolf hung. The crowd began to separate. They shouted at him, their blood high from the sight of the hanging wolf. McVay paid no attention to them. He drove to the wolf and under it. When he got out of the pickup, a cowboy moved toward him, but when the man saw the look on McVay's face, he did not say anything. McVay vaulted easily into the rear of the truck. The crowd was silent as he reached out and touched the wolf. The feel of it made him close his eyes. He slowly drew out his boot knife and cut the rope that held the wolf. It fell heavily onto the bales of marijuana in the bed of his truck.

Now the crowd came alive. They jeered at McVay, standing tall against the fiery sky. No one was silent, except Sheriff Bailey, who stood off to one side and watched. Finally Simmons started to climb into the pickup box with McVay, shouting that the wolf was government property. But when he looked up, McVay's knife was only an inch from his face, and seeing the fire reflected in McVay's eyes, he backed down. Now the town was silent. No one moved. McVay jumped down from the pickup box and got back behind the wheel.

The crowd parted for him, and for an instant no one spoke. Then the whispers began, and finally Stockton turned to find Bailey standing against the wall of the café. "Well, go get him," he shouted. "You're the sheriff. Go get him." Bailey stared blankly. Then Simmons joined Stockton.

"He can't do that. It's your job to stop him."

Bailey looked at them and began to nod. He nodded for a long time, then he began to move toward his car. When the engine started, he looked into the rearview mirror at the town and mashed the accelerator to the floor. He was doing seventy miles an hour by the time he saw the huge rooster-tail of dust from McVay's pickup. McVay had turned at the intersection west of town. He was no longer on the main road. Now he was on gravel, and the dust billowed in the fire-bright sky. When Bailey came to the intersection where McVay had turned, he was doing eighty. But he did not slow down or even look in the direction McVay had gone. He looked straight ahead. Then he reached into his glove compartment, pulled out the eight-track tape, slid the seat back, and turned the volume up as far as it would go. The sound of lightning fingers on the piano filled the car. It reminded him of icicles being knocked off the eaves on a cold day in January.

In 1986 Dan O'Brien received the prestigious Iowa Short Fiction Award for his short story collection *Eminent Domain.* Dan O'Brien is the recipient of two National Endowment for the Arts awards for his fiction. His works have appeared in a variety of journals, ranging from *Redbook* to *Prairie Schooner,* and he has taught creative writing at the University of Colorado. As a cattle rancher and an endangered species biologist living in South Dakota, Dan O'Brien possesses an intimate knowledge of the rugged landscape that comprises the *Spirit of the Hills.*